INCUBATION

BOOK ONE OF THE INCUBATION TRILOGY

LAURA DISILVERIO

ISBN-13: 978-0692680728 (diAgio Publishing)
ISBN-10: 0692680721

Printed in the United States of America
First Printing: 2016
20 19 18 17 16   5 4 3 2 1

diAgio Publishing
To order, visit www.lauradisilverio.com.

Layout by Penoaks Publishing, penoaks.com

ACKNOWLEDGMENTS

I am beyond grateful to the young adults who encouraged me to write this story and helped by commenting on early drafts, including Lily and Ellen DiSilverio, Jake Hullings, Gretchen Gaebler, Daniel Moody, Audrey Miller, and Caili Downs. All the good stuff came from them. This story wouldn't be nearly as good if they hadn't shared their ideas, thoughts, and imaginings. I am blessed to have a brain trust like this.

I also owe more than I can ever repay to Glenn Miller who pushed me to get outside my comfort zone and try something new. He made me remember you cannot discover new oceans unless you have the courage to lose sight of the shore. I haven't seen the shore in months. Thanks, Glenn.

PART ONE

CHAPTER ONE

I've never seen a bird, of course. Not a live one. So this discovery washed ashore from who knows where makes my breath catch in my throat.

Stooping, I free what I'm almost sure is a feather from the damp sand. Platinum strands fall into my face as I brush sand grains from the bedraggled feather and smooth the barbs. It tickles my palm. I've never found anything this exciting in all the years I've been sneaking down to the beach, not that I can steal away more than once a month, if I'm lucky. It's shells, mostly. There was a dolphin last year, her skin slick rubber, her eyes liquid and pleading, that Halla and Wyck helped me drag to the waterline. And the mine I almost stepped on six years ago, days after my tenth birthday. The mine had made my pulse race like this, but it was unnatural and ugly; mines are why the beach is off-limits. I'd been restricted to my room for a week after reporting it. No good deed goes unpunished, right?

I stroke the foot-long feather, dark gray near its base fading to cream at the tip. It is proof, proof that birds still exist . . . somewhere. Shading my eyes, I scan the sullen Atlantic, darker than the feather, and then the steel wool sky, as if I might spot the bird that dropped my feather. Ridiculous. The feather has surely drifted from hundreds or even thousands of miles away, from some tiny island or rocky atoll that has, miraculously, escaped the avian flu. Excitement bubbles inside me. I can't wait to show Dr. Ronan.

A heavy hand lands on my shoulder. I whirl. A frowning border sentry blocks my way, hand on his Electrical Signal Disruptor, beamer slung across his back. He's young and new—I've never seen him. His stern expression says he takes himself and his duties seriously. That won't last any longer than it takes for the elements to dull the shiny brass of his belt buckle and uniform insignia.

"This area is off-limits." He nods at the sign wired to the fence. It warns of disease-bearing immigrants, toxic flotsam from wrecked boats, and mines buried on the beach and floating offshore. The sign's red letters have weathered to pink. Immigrants aren't much of a threat anymore—most died off years ago—and I've only ever seen the one mine.

"Right. Sorry. I'm going." I turn, hoping he'll let me slide.

"You belong at the Kube." Figuring that out doesn't make him a genius; my sky blue jumpsuit with the stylized leaf stenciled over my left breast gives that away. "I have to report you. Name?"

I can't afford another report, not two days before Reunion Day. "Hey." I try a smile. "I goofed, wandered too far by accident. You know how it is. I must have missed the sign."

"And the fences and the warning beacons?" His expression says "gotcha." He starts to draw his ESD out of its holster.

Before I can answer, another sentry emerges from the path that cuts between the dunes, spots us, and strides our way, booted feet scuffing up sand.

"Recruit, what's going on?" Without giving the sentry a chance to respond, Corporal Airrick Risenor, who lived at the Kube before being inducted into the Border Security Service, fixes his gaze on me. His eyes are blue, filled with exasperation. "Jax, didn't I tell you last time that it was the last time?"

"I know. I'm sorry. It won't happen again."

"Until it does."

We both know I'll be back, that I can't stay away from the beach no matter how hard I try. Which I pretty much don't. I need the beach. Sometimes, I think I hear my mother's voice here, blending with the waves and wind. Her voice is husky, low-pitched, infinitely loving as she sings me a wordless lullaby. Intellectually, I know I can't possibly remember her voice—I was only a week old when the government repossessed me—but here, it's possible. My eyes plead with him. He's caught me twice before.

He heaves a sigh. "Get out of here."

"But, sir—" the recruit objects.

I don't need a second invitation. Shooting Airrick a grateful smile, I take off over the dunes, slip-sliding up the sandy incline.

"Don't let me catch you down here again, Jax," he calls after me.

Once I reach the road, I half-jog toward InKubator 9, four block-like stories rising above the walls and the dome. Usually it stands out against the sky's hazy blue, but today it blends with the steely hue. Wind gusts tug at my feather, and I cradle it in both hands. With my hands occupied, I can't brush the windblown hair out of my face and it catches in my eyelashes and at the corners of my mouth. I try to push the strands out with my tongue. I near the Kube, hoping I can sneak back in without getting spotted, and hoping against hope that no one pinged my locator while I was gone.

Vaguely aware of a distant hum, like electrical current running through a wire, I avoid the Kube's main entrance by circling the fence until I reach an auxiliary gate that leads directly into the lab and the dome. The humming grows louder and I suddenly know what it is. I jerk my head up and scan the sky. *There.* A dark cloud looms in the west, growing and spreading until it blocks out the sun. Locusts. I need to get inside. I lean in to the iris scanner, but blink nervously, causing it to say with irritating calmness, "Not recognized."

"Damn it." I can't help but look up. The swarm is closer, almost upon me. Willing myself not to blink, I put my eye to the scanner again. This time, the gate clicks open. I push through it, and pound across the hundred yards of open space that separate me from the dome. I can tell by the sound, swelling so my ears hurt and my body seems to vibrate, that I'm not going to make it. I'm still twenty yards from safety when the swarm overtakes me.

Dropping to the ground, I put my arms over my head with my right upper arm pressed against my ear and that hand reaching over to cover the other ear. My left hand lightly covers my mouth and nose. I squinch my eyes closed and fold my lips in. The small, solid bodies thud against me. They tangle in my hair. I can feel some of them light on me momentarily, before they decide I'm not plant matter, and lift off again, buzzing onward in search of food. Something pinches the back of my hand. There are millions of them. They smother me. I force myself to inhale and exhale evenly through my nose, keeping my hand cupped over it. I'm not afraid of dying—I've only ever heard of one person killed by a swarm of locusts and that's because he forgot to cover his nose and mouth and asphyxiated when the bugs clogged his airways—but it's freaking unpleasant and I'm relieved when the hits come farther apart, then slow to a trickle, and then cease. The swarm has passed.

I open my eyes and take a deep breath. All clear. Slowly, I stand. My neck prickles and there's another pinch. I slap a hand to it and fling away the locust. There's no chance I'll make it back to the lab before Dr. Ronan misses me; I'll have to go through decontamination to ensure none of the bugs gets inside. It would be catastrophic. At the thought of the locusts munching their way through the crops in the dome, the food we work so hard to cultivate, I glance toward the dome and am startled to see it has turned black. It takes me a split second to realize the locusts have settled on it, perhaps attracted by the green within. It's made to withstand the weight, but the usually transparent dome rendered black by the shroud of insects makes me shudder. It's a sinister, huge, black orb.

Shaking off the uncharacteristically fanciful thought, I hurry to the airlock and ready myself for the tedium of decon. The deconner is standing by when I step into the small, tile-lined room, telling me through the speaker to strip off my clothes and boots and put them in the locker, and then step into the shower. It's embarrassing standing there nude, but we've all done it, in drills and occasionally for real, and we all pull decon duty as an additional service on a rotating schedule. I conceal the feather under a hand draped casually down my thigh and scrub myself in an awkward, one-handed way with the special soap while water blasts from the six shower heads. Obedient to the instructions still coming from the speaker, I bend, flip my hair over my head and shampoo hard with the anti-insecticide gel. When I fling my hair back, it splats coldly between my shoulder blades. The locust-blackened dome looms outside the porthole window. Creepy.

As I watch, sparks travel up the dome's ribs and spread. Dr. Ronan has activated the electric web running through the clear polyglass, usually used to discourage outlaws after our crops. Locusts explode in bursts of goo and catch fire. For a moment, the dome is ablaze with a thin ripple of fire, but then the bugs cascade from the sides, a waterfall of flame that sputters out as it hits the concrete apron. Many more locusts lift off and buzz away than were incinerated.

A door slides open and I cross into an equally small room furnished with a chair.

"That was just gross." The voice sounds from behind me, with the rich, slow syllables of the Delta Canton. The deconner has entered, holding a paper robe for me.

"Halla?" I recognize my friend's voice through the distortion of the mask. She was five when she came to the Kube after her grandmother disappeared, and her drawl has diminished but not vanished. The body in the bulky decon suit is short and round. I slip into the paper robe and tie it. Not cozy, but better than naked.

Halla pulls off the mask, revealing her curly black hair, loam-brown skin, and plump cheeks. "It's me. Let's do your hair. Sit."

I sit and she stands behind me, raking through my hair with the fine-toothed steel comb that will ensure no locust egg uses me as transport into the Kube. The comb's teeth score my scalp.

"You were at the beach again, weren't you?" Halla's voice is resigned, not accusatory.

"I found this." I hold up the feather.

"Is that a *feather*?" She reaches to touch it, but draws her hand back as if afraid of being stung. "I can't let you take that in. You know the rules."

"It's deconned," I say.

"Ev, I can't—"

She's going to refuse me a couple of more times before she gives in, but a blast through the intercom interrupts her. "Everly Jax report to Proctor Fonner's office ASAP." The message is repeated.

"I had to file the decon report," she says, worried I'll blame her for the summons.

"I know. Not to worry." Outside I'm calm. Inside, I'm more nervous than usual. Reunion Day is April twelfth, only two days away.

Brown eyes wide with worry, Halla hands me a jumpsuit. I quickly slather on lotion, noticing a red mark on my hand, and scramble into the clean clothes. I can't take the feather with me to the Proctor's office.

"Hide this for me. Please," I beg Halla, thrusting the feather at her before she can decline. "*Please.*" I'm out the door before she can respond.

Supervising Proctor Fonner makes me think of a praying mantis. He's tall with a lanky build and an abnormally large head. He even holds his hands like a praying mantis, clasped gently together at belly-button height. It's his expression, though, that really gets to me. His face is always smooth and calm, but with something watchful, almost predatory, going on behind his eyes. He's wearing a white jumpsuit, the staff uniform, and standing by his window when I enter. He doesn't turn immediately, but continues staring down at the dome which is clear again, the crops and orchards within a vigorous green. I think I spot Wyck in the group of workers shoveling up locust carcasses. If they were edible, we'd be feasting tonight, but over the years they've evolved to emit an alkaloid that induces vomiting in mammals. I wish I were in the dome, working on my locust virus. I bite my lip and try not to shuffle my feet. He's trying to un-nerve me by ignoring me and I refuse to let him see I'm uncomfortable.

"I think the swarms are getting larger," he observes, still not turning. His voice is melodious, and he seems to put equal weight on each word, which makes his speech measured.

"Yes, sir." Always nice to be able to start out on an agreeable note. He was right.

"Disturbing. Pragmatist scientists have been saying for years that the swarms would dwindle when their usual food sources disappeared. Instead . . ."

"They've shown they're adaptable, sir." I was thinking of the way the super locust had developed in the first place, by adapting to the insecticide developed as a last-ditch effort to eradicate them. Boy, had that backfired.

"And you, Jax, are you adaptable?" He swivels to face me finally, his gaze boring into me. His eyes are a curious light gray, almost silver. Compelling. He's in his early sixties, too old to be geneborn, although his jet-black hair and virtually unlined face make him seem younger. The anti-aging properties of telomere stabilization at work. I've heard that the proctors at some Kubes are almost father figures. I can't imagine it.

"I believe so, sir." What is he getting at?

"I'm not so sure. You've been here sixteen years, and yet"—he taps the tips of his fingers together—"and yet you don't seem to have adapted to the *ethos*, if I can call it that, of InKubator 9. You flout the rules, which are put in place for your safety and the safety of our entire cadre, and you lack respect for those in authority—those who are trying to guide you toward becoming a useful citizen of Amerada."

"I'm sor—"

He stops me with an upraised hand. "Don't say you're sorry. I know you're not remotely sorry. What were you doing on the beach?"

Damn. They'd pinged my locator. I have to stop myself from rubbing the spot on my inner arm where the microchip is lodged. Although we all have locators implanted at birth, the satellite system that can track them has degraded over the years. With almost all of Amerada's resources going to food production and security, the country hasn't had the money for launches or developing new technologies in decades. Pings are random, unless an official makes a special request to locate someone. Of all the bad luck. "Walking, sir. Thinking."

He raises thin brows a tiny bit. "Thinking? About what?"

"About a way to deliver the virus I'm developing into the locust popu—"

"You couldn't do your thinking here?"

"No, sir." So far, I haven't had to tell a single lie, which is gratifying.

"Why not?" He seems genuinely curious.

"Why not?" I hesitate. Telling the truth hasn't been a total calamity so far, so I decide to stick with it. "I feel smothered here sometimes, like someone has wrapped my brain in cotton. It's having people around all the time, and never having silence. Sometimes, I can't breathe here, never mind think. But at the beach"—I feel lighter just thinking about it—"ideas come popping into my head, so fast I can't keep track of them all." I make little popping gestures, flicking my fingers outward.

He nods, as if what I've said doesn't surprise him. "Acorns," he says inscrutably. Before I can ask what he means, he continues, "You know Reunion Day is the day after tomorrow."

I nod, too apprehensive to speak.

"You also know that the opportunity to reunite with your birth parents, should they be willing and able, is a privilege and not a right. A privilege I can take away." With an elegant turn of his wrist, he opens his hand upward, as if releasing something ephemeral.

Sometimes I'm sure that's why the government began Reunion Days. It's a carrot and a stick. If the parents don't object when their child is repossessed, if they continue with their service and don't commit any crimes or do anything to de-stabilize the Prag government, they get to reunite with their kid. Ditto for the repos. Behave, and you'll get to meet your parents when you're sixteen. Rock the boat and . . . My throat tightens. "You can't—"

He steps closer so we are mere inches apart and I have to look up at him. "I can and I will. Don't push me, Jax. You have potential, abilities Amerada needs if we're going to rebuild our population and increase our food production. You're a five-percenter. I've cut you a lot of slack because of it. However, if you set one foot—one *toe*—out of line from here on out, I will deny you the opportunity to participate in Reunion Day. Do not doubt it."

His mouth is set in a grim line and a blood vessel pulses below his bony jaw. I'm getting a crick in my neck, but I can't look away. "I don't, sir." It dawns on me that he isn't taking Reunion Day away—yet. "My punishment?" Probably massive demerits. I'll be churning the biodegradable nappies from the nursery into the compost heap all week and confined to my room when not serving, but I can live with that. I have before.

"To be decided," he says. "You'll be informed when I've made my decision."

"Thank you, Proctor Fonner."

"From here on out, do your thinking in the lab." He turns to the window; I'm dismissed.

In the anteroom, an AC I don't know is reporting the theft of a ring to Proctor Fonner's aide. There's been a rash of petty thefts recently and Proctor Fonner has admonished us as a group, directing the guilty party to come forward so "the fabric of our communal life can be mended." I'm grateful now that he didn't steal my Reunion Day and I jump into the elevator before he can change his mind.

CHAPTER TWO

So relieved I feel like I'm floating, I collect my feather from Halla—I knew she'd save it for me—and tell her what happened. She seems anxious, edgy, but I'm too wound up to draw her out. Telling her I'll see her during Assembly, I take refuge in the dome. Walking through the doors that *whoosh* open after an iris scan, breathing in the moist, loam-scented air, I feel like I'm home. My shoulders relax. Even though I've lived at the Kube ever since the government repossessed me from my unfit or unlicensed parents, except for the couple months I was fosted out, it's only in the labs or the dome that I feel truly at home. I was first allowed in the labs when I was eight, after tests showed my aptitude for biology and chemistry. I'm sure that stacked against geneborn students I'd be nothing special. It's just that in the Kube, where all the kids are nats—natural-borns—I have some sort of freak ability. I think in chemical equations the way most people do words.

The dome is cavernous—a hundred acres—and I hop on a battery-powered ACV scooter to get to the lab which is at the eight o'clock radii if the interior entrance I'm at is at six o'clock. Passing experimental rice paddies, a citrus grove, and the new strain of wheat we've developed with a bitter taste we hope the locusts won't like, I arrive at the lab, a building all stainless steel and tile. Leaving the scooter at a recharging dock, I burst into the lab waving my feather. "Dr. Ronan!"

"Where the hell have you been, Jax?" Dr. Ronan looks up from the slide he's preparing and glares at me from under bushy brows. Wiry hairs stab in every direction.

He always greets me like that, even if I've only been gone a few minutes. "Look what I found."

"I'm busy." I get his white-coated back and a view of his luxurious, collar-brushing hair, dyed a dark blond that might have been his natural color a half-century ago. Now approaching ninety, with long, fleshy ear lobes and wrinkles to prove it despite the telomere stabilization processes perfected in the 2020s, the hair is a strange vanity.

"It's a feather. I found it on the beach."

I can tell from the way he stills that I've caught his attention. He doesn't turn, though.

"It must mean there are still birds, somewhere."

"Of course there are birds somewhere," he says irascibly, looking up from the microscope finally. The eyes beneath the lively brows are shrewd, despite age-yellowed corneas. "It is statistically unlikely that every bird on the planet perished from the avian flu. There are too many different species and habitats. Use that brain God gave you and don't believe everything you hear. Analysis. Skepticism. Why have I wasted eight years of my life on you? *Hunh.*"

I'm unoffended and undismayed by his scathing tone. He says something similar on a weekly, if not daily basis. "Well, they're gone here."

He plucks the feather from between my fingers and studies it. "Something with a big wingspan. *Diomedea epomophora*, maybe, or *fregata*. Did you know that perhaps eighteen percent of the world's population suffered from ornithophobia? Hard to imagine. Beautiful creatures, birds. Maybe it was the beaks, or the fluttering. Now, if only spiders had died out, instead of birds, imagine the relief, although that would have had a negative impact on the ecosystem, as well. Spiders are important little buggers." He hands the feather back. "You can research it later, if you like, on the computer."

I commit the Latin names to memory. "Thank you. I'll let you know what I find out." Computer time is a gift and I'm excited. It's hard to believe, but in the early twenty-first century, everyone had a computer and could communicate with people all over the globe. Since the Pragmatists took power, only government entities and a chosen few have computers and even they don't have access to international networks, if such still exist.

He takes my hand and lifts it. Startled, I start to tug it away until I realize he's squinting at the red welt near my wrist. "Where did this come from?" he asks.

"I got swarmed. I guess one of the locusts mistook me for a tasty leaf by accident," I say, trying to reclaim my hand. "Or, I banged it on something when I hit the ground."

He lets go reluctantly. "The locusts have adapted disturbingly quickly to our countermeasures, but this . . .."

"'This?' What—you think they've become carnivorous?" I stare at him, incredulous. "Locusts are herbivores."

"I don't think anything, not in advance of the evidence. The welt could be an anomaly, not related to your encounter with the swarm, or it could be something more. The provisional hypothesis, however, deserves consideration and study. Speaking of which, wouldn't it be lovely if you actually got some work done before Assembly?"

Knowing that tone, I put the feather aside, don my lab coat, and return to the data I was analyzing before lunch and my unauthorized beach visit.

Assembly time rolls around and I carefully lock up the samples I was working with before hurrying to join Halla at the transport station. The monthly Assembly is the only regularly authorized out-of-Kube expedition and it's exciting to join the other residents of Jacksonville in the arena for the broadcast. I look for Wyck on the platform and disappointment prickles when I don't see him. He's probably at the arena already. IPF troops file into one compartment, booted feet clanging on the metal flooring. No train travels without an IPF contingent. Halla and I settle onto the bench seats of the train, thigh to thigh with the others kids from the Kube, and head into the city.

You can tell by the number of buildings rising on the horizon that Jacksonville was a big city before the pandemic. Now, though, only a few thousand people live here, most of them within a five mile diameter of the Kube and arena. They get their rations from our dome, so it wouldn't make sense to live far. Half of them work in the desalinization plant, turning sea water into drinking water since many of the land-locked water sources were poisoned by the insecticides two decades back. Half of them work in the fish farms, harvesting and drying the country's most reliable form of protein. The impressive-looking skyscrapers—hard to believe there were once enough people to fill them—are empty shells, unstable, one strong breeze from collapse. Hurricanes have demolished many, and rubble blocks the streets with no one to haul it away. Only a handful of urban outlaws live in the city center, scavenging to survive.

As the train hums toward the arena, I stare out the window at old wheeled automobiles grown over with kudzu, a vine that has adapted so the locusts won't eat it. It's a poisonous chartreuse color now, and secretes a small amount of acid that makes it inedible for the locusts and, unfortunately, for us. I wonder yet again what genomic factors enabled it to mutate so quickly and effectively. Something to do with the alternative respiratory pathway of the kudzu's mitochondria? I file the thought away to discuss with Dr. Ronan. The cars are unrecognizable except for a rusted tailpipe sticking through the vibrant leaves, or a glint off a broken windshield. Hillocks of kudzu mound beside the tracks, evidence of homes or warehouses that were bombed out in the resource wars, abandoned, devoured by termites, or all of the above. It's eerie, the way the vines have taken over, growing a foot a day, impassively strangling the damaged and the intact alike, utterly undiscriminating. I spot what seems to be a mast rising out of the kudzu sea, with a tatter of sail sagging from it. It's a boat washed inland by a hurricane, maybe. The sight depresses me and I turn away.

"Dr. Ronan thinks my feather is from a frigate bird or an albatross," I tell Halla, having looked up the Latin names.

"Great," she says, clearly distracted. Her fingers pluck at the sky blue fabric stretched over her thigh. She leans in, her shoulder pressed against mine, until her mouth is an inch from my ear. "Can we talk, Ev? When we get back from Assembly. I've got to talk to someone, and you're the only one I—" She stops on something suspiciously like a sob.

My brow furrows. Halla is the most upbeat person I know. "What's wrong?" I whisper.

She shakes her head hard. "Not now. We're here."

"Here" is the arena, a former Baptist church built to allow ten thousand people to worship at once. The Pragmatists aren't against religion, but most citizens stopped going to church—or to any other gathering place where they might get infected—round about the second wave of the pandemic. Most never went back, even when the flu threat diminished, because they were out of the habit, or maybe because they'd quit believing. With almost every citizen in the area in attendance, the arena is less than half full. The seats are raked so everyone has a good view of what used to be an altar but is now a podium with a huge screen behind it for the broadcast from Atlanta. It smells faintly of old candle wax, or maybe that's my imagination.

The arena is segregated as usual, with geneborns and their families on the left side of the aisle and nats like us on the right. The proctors have herded everyone from the Kube toward the back and Halla follows me to the second-to-last row. As I crab my way toward the middle, Wyck sidles around the students approaching from the other end and snags the seat beside me. I get a little flutter in my tummy and smile.

"Missed you at the station," he says, dropping into the chair with loose-limbed grace. My age, he has curly brown hair and hazel eyes that seem greener when they sparkle with mischief and browner when he gets moody. He came to the Kube relatively late, when he was almost seven, with a broken arm and lots of bruises, and he was a holy terror initially. He still manages to rack up more demerits than any other kid in the place, and Proctor Fonner told him last month that he's arranged for him to enter border sentry training with the next class. The proctor says the military discipline will be good for him. Wyck says the Atlantic will freeze over before he becomes a border sentry. He's smart enough to be in the Infrastructure Protection Force instead, but he refuses to take the aptitude tests. It might have something to do with his father being an IPF soldier.

"I was late leaving the lab. I was researching this. Look." I pull out the feather and tickle his neck with it.

He scrunches his shoulder up and takes the feather from me. I like the way he handles it, almost reverently. "Wow. It's twink. This means—"

I nod enthusiastically. "I know."

"I'm going to find them one day," he says fiercely, handing the feather back. "Birds. Other people. I'm not staying in Amerada. We can't cower here forever, afraid that if we set foot out of the country we'll bring home a new flu or plague. Who knows what's still out there? There's got to be something, some*one*. You know, in the last century and the first part of this one, we actually traveled in *space*, went to the moon, thought about going to Mars. Now, because we let a bunch of chuffers tell us what to do, we can't even go to Europe or Africa." His eyes burn greenly.

The student on his other side hushes him nervously. He's coming close to criticizing the Pragmatists which is a very, very dangerous thing to do. I squeeze his arm, trying to tell him to pipe down. He jerks away and slumps as a march plays and the screen comes alive. On my other side, Halla crosses her arms and lets her chin drop; no one pays much attention to the propaganda blasts that open each Assembly. There's a montage of IPF troops putting down a Defiance attack against a power generation facility; providing security for Pragmatist ministers traveling through Atlanta; and using full bio-chem intelli-textile suits and breathing gear in a training exercise.

Wyck tenses beside me. "IPF," he mutters. "Automatons. Robots. No minds of their own. Kill first and ask questions later."

"Ssh."

A pregnant woman, wholesome and round, replaces the soldiers on the screen and begins to talk about how privileged she is to serve Amerada as a surrogate. Blah, blah . . . the usual song and dance. We all know how important it is to help rebuild the population, but I can't even imagine being pregnant. I've known several girls from the Kube who volunteered for surrogacy, though. The on-screen woman says how wonderful it is to bear a child for Amerada, and then turn it over to approved parents before pursuing her studies or career with a government stipend.

I glance casually around the arena and my gaze snags on a young man seated a row in front and off to the left, the geneborn side. The way his auburn hair breaks over his ears is familiar, as is the slope of his nose. I tense. It can't be him—they don't live near Jacksonville anymore. I can't look away. Finally, he turns his head slightly to talk to the man beside him. He's got the gold eyes of a geneborn, the engineered genetic marker that sets the geneborn apart, but it's not Keegan. The breath I've been holding wheezes out of me. Even after all this time—twelve years—the possibility of being in the same room, even in a crowd, makes my hands damp with sweat.

A bagpipe flourish announces Premier Dubonnet. Her face fills the screen. Blunt-cut gray bangs brush thin brows, crowding her large features into too small a space. Dewlaps waggle when she talks. The imaging unit pulls back and we can see she is seated at a conference table, surrounded by several stiff-backed ministers. The seal of Amerada above them with its eagle imposed over a maple leaf provides the only color in the room. In the background, IPF troops are ranged along the wall, alert as always.

The Premier speaks enthusiastically about the progress made in cleaning out Amerada's lakes and rivers. Beside me, Halla is unusually still and I give her a worried look. Whatever is on her mind is keeping her from poking fun at the propaganda ads like she usually does, and she hasn't once whispered a comment about the address, or asked me about any of the technical terms the Premier used about the water situation.

Premier Dubonnet talks for another ten minutes before asking the Minister for Science and Food Production to speak. Slim and severe looking, with blond hair scraped back from a high forehead, Minister Alden looks into the imager and explains experimental techniques under development for eliminating the super locust and other crop-devouring insects, and improvements to the crops themselves. I lean forward, interested. Her voice is crisp as a radish and I'm sure she keeps everyone working for her on their toes. Dr. Ronan has spoken about her a couple of times, calling her ambitious and impressive; he taught her at university, I think.

Her remarks about locust eradication fire my imagination, and before I quite realize what I'm doing, I'm on my feet to ask a question. "Minister Alden, Apprentice Citizen Everly Jax from Kube 9. May I ask a question?"

Minister Alden sits taller and sucks in an audible breath, taken aback at my presumption, I assume. There's rustling around the arena and I feel everyone's eyes on me. I wish I hadn't leaped up, but in theory anyone is free to ask questions during an Assembly. No one ever does, though—not without pre-approval. Still, I remain standing. Minister Alden studies me, her lips slightly pursed. She's older than I thought, in her sixties.

"Go ahead, Jax," she nods. Her frown tells me she won't hesitate to rake me down publicly if she thinks I've wasted the Assembly's time.

"You mention trying to eradicate the locusts by inserting sterile males into the population. My experiments suggest that the radiation required to sterilize them frequently leaves them at a competitive disadvantage against non-sterilized males. If that's also your experience, have you found a way to overcome that problem?"

She doesn't answer right away. "That's a superior question, and as you probably can guess, I don't have a full answer yet. I can tell you that we're experimenting with recombinant DNA approaches that might solve that problem." She leans in. "Where did you say you're from?"

"Kube 9." I whisper now, regretting my impulsiveness.

"Perhaps Proctor Fonner will be kind enough to forward me your file." I can tell it's an order, not a "perhaps." "I'm always looking for the best and brightest."

Flushing with relief and gratification—the Minister for Science and Food Production might want me to work for her!—I sink into my seat. The Assembly goes on, but I take in nothing.

Wyck socks my upper arm surreptitiously. "Brass ones, Ev," he whispers.

I shrug, and am relieved when the Premier wraps up by leading us in the pledge of allegiance. We all proclaim, "Amerada before family, before friends, before self. Amerada over all!" before filing out.

Over the babble of conversation on the transport platform, Halla says, "You were so brave. I would never have the nerve to speak up in Assembly."

"I didn't really plan it," I admit.

She giggles, her face momentarily lightening, and says, "Everly Jax spoke before thinking. Aren't you stunned, Wyck?"

He nods solemnly, playing along. "Stunned."

I make a face at them. "Fine. Make fun. But maybe by this time next year, I'll be working for the Ministry of Science and Food Production. You'll be a border sentry repelling immigrants on the Cali-Mex border, and Halla will be—" I don't know where I think Halla will be, but it doesn't matter because something has recalled her worries and she looks like she's trying not to cry. Wyck is pissed that I've brought up his impending sentry duty, and we step onto the train in silence.

There's the usual post-Assembly hubbub of conversation, but my friends are silent, so I stare out the window, almost hypnotized by the train's movement. A girl across from me complains to a friend that she can't find her little pocket mirror. It's silver-backed, special to her. They search the floor. Suddenly, the brakes squeal and a huge impact slams me forward. I grab the underside of the seat as the train lurches to a halt. The force strains my shoulders. The girls across from me sprawl on the floor.

"What the —?" Wyck asks.

I make sure the girls are okay and then stand and press my face against the window's cool surface, straining to see. We're in the second car, close to the front, and I can see something on the tracks, but can't make out what it is. Maybe we've hit a fallen tree.

"I think it's a tree on the tracks," I'm saying when a movement in the kudzu catches my eye. The wind must really be rising. No. The kudzu is creeping up on us, mounds of it detaching from the sea of vines and moving toward the train. "Outlaws!" I gasp.

CHAPTER THREE

Brr-*boom!* The train rocks; we've been hit by a weapon. Something big. I brace my legs wider. Repos who were previously trying, like me, to see what was happening, drop to the floor. Only Wyck and I remain standing. IPF troops deploy from their compartment two behind us, firing as they drop to the ground. A clump of kudzu comes close enough that I can see the face beneath the camouflage. It's all beard and rage, and then it's gone as a particle beam from a soldier's weapon blasts it away. Red mists the window. I jerk back involuntarily.

"Bastards," Wyck screams. He thumps on the window. "You didn't have to beam him."

I'm startled to realize he's yelling at the soldiers. One passes beneath us, anonymous and insectoid behind his bio-chem mask and helmet. I don't suppose he can hear

Wyck, but I'm not taking the chance. Hooking an arm around his shoulders, I say, "Get down."

I drop, taking Wyck with me and bruising my knees. Most kids have their arms over their heads. Two or three of the younger ones are crying. Halla's got her arm around a little boy, trying to comfort him, even though her face says she's as scared as he is. He clings to her, calmed by that quality in her that makes all the under-tens love and trust her. She starts singing a simple melody I imagine she learned from her grandmother and some of the little ones join in. "Jesus loves the little children . . ."

"Why would outlaws attack us?" I ask Wyck. We're huddled together, and even in the chaos of the attack, I'm conscious of his bony shoulder knocking against mine, and of his breath on my cheek. "We don't have any food."

"Not outlaws," Wyck says. "Defiers."

"Here?" He's wrong. The Defiance operates much farther west, harassing the government troops defending pioneer outposts and generally being a nuisance. They wouldn't dare come this close to Atlanta. The government has this area secured.

"They've been moving east and I heard they captured a weapons depot north of New Orleans," Wyck says. An almost admiring note in his voice makes me uneasy. Surely Wyck doesn't sympathize with—

A crack, as of a window shattering, sounds from the first compartment and the floor shudders. I hear screams.

"What's happening?" someone calls out, hysteria pitching her voice high.

The distinctive whine and blast of beamers drowns her out. I risk a peek and see soldiers' gray backs as they pursue the attackers into the dense undergrowth. Micro-drones are overhead now, tracking the fleeing men. An outlaw—or a Defier, if Wyck's right—lies near the tracks, shredded kudzu leaves forming a corona around him, limbs flung out. There's a dark splotch in his mid-section and, as I stare in horror, his chest heaves in and out rapidly, six, eight times, and a bloody froth bubbles from his mouth. His muscles seize, and then he stills. I'm willing him to breathe, watching for his chest to inflate again. *Come on*, I urge silently. Nothing.

I slump, and stare blindly ahead. *He was an outlaw*, I tell myself. That doesn't make me feel any better. Wyck puts an awkward arm around me, but I stay stiff. The fight has moved away from the train and it's quiet now, except for sniffles and heavy breathing. Dusk is falling and soon it's hard to make out faces. We're all still, waiting. Halla, two toddlers sharing her lap, slips her hand into mine and I squeeze it.

"'I will fear no evil, for you are with me; your rod and your staff, they comfort me,'" Halla recites quietly under her breath.

Wyck jumps up like a spring compressed too long. "I'm going to find out what's happening." Before he can move, the train's announcement system crackles and Proctor Fonner's voice flows calmly through the speaker.

"Everything is fine. There is nothing to worry about. Our IPF commander assures me the threat is neutralized. Resume your seats. The train will start up again momentarily. Our Kube medical team will meet us on the platform and assist those needing medical care. All others are to report directly to their rooms and remain there. Curfew is in effect until zero-six-hundred tomorrow morning. Anyone caught breaking it will be subject to severe discipline. Thank you for your bravery and control under difficult conditions. Well done."

Like robots, we push ourselves up and settle on the bench seats. It's too dark now to assess the damage to the compartment that was hit. Apparently it wasn't knocked off the tracks because we're underway with a grinding sound within ten minutes. At the Kube transport station, we file off the train quietly. The proctors are waving us along, directing us into the Kube, but I glimpse the starburst hole in the side of the first compartment, the metal curved inward in sharp, jagged triangles. I see splattered blood and someone's lower leg jerking before the medical cadre hustles up and sets a screen between us and the damaged train car. I swallow hard.

"—damn laser scalpel is cutting out," a tense voice growls from behind the screen. "The energy pack isn't—"

On the words, Wyck darts away and around the screen, pulling the ever-present tool pouch from his belt. The proctors let him through; everyone knows that Wyck can fix anything.

Looking around as I follow Halla inside, I try to see if anyone I know is missing. I don't see Yuna—her ginger head is usually easy to spot—or the six-foot-seven Dal. They're already inside, I tell myself. Safe.

The Kube's living quarters are laid out with four towers connected by a central dining and common area on the first floor. "Tower" is something of a misnomer, since the complex is only four stories high, but that's what we've always called them. The building was once an office complex, but the government repurposed it as an InKubator, which helps explains why the vibe is impersonal and utilitarian rather than homey. Proctor Fonner's personality has a lot to do with that, too, I've always suspected. The northeast tower holds the infants and nursery children. The southeast tower houses repos five to ten years old, and the southwest tower is for the proctors and staff. Halla and Wyck and I, along with the other eleven- to sixteen-year-olds, live in the northwest tower. Gleaming white subway tiles lit by overhead fixtures make the common area, the building's former lobby, almost painfully bright. I blink. Obedient to the direction of the proctors, who seem tenser than normal, I let myself be herded toward the elevators. I get into the glass capsule, squished against Halla and some younger girls.

When the doors *whish* open on Halla's level, she gets off slowly. When the others have passed her, she turns around and mouths "Please" to me before the doors shut again. Her brown eyes shimmer with unshed tears. For a moment, I'm puzzled, but then I remember her plea to talk. We're under curfew—there's no way we can get together.

"Do you . . . do you think anyone was badly hurt?"

It takes a moment for the words to register, but then I look at the fourteen-year-old whose room is two doors down from mine. Her fingers twist a hank of mousy hair.

She's looking at me hopefully, as if I'll deny what we both suspect.

"There's no way to know if—" I start to say, but then switch to the truth. "Probably."

The word hangs there for a moment, but then Shaliqua, who lives at the end of the hall, spits out, "Damn those outlaws! Damn them. I hope the IPF shot them, every one of them." Her fists are clenched at her sides and her thin frame is trembling with fury, or reaction to the day's events. The two boys standing behind me murmur agreement.

Remembering the outlaw I saw die, I say nothing, merely stepping off the elevator when it opens, and walking directly to my room. It's tiny and utilitarian, with a single bed and nightstand, hooks and shelves for clothes and my few personal items, including my *Little House on the Prairie*, and a toilet and sink in an alcove. Hygiene facilities with showers are communal, down the hall. As one of the oldest repos, I've got a corner room with floor to ceiling windows on two sides. During the day, I can glimpse the sea. It's dark now, though, and all I can see is the dim glow from the dome and the harsh glare of the perimeter lights. There's a lot of activity at the IPF compound, a stone's throw away, and it seems there are more soldiers than usual on patrol.

Hungry, I eat a vegeprote bar, then sponge bathe rather than go down to the hyfac. I try to read a paper on epigenetics that Dr. Ronan assigned me, but I can't focus. Halla's face keeps intruding. *I can't violate curfew*, I tell her image. *I can't. Day after tomorrow's April twelfth. Reunion Day. I can't risk it. Surely whatever you want to talk about will keep until morning*. I keep seeing her mouth form the word "Please." Damn it. I fling my reader onto the bed and knuckle my eyes until lights flash behind them. In my mind, the ghostly shapes of my parents struggle with the solid form of my best friend.

I pick up my *Little House on the Prairie* and hold it loosely. It's the only thing I have from before the Kube, my only link with my parents. It's an actual book with a picture of a little girl in braids on the cover, her parents and a log cabin in the background. I've read it so many times I can recite large chunks, and I don't read it now. Just holding it comforts me and brings me closer to the parents who sent it with me for some reason. I've searched it for messages, but there's not so much as a name on the flyleaf or an underlined passage. I wonder sometimes if it means my parents were pioneers at an outpost. Mostly, though, I think they were trying to tell me that they love me like Ma and Pa Ingalls loved Laura. I stroke the cover and put it back.

I can't not go. I can feel that Halla really needs me. Mind made up, I remove my boots, sling my bag across my chest, and cross to the door. I ease it open. The hall is dark, but not black, with dim biolume fixtures set on the wall every fifty feet. Scanning left and right, I see no one. The stairs are six doors down. I glide toward them.

I try the stairway door. Locked. I'm not surprised. This isn't exactly the first time I've gone sneaking around after hours. I pull the mini EMP gadget Wyck built me from my bag and hold it against the maglock armature. He talked about solenoids and soft iron cores when he gave it to me, but the only part I care about is that the electromagnetic pulse disrupts the lock's power supply for a half-second. *Bzzt.* I pull the door open, mildly triumphant. The stairwell is can't-see-my-hand-in-front-of-my-face dark. Putting one hand on the wall, I step down. I grope for the door when I reach the next landing.

All is silent and still on Halla's floor, and moments later I'm tapping gently on her door. It opens immediately and then Halla is hugging me. I catch a whiff of body odor under her natural cinnamony scent. She hasn't washed or changed.

"You came," she breathes. The fruitiness of ketosis tells me it's been a long time since she ate.

I hug her back hard. "Of course I came," I say, as if there was never any doubt. I'm glad I did. In the dim light from the table lamp her eyes are red and swollen. A pile of sodden tissues on the bed testifies to quarts of tears; she should be dehydrated by now. "Did you eat anything?"

She shakes her head and blinks back more tears, trying to speak. Pulling a vegeprote bar out of my bag, I hand it to her. "Eat first," I insist, whispering. We can't afford to be heard and informed on. *I* can't afford it.

She sags onto the bed and bites through the edible wrapper. I fetch a glass of water and hand it to her. It chatters against her teeth as she drinks. I take it, place it on the nightstand next to her open Bible, and sit beside her. She takes another bite of the energy bar, and says something unintelligible.

"What?"

She swallows hard.

"I'm pregnant."

"What!" I jerk and my elbow smacks the water glass. It falls to the tile floor and smashes.

We freeze, listening for any indication that someone heard us. There's no sound from the next rooms. Glass slivers glitter on the floor, but neither of us makes a move to sweep them up.

I relax slightly, ashamed that my first reaction is hurt that Halla didn't tell me that she and Loudon were even having sex. What do I say now? "How pregnant?" Stupid question. Pregnant is totally pregnant, no gradations.

"Six months."

"Oh, Halla." I'm sad that she's kept this secret alone for so long. I'd noticed she was getting a bit plumper, but she's always been on the round side, so I hadn't thought much of it. "Does Loudon know?"

She shakes her head and the tears stream again. Last time I saw her this upset was the day Loudon left to start his IPF training. Coincidentally, that was six months ago.

Handing her more tissues, I say, "It isn't the end of the world. You'll have the baby, it'll be sent to another Kube, and you can—"

"I want to keep my baby." She puts a protective hand on her belly. "Our baby—mine and Loudon's."

Oh. Different story. No way is that possible. She doesn't have a husband or a procreation license, and hasn't contributed the mandatory nation service that would earn her the right to have a baby and keep it. This baby was conceived without a license: the law says it belongs to the state. I don't bother telling Halla that—she knows it.

"This baby is God's gift to me, me and Loudon. The government shouldn't be able to take him away because we don't have a license and haven't done our service yet." Her lower lip sticks out. "I'm not going to let them. I'll die first."

Normally a gentle person, Halla has a stubborn streak and I know she means it.

"What are you . . . how do you plan to—?"

She looks me in the eyes, her own red-rimmed, but determined. "I'm running away."

"You can't!"

"I have to."

The difficulties that will confront her swirl in my mind. How will she find food? What about shelter? She'll be an enemy of the state—hunted. Her family is dead, so they can't help. Her parents died when she was one and her grandmother took her in; she lived not far from the coast in the Delta Canton, a land of swamps, drawling speech, hurricanes and religious enclaves that were among the last hold-outs against the Pragmatist government. When her grandmother disappeared and was presumed dead, Halla came here. She's soft and gentle, not a fighter. She'll fall prey to one of the roving bands of outlaws. Horrible images hold me silent. "Where will you go?" I finally ask.

"To Loudon." Her soft mouth sets mulishly. "I heard from him a week ago. He's finished his training and been assigned to an IPF base outside of Atlanta."

"You haven't told him?"

She shakes her head, dense curls dancing. "How could I? You know the Prags are reading and listening to everything."

I nod. I wonder what Loudon's reaction will be if she reaches him. I know he loves her; I watched their friendship turn into something more in the year before he left. But it takes a special kind of love to give up everything familiar and safe, and make yourself a fugitive for your beloved's sake.

"He loves me," she says fiercely, as if reading my mind.

"I'm sure he does," I say, "but that doesn't fix anything. Even if you get to him . . ."

We both know her troubles aren't over. Even if she manages to find Loudon, he's still an IPF recruit with six years to serve on his mandatory enlistment, not allowed to marry until he's done. They still don't have a procreation license.

"We'll go west," Halla says, "to a pioneer outpost. They need all the people they can get." She nods hard twice, more assuring herself that her plan is workable than trying to convince me. "Loudon and I are strong—we'll be good pioneers."

Yeah, right. The chances of a pregnant woman and a deserter reaching an outpost are non-existent. They'll be hunted down and captured before they reach the Mississippi.

"There's got to be another option. Let's think abou—"

"I have my semi-annual physical day Thursday," Halla says. Today is Monday. "The doctor will find out. I have to leave before then. Will you help me?" Her eyes plead with me.

I'm sure the most helpful thing I can do is talk her out of this insane plan. I try. I bring up the hardships she'll face traveling to Atlanta, the dangers, the very real possibility of her being tracked down and captured. I imagine she'd get prison time, or worse. She listens with an expression that says she's hearing me out to be polite, but her mind is made up. I need to jar her back to reality.

I stab her with, "You're going to kill this baby. You won't have enough to eat, so the baby will starve. It's little better than murder."

When she pales, I'm immediately ashamed. "I'm sorry. I didn't mean—"

She stands, looking shaken but resolute, and says, "I have to do this."

Suddenly, I'm angry. "You don't! You're going to end up dead and your baby with you. Or you're going to end up in prison and your baby will end up who knows where. How is that better?" I try to sound calm and reasonable when inside I'm so afraid. "You're not thinking this through. You're making an emotional decision, not a logical one. The Prags have the best plan, one that benefits the baby and the country. Let them raise the baby. They did okay with us. They'll make sure the baby is educated so it can—"

"Him! Not *it*—him!" Halla's chin juts out. "You say 'emotional' like it's a bad thing. It's not. Everything's not about smart and rational and intellectual and data. Some things are about *feelings*. Love. Not that you would know.

And don't bother to hit me over the head with science and tell me my hormones are out of whack, because I know that. I've been puking my guts up and crying for no reason for months—I freaking know that. But they haven't changed who I am or messed me up like a Dr. Jekyll potion. There's science for you! I love Little Loudon and I know—I *know*—that he belongs with me. We belong together. I thought you would help me. I thought you were my friend." She breathes hard through her nose, her chest rising and falling.

"I am your friend." It comes out as a whisper, even though I mean it with all my heart.

"Not the friend I need right now. Go, Everly. Just go."

"Halla, I can help. I'll—"

She shakes her head vehemently, unable to speak. When I don't move, she walks around me and opens the door. Her head tipped down, she motions for me to leave.

I get to the threshold and hesitate. When she doesn't look up, I step into the hall. The door closes behind me with a snap that should have me looking over my shoulder, hoping no one heard it, but I'm on the verge of tears, choked up about losing Halla. Part of my sadness is for her, and part for me. I'll never see her again if she runs away. I can't stand it. I rest my forehead against her closed door. "Don't go," I whisper.

Nothing happens. Halla doesn't emerge. I don't knock.

I make the stealthy trek back to my room, thinking about Halla. She's been my best friend forever. We played pretend together when we were little, with me the daughter and Halla the mommy, or me the scientist making save-the-world discoveries and Halla sometimes my lab assistant and sometimes an insect I was dissecting. The world's only giggling cockroach: "Being dissected *tickles*," she used to say. When we got older and spent more time in classes, we always sat side by side until one exasperated proctor or another separated us to keep us from talking. I helped her keep up in science classes so we wouldn't get split up. She smuggled me rations when I did something that got me confined to quarters. I can't imagine being here without her.

As I enter my room, I have a thought that makes me let go of the door so it bangs shut. I wince. I can save Halla by telling Proctor Fonner about her plan. They'll keep her under guard until she has the baby, and then take it to another Kube. That would be the right thing to do, for the baby, Halla, and the nation, but it feels incredibly wrong. *Amerada over all*, I remind myself. She'll hate me forever for separating her from Little Loudon, but wouldn't that be better than letting her go off to die somewhere between here and Atlanta? I worry about it for hours, tossing and turning so much the covers wrap me like a mummy and I have to get up to untangle them. Yes, I finally decide, it would, but can I make myself do it? Can I betray her to Proctor Fonner? I punch my pillow. I'm ninety percent certain she'll die if she runs away on her own, her and the baby both. I can't have that on my conscience, even though keeping her here against her will, hating me, will be unendurable. I can't understand why she wants to keep the baby so badly, but I understand that she does, and I know she'll never, ever forgive me for what I'm going to do. I cry myself to sleep.

CHAPTER FOUR

At breakfast the next morning after the mandatory physical fitness period, I'm heavy-eyed and draggy, uninterested in food. Halla and I exchange a brief, unsmiling look when we enter, and she chooses to sit across the table and well down from me, rather than at my side. She looks as bad as I feel. It's painful to think that we've probably exchanged our last words, because she'll never talk to me again after I tell. Proctor Fonner glides in after we get seated and steps onto the small dais where the proctors stand to read to us or lecture as we eat. His presence is unusual and his aspect solemn. From the thick silence that smothers conversation, I think we all know what's coming.

Looking down his long nose, and with his hands clasped at waist height, Proctor Fonner says, "I regret to inform you that our Kube community, our nation, has lost two of its valuable members, Dal Spaeth and Yuna Nieves. They were killed in yesterday's unconscionable attack on our train. Additionally, Proctor Jeffson suffered serious head and spine injuries—she's paralyzed from the neck down—and has been transported to Atlanta for treatment."

There's a collective gasp. Yuna was four years younger and I didn't know her well, but she seemed to be a sweet girl, always smiling, with a gap between her two top teeth that somehow made her smile infectious. Dal was my age, but a little slow, almost simple, so we hadn't been in the same academic track. Still, I've known him forever and I feel his loss more keenly than I would have expected. I push my plate away. Muffled sobs and sniffles sound from all sides.

"The Premier and her ministers are outraged by the increasing boldness of the Defiance and she has promised to send an additional IPF contingent to find and neutralize the individuals who participated in yesterday's lawless attack," Fonner continues, letting righteous anger creep into his voice.

"It was the Defiance, then?"

Oh, no. The voice is Wyck's, too interested, and I turn my head to see him half out of his chair. *Sit down and shut up.* I scrunch my eyes closed as if that will keep the inevitable from happening.

"Has the Defiance—"

"The perpetrators were murderers, plain and simple," Fonner interrupts him coldly. "Report to my office after classes today, AC Sharpe." His voice smoothes out again. "Every premature death is a blow to our nation's stability, but especially so when the deceased were so young and vital and still had so much to contribute. This is a very sad day, a tragic loss. We will have an appropriate memorial for our lost colleagues on Friday, but for now I ask for a minute of silence on their behalf."

I bow my head and think about how Dal, always big for his age, used to pick me up under the arms when we were six or seven, and swing me around so my feet flew out and it felt like I was flying. He'd laugh and I'd laugh and he'd spin me until he got dizzy and we both fell. I haven't thought of that in years. *Poor Dal.* I'm lost in my memories when the sound of my name startles me.

"—and AC Jax report to my office before the afternoon service period." He descends from the dais and leaves, his straight back telling me nothing.

Why have I been summoned? Who else's names did he call? I look around, and the girl beside me gives me a tiny, puzzled shrug. Maybe it's for the best. I can tell Proctor Fonner about Halla when I see him.

I get nothing out of my morning class, a physics lesson with Proctor Lutz who stammers. I'm too busy agonizing over Halla, mourning Yuna and Dal, and worrying about my summons to the Supervising Proctor's office. When he wraps up the lesson, Proctor Lutz reminds me of the appointment and I get into the elevator nervously. Has

Proctor Fonner decided on my punishment? *Not Reunion Day, not Reunion Day,* I think. *Don't let him take it away.*

Wyck is waiting in the anteroom when I arrive, chatting with Proctor's Fonner's aide as if he doesn't have a care in the world. My first thought is that I can't tell Proctor Fonner about Halla if Wyck's there. He winks at me as I come in. Rolling my eyes, I enter Proctor Fonner's lair. He's seated behind his desk, erect and severe as always, and he eyes us dispassionately as we stand in front of him. He gets right to it.

"AC Sharpe, AC Jax. I've selected you to carry out a special task this afternoon during service hours."

Is his pause to gather his thoughts or heighten the tension? I'm guessing the latter.

"Someone must undertake the sad duty of inventorying and packing up AC Spaeth's and AC Nieves' effects. I have selected the two of you."

Relief whooshes through me. This is my punishment for the beach. It's a sad task, but he's not taking away Reunion Day. I sneak a sidelong glance at Wyck who seems equally relieved that he's not being disciplined more severely.

"I trust you will carry out this duty with decorum and thoroughness."

I nod and Wyck says, "Yes, sir."

A slight lift of Proctor Fonner's brows dismisses us. Wyck holds the door for me. I hesitate for a moment, but Proctor Fonner is engrossed in work on his desk and Wyck is waiting. I'll tell him later. Feeling cowardly, I hurry out.

Back in the anteroom, we let out simultaneous sighs of relief and it almost makes me giggle. Then I remember what we're tasked to do and I sober up. The aide gives us the room locations and we head for Dal's room first. Two empty cartons are stacked in the hall. Only two. A palm sized imager for making an inventory record sits atop them. Wyck immediately grabs up the gadget, along with a box. I lift the other box. Wyck pushes open the door without hesitating, but his movements are jerky and I know he's as uncomfortable as I am.

Dal's room is furnished like all the rooms, but his is messier than most, with the bedclothes draping onto the floor, spare jumpsuit crumpled beneath a hook, and oddments piled high on shelves. Scraps of paper, pinecones from the dome, funny shaped rocks, used up toothpaste tubes and other things I'd classify as junk litter every flat surface.

Wyck looks around. "Dal was quite the collector."

I nod, set my box down, and open the top drawer of the nightstand. Wyck scans the shelves with the imager, and then picks up the other box and looks at the litter, irresolute. "Should I box this stuff up or just throw it away?"

"Box it," I say without hesitation. "It was important to Dal."

"I wonder where it goes?"

I don't know, so I don't say anything. The top drawer contains nothing but underthings and I layer them into the box, not sure why I'm not just flipping the drawer over and dumping the contents. The bottom drawer contains more "treasures," I see, but Wyck distracts me from inspecting them.

"They died instantly," he says, not looking at me, seemingly focused on putting what seems to be a kudzu leaf collection into his box.

I remember that he went behind the screen to fix something when the medics were trying to save Yuna and Dal. I hadn't thought about his seeing them.

"The explosion got them both. Yuna had a two-foot piece of metal straight through her heart, and Dal's neck was broken by the force of the explosion. Proctor Jeffson wasn't so lucky. I'd rather die quick than end up like her. Not being able to walk or feed yourself—" He shudders. "I want it to be quick when it happens. No pain, no lingering, and for certain sure no fire. Drowning might not be so bad."

My lungs ache and my throat closes against the water. It invades my nostrils and I watch little bubbles drift to the surface. My limbs thrash. The gold eyes above me, blurred by the water between us, seem full of dancing flames. Need to breathe . . . I suck in a breath, and blurt, "Drowning's horrible."

Wyck gives me a look, startled by my vehemence, and says, "How do you want to die?"

"This is a morbid conversation." I fling items in the box, completely unaware of what they are.

Undeterred, Wyck says, "I could die a hero's death, throw myself on a vaporization grenade to save my troops. Gone"—he snaps his fingers—"just like that. That wouldn't be a bad way to go."

"I thought you didn't want to be a soldier."

49

Wyck shrugs, annoyed, and a handful of dried kudzu leaves flutter down. "A sergeant in my dad's unit died like that the week I got repoed. Not my dad, that's for sure. I want my death to mean something, that's all."

"Better for your life to mean something." A glint from the bottom of the drawer catches my eye. It's a mirror. A palm-sized, silver-backed mirror like the girls were searching for on the train. There's a bracelet, too, with heavy links; a knife with a short, shiny blade; a six-inch square remnant of reflective mesh; and a ring made of intertwined metals. *Uh-oh.* I rock back on my heels. Dal was the thief. My brow crinkles as I try to reconcile the happy, somewhat simple Dal I knew with this evidence. I use a forefinger to rearrange the objects; they are all so shiny. I know suddenly that it's the shininess that attracted Dal. I can see him when we were younger, fascinated by a hematite specimen that the geology proctor passed around. Dal turned it over and over, staring at it, mouth agape, until the next kid in line wrestled it away. I scoop the objects into my messenger bag. Wyck's busy imaging the items he's packed up and doesn't notice. I'll get these things back to their owners somehow. I'm not branding Dal as a thief. He wasn't, not in his heart. I don't want him remembered that way.

Wyck approaches with the imager and inventories the items in the box. "Not much, is it?"

"No." I think of the feather, my *Little House* book, and the clothes and toiletries in my room. What would someone sorting through my effects think about me? Would my feather be dismissed as "nature junk," the way Wyck and I

50

have written off Dal's treasures? Would the person dropping *Little House on the Prairie* into a box assume I was slow, that I read on an eight-year-old level? Stuff lies, I decide.

I stand, and the items in my bag clink. I must look funny, because Wyck asks, "You okay?"

There's concern in his voice and I tear up, even though I didn't know I was feeling so sad. That's the thing about Wyck—one minute he's talking about how cool it would be to get vaporized, and the next he's tuned into my feelings, sometimes before I am.

"Yeah," I sniff. "Okay enough."

He puts an arm around my shoulders and hugs me against his side. "I can do Yuna's room by myself."

I let myself lean into him for a moment. He's warm, comforting, skinny enough I can feel individual ribs. Before the embrace can get awkward, I ease away, saying, "Thanks, but I'll help."

There's something indefinably feminine about Yuna's room, even though she has the same furniture as Dal. Maybe it's the neatness, with every toiletry item carefully aligned on the shelf, or maybe it's the scent, a hint of baby powder in the air. It takes us less than twenty minutes to inventory and pack her things.

"She was only twelve," Wyck mutters, imager held high to document it all. "Twelve." Laying the imager on a shelf, he crosses to the door and closes it. He returns, halting only a foot away from me, his expression intense.

He's going to kiss me. Finally. Anticipation rises in me like helium, making me light-headed. I angle my face slightly and sway—

"Halla told me she told you."

I stagger back a step. I feel stupid for thinking— "She told you? When?" I immediately realize how stupid it is to care whether Halla told Wyck about her pregnancy before she told me.

He sits on the bed. "This morning. She says she's leaving. I'm going with her."

His announcement hits me like an axe in the stomach. I deflate onto the bed beside him. "What?" I whisper.

"She needs me," he says, almost angrily. "No one needs me here."

"That's not true!" *I need you.* "You fix—"

He grabs my shoulders and makes me face him. His eyes burn greenly. "Halla *needs* me. She'll probably die out there on her own—"

At least we agree on something.

"I mean, what are her chances? She's not tough to start with, and she's pregnant."

"Did she say anything else?" *About our fight?*

"Like what?"

I guess not. My fingers pluck at the coverlet hard enough to yank fibers from the decorative tufts. "She shouldn't go."

"Of course not, but she's going to. And so am I." He firms his mouth into a thin, resolute line.

With Wyck along, Halla has a chance. Maybe fifty-fifty. Not great, but good enough that I let go of my plan to tell Proctor Fonner, a plan I hated anyway. But they'll both be gone . . . I'll be alone. *Halla's stealing Wyck away. I wasn't a good enough friend to offer to go with her. I'll have nobody.* The thoughts stream through my mind, a jumbled mix of panic and fury. "Wyck, don't—"

"Fonner handed me my orders for border sentry training last night," he says. "I've got a ticket on tomorrow's train to Base Kestrel."

"Oh, Wyck." He's always said nothing could make him undertake military duty of any kind. "Oh, Wyck. There's got to be another option. Running away—"

"There's not." He tucks a strand of hair behind my ear. "You're needed here, Ev. You're going to be the one who finds a way to eradicate the locusts—I know it. Me . . . yeah, I come up with some useful gadgets now and then, tinker with stuff and fix it, but no one will miss me anymore than they'll miss . . . than they'll miss Yuna."

"I'll miss you." *He can't go.* I lean forward an inch, almost working up my nerve to kiss him. I don't know if he likes me that way. Kissing him might embarrass him and then I'd be humiliated and he'd leave with the awkwardness uppermost . . .

He rises, and my shoulders slump. The moment is gone. Picking up his box, he crosses to the door. "We should go."

"Just a minute."

Yuna's bed is rumpled, an offense against her evident neatness. I make it. Wyck hovers in the doorway while I plump the pillow. As I smooth the last wrinkle from her coverlet and scoop up the threads I pulled loose, I wonder who will miss her, who will remember her a year from now, five years from now. You're not really gone until no one remembers you. I lift my box, join Wyck, and close the door softly.

CHAPTER FIVE

Sunshine knifes through my window to wake me on Reunion Day. Despite lack of sleep, I hum with excitement. Worry and sadness about Wyck and Halla take the edge off my anticipation and for a moment I resent Halla for stupidly getting pregnant, for insisting on keeping the baby, for leaving and for taking Wyck with her. I'm ashamed of those feelings and try to make them go away.

I take extra time getting ready after morning calisthenics. I'm stuck wearing the sky blue jumpsuit, but I brush my blond hair until it gleams, wondering if my mother, or maybe someone in my father's family, has hair this color. I lean in toward the small mirror. My eyes with the charcoal ring around the marine blue irises . . . do I have aunts or uncles or a grandparent with that same dark gray ring? I abandon preening and ride down in the elevator, stomach clenched, ignoring the buzz of conversation around me. I don't see Halla in the cafeteria. I sit by myself, too keyed up to chat with friends, even Wyck who is letting his breakfast congeal while he uses the miniature tools he invented to tweak something in Johan's prosthetic hand. Johan twists and bends his wrist and claps Wyck on the back with a broad grin when he's done. I eat without tasting anything, and jump when the announcement booms loudly: "All apprentice citizens participating in Reunion Day, report to Room 104."

I go to stand, but my knees tremble so badly I sink down again. *Get a grip, Everly.* I push back up and make my way with the others—twelve of us total—to Room 104. Wyck gives me a thumbs up. I smell nerves the moment I enter the room. It's small, square, white, and brightly lit, although one bulb is flickering. My first Amerada History class was in this room, and I flash on my seven-year-old self taking a quiz, trying to remember if the capital city was spelled "Atalanta" or "Atlanta." There's still a series of maps projected on the plasma wall, showing the old United States and Canada with their states and provinces, a map of the country during the Between with its secessions and ever-changing alliances, and the current Amerada with its cantons and outposts. My gaze flicks off the maps to the other repos.

Everyone is as nervous and excited as I am. We're evenly divided, boys and girls, sitting in chairs spaced along the room's perimeter. One boy's foot jitters hard and fast enough to churn butter. Another gnaws on his cuticles. A girl is blinking repeatedly. No one talks. I know them all, of course. Some I like, some not so much. We know the drill. We're to sit here quietly and wait for a summons. Someone will come for us and lead us to a room where our parents will be waiting. We have two hours to get acquainted. Two hours! It might as well be two seconds. Still, it's better than nothing. We're allowed to stay in touch with our families once we've been reunited, and can earn passes to visit them until we leave Kube 9 for advanced training and our first service posting.

The door opens. Twelve pairs of eyes lock onto the proctor standing in the doorway. She pauses a beat to ratchet up the tension, I'm sure, and then says, "AC Danza Myring."

Danza, a delicate girl with flyaway copper hair, gasps, pops up, and hurries to the door. She trips, but catches herself on a chair. Then she's gone and the door closes again. *Click.*

We wait. I wonder if the waiting is to teach us patience, or if our parents are arriving at different times. Some of them have traveled from a distance, I guess.

It's at least fifteen minutes before the door opens again and another name is called. The remaining ten of us watch enviously as Bram saunters out, the tic under his left eye belying his seeming cool. *Click.*

The floodgates open and six names are called within ten minutes. Six excited repos disappear through the door. Two more go half an hour later. There are only two of us left. Patam and I exchange sidelong glances and go back to staring at our boots, our fingernails, anything but each other. It's been over an hour. My anticipation is turning to worry.

A footstep sounds outside the door. My head jerks up. I watch the knob turn. The door sighs inward. A proctor steps in. There's a rushing sound in my ears. I can't hear what she says, but her lips move. Did they form the words "Everly Jax?" I'm sure they did. I lean forward, start to push up. Patam stands, relief lighting his face, and strides toward the proctor. *Click.*

I am alone.

Where are they? My tummy growls and I put a hand to it. *Why aren't they here yet?* I push back my cuticles with a thumbnail, rub a smudge off my soft boot with spit, and climb on a chair to tighten the sputtering light bulb. I sit again. My gaze lights on the maps and I mentally reel off the key dates we had to memorize in Amerada History: 2020, First Wave of avian influenza begins; 2022, international travel suspended; 2026, official proclamation of famine; 2030, dissolution of United States; 2045, Pragmatists come to power. I recite the names of Amerada's six premiers in order. I finally resort to counting off the minutes in my head: one-Amerada, two-Amerada, three-Amerada . . .

I don't know how long it is before I know. My parents aren't coming. I know it long before the proctor opens the door, gives me a sympathetic look, and says, "I'm sorry, AC Jax."

She leaves.

Click.

People's parents always show up for Reunion Day, unless they're dead. Parents dying is not an unusual reason for kids to end up in the Kube, especially kids my age because there was still a lot of flu when we were young. It's almost as common as parents being unlicensed or unfit. A few kids, like Wyck, opt out of Reunion Day. I suppose it's remotely possible someone's parents could die after their kid is repoed and Proctor Fonner not be informed, but DNA is logged for every birth, marriage and death, so it's an extremely rare death that doesn't get entered into the system. I try to think of others reasons for their non-appearance, but my brain won't work. Heartbreak is short-circuiting my synapses. Tears prick behind my lids, but I will them back. I meet two of the repos who met their parents today and brush past, pretending I don't hear their questions about my reunion.

I'm going to the beach. I need the surge and splash of the waves to fill up this gaping hole that has opened within me, this emptiness that is like nothing I've ever felt. Sentries and being put on report be damned. What are they going to do to me now? They can't take Reunion Day away from me. Someone's already done that. I blast into the dome, planning to sneak out the east gate closest to the beach. I'm imagining the sand abrading my bare feet, when Dr. Ronan approaches, lab coat flapping around his knees. Damn the luck. I try to wipe the tears away with the back of my hand.

"There you are, Jax," he says. "Where the hell have you been? I'm afraid the data from the histocompatibility experiment were corrupted. I need you to re-run the last hundred samples through electrophoresis again. Come along."

My swollen eyes and dejected aspect completely escape him. Dr. Ronan doesn't notice anything that's not on a slide or growing in a Petri dish. Part of me is relieved, the other part hurt or maybe pissed off. I've spent more time with him than with any other single person in this Kube and my unhappiness should matter to him.

"Today was Reunion Day," I say pointedly, hurrying after him. We're passing the tanks where other scientists are working on a new fertilizer and it smells rank. Holding my breath, I say nasally, "My parents didn't come."

"Of course not," he says tetchily, disappearing into a field of gold-tinged genetically modified wheat. "Really, Jax, use that brain God gave you." He breaks off a head, pops it in his mouth, and chews it thoughtfully. Despite his height and leonine appearance, he looks like a cow working a cud.

I stop dead. "What do you mean 'Of course not?'"

"Definitely bitter enough to discourage the locusts, I would think," he says. "We'll need to see if the flavor dissipates with cooking heat, however, like we postulated. We need to name the new strain—any ideas?"

"What do you know about my parents?" I ask, stopping him by tugging his sleeve.

"Why, nothing, of course. No one does."

"That's ridiculous. The Ministry of Reproduction couldn't have repossessed me without having a file on my parents, my mother at least." It isn't possible.

"That's just it," Ronan says. "They didn't repossess you. Your parents left you at the Kube when you were an infant. Abandoned you. Well, someone did, at any rate. We have no empirical evidence that it was your parents." He breaks off another head of wheat and tastes it with his tongue, as if he hasn't brought my world crashing down.

I sway. "What?" It comes out as a whisper. I clear my throat and say louder, "You're lying."

He turns an astonished face to me. "Lying? Leaving aside the impugning of my integrity, what would I have to gain by lying to you? I can't recall that I've ever bothered to lie." He pauses to consider, shakes his head as if nothing comes to mind, then continues. "Things that happen outside the lab don't always catch my interest, but there was such a kerfuffle about your arrival, in *such* a way, that I took note. Why, it was the talk of the staff dining room for a month. Boring, I thought it at the time. Another baby. I failed to see why you caused such excitement. However, I'm pleased to report that you have turned out to be a most satisfactory addition to InKubator 9. Most satisfactory." He gives me a small, approving smile, and begins to talk about the wheat again, as if the matter of my birth and arrival at the Kube is now closed.

"Why wasn't I told?" I burst out. How many *years* had I spent looking forward to Reunion Day, imagining what my parents would look like, what they would say? Imagining the first hug from my mother, the way she would smell of gardenia or maybe vanilla. A day Proctor Fonner and Dr. Ronan and who knows how many others must have known was an impossibility.

"Really, Jax." Dr. Ronan is impatient now. His bushy brows twitch together. After a moment, he shrugs. "Doesn't really matter, does it? Either way, you got a first-class education, food, shelter, all the necessities." He gestures to indicate the dome. "You've had access to the finest research facilities anywhere, as well as the most brilliant bio-chemist in the land, probably on the planet, to teach you, shape your thought processes, urge you to think past your first simplistic responses, to examine all the data and draw proper conclusions. You were different from your peers from the start. Where they saw *what*, you wanted to know *how*. You were worth my time."

I'm too gobsmacked by his news to appreciate his backhanded compliments.

"So you need to put this behind you. Don't waste effort trying to track down your biological parents, or worry about who they are, or were." He dismisses my parents with a wave of one gnarled hand. "Clearly, they were highly intelligent people and probably attractive, because you're not ill-looking. Your genetic legacy is the same whether you know their names or not, so let's move on, hm? You can't let this distract you from what's really important."

He doesn't need to spell out what's really important: the work we do in the lab, trying to improve food production techniques and defeat the super locust. Nothing matters but the work, serving Amerada. Well, not today. I turn on my heel and stride away, not even bothering to make up an excuse. Anger seeps into the layers of confusion and disappointment gripping me. I become conscious of pain; I've been clenching my fists so hard my nails have left deep half-moons on my palms. I flex my fingers.

I can't sneak away to the beach now, so I return to the Kube proper, leaving the dome behind. My boots slap on the floor and an oncoming line of eight-year-olds falters when I pass. One thought blazes in my mind: they have lied to me. All my life I've been promised a reunion with my parents if I behave, study hard, contribute to the Kube and Amerada. Well, I've done all that and now the prize I've been promised—family—is wrenched away. Maybe it never even existed. I know who to blame.

CHAPTER SIX

In the Supervising Proctor's office, I don't even slow down for the aide. He's only half way to his feet when I blast past.

"You can't—" he starts. He squawks as I bang open Proctor Fonner's door. I slam it behind me, cutting off the aide's gobblings.

Proctor Fonner displays no surprise at my entrance and that takes a little of the wind out of my sails. I halt three steps inside the door. He looks up from the screen he's reading from, taps it closed, and raises his thin, dark brows a hair. "AC Jax. Apparently we need to re-work our etiquette curriculum."

The words are calm and measured, and in that instant I know he knows exactly why I'm here. He's been expecting me all day. His flip comment about manners enrages me further and I'm suddenly at his desk, palms flat on the polished surface, leaning forward. This close I can see the fine lines mapping his skin, a hint of chapping on his thin lips. "Why didn't you tell me? Why did you let me think—?"

He doesn't try to make out like he doesn't know what I'm talking about. "I can see you're disappointed by the outcome of your Reunion Day, Jax. I don't altogether blame you." He steeples his fingers and leans back, large head heavy on his thin neck.

"You lied to me!" I slap a hand on his desk and my palm stings.

He doesn't flinch. "As with all decisions related to the upbringing and training of apprentice citizens, we did what we thought was in the best interest of the state and the apprentice."

"What the *hell* does that mean?"

"It means," he continues with the same calm tone, "that we decided it would only unsettle you to know that your arrival here was in any way different from your peers'. We wanted you to fit in, to bond with the other apprentices; in short, we didn't want you distracted or distressed by the knowledge that your parents—"

"Didn't want me."

"—chose, due to circumstances we cannot evaluate, to provide you with a safe life, a good life, by leaving you at this Kube."

His unceasing calm inflames me. "You let me sit in that room all morning, hoping they would come!"

"I couldn't know for sure that no one would come. I was hoping she—they—would." There's no hint of apology in his voice.

Head cocked slightly, I study his face and I suddenly understand. I draw back. "It was punishment, wasn't it? You let me sit there to punish me for—what? The beach? For not always keeping curfew? For not kowtowing sufficiently?"

His eyes shift left briefly before returning to mine. Ignoring my accusation, he rises. "Stand down. I will not tolerate this insubordination, AC Jax. I have given you some leeway because I understand—"

"Who are my parents?"

For the first time he hesitates. "I don't know."

"The DNA registry. Surely you ran my sample through the database. Who are they?" I'm almost pleading. "You know my name, so you must know—"

"Your name. Ah. Wait here." He glides to the door and is through it almost before I register his movement. I turn. He silences his affronted aide with an uplifted hand and then says something I can't hear. He returns to his desk, sits, and engages himself with Kube business while I fidget, unsure what's happening. Just when I'm about to ask him why I'm still here, an older proctor appears in the doorway, holding a hinged orange cube. He's elderly, and his arms are shaking. At Proctor Fonner's nod, he sets the box down on the desk. "As you requested, sir," he says, giving me a curious look from rheumy eyes.

"Thank you. We'll only be a few minutes."

The other proctor nods and shuffles out, closing the door.

Curiosity overcomes my nervousness and I approach. Proctor Fonner taps in a five-digit combination on the lid's lock pad, and a click signals that it's open. He waves me forward. "You were curious about your name."

With the sense that I'm opening Pandora's box, I lift the lid. Inside is a soft-sided olive-green bag with wheels and an extendable handle. I study it.

"From before," Proctor Fonner says, "when commercial air travel was popular. I had a suitcase like this, only red. You've seen images of airports? People used to hustle through them, pulling their suitcases, traveling from Texas to California, or New York City to Europe. Doing business, visiting friends and family, exploring exotic nations and cultures. Before we shut down the airports and international travel, of course."

He sounds uncharacteristically wistful and even though I'm anxious to examine the suitcase, I ask, "What was it like, sir? Flying?"

"Efficient." His brusqueness suggests he regrets his moment of openness. "An efficient way to get from A to B. Unfortunately, it was also an efficient way to spread disease. After the flu came over from Asia, the government had no choice but to ban air travel. Isolation was our only protection. Still is. You arrived here in that." He points to the suitcase.

At his nod, I lift it out of the box, lay it on the floor and kneel beside it. A zipper runs around three sides and I tug on it. It unzips with a metallic purr. Holding my breath,

I flip the top of the suitcase back. It's empty. The gray liner is faded and torn. I run a hand over it and tuck my hand into the mesh pockets. Nothing. The lid has an interior zippered compartment and I unzip that and search it as well, not sure what I'm looking for, but wanting to find something. Something personal. Something that would tell me even a little bit about my parents.

"There's nothing there," Proctor Fonner says after I've already figured that out. He forestalls my next question. "Never was. The suitcase was placed outside the main entrance, partially unzipped, with nothing inside it but you and that book. You had nothing on but a diaper. The doctors' best guess was that you were perhaps a week old."

"But my name?"

Proctor Fonner flicks a tag rubber-banded to the suitcase's handle. I turn it over slowly. It reads "JAX."

"The old code for the Jacksonville airport," Fonner explains.

"So, it's not even a name?" I'm beyond tears now, blank.

Something like compassion flits across his face. "It's *your* name."

"But it's not a family name. It's just . . . nothing."

He sighs, impatient. "Let's not indulge in hyperbole. The immortal bard was right: there's not much in a name. I've shown you this hoping that you'll be able to move on, to accept that you are unlikely to ever know much about your biological parents. I know you think being part of a so-called 'traditional' family would complete you in some way—Oh, yes," he says in response to my startled look, "I notice more than you realize. My point is that having a family is not always desirable. Surely you recognize that from your brief time with the Ushers. You were very young, but still."

Keegan's lean, malevolent face flashes in my mind's eye and I go cold. Fonner doesn't notice.

"Children do not fare well when one or both parents are abusive, or addicts, or neglectful, or simply ignorant. That's why the government has to step in sometimes, why the InKubators exist. Children are the future of the CSA and it is our duty to see they have the best chance possible to become productive citizens. The Pragmatists recognize that and they are right."

"Are you saying that my parents—?"

Folding his hands at his waist, he continues, "I'm saying you need to accept the situation as it exists and not fool yourself into thinking that you can either identify your parents or that you would necessarily be happier if you did so. Despite what Dr. Ronan may have taught you in the lab, there are things better left unknown."

He seems to be warning me, but he has only made me more determined than ever to identify and locate my parents. "What about 'Everly?'" I ask

"Ah." He almost smiles. "Proctor Mary in the nursery named you Everly. She said you were 'everlastingly fussing' and she shortened it to Everly. I've always thought it was pretty."

The personal comment unnerves me and I'm silent. As if to make up for the compliment, Proctor Fonner adds acerbically, "And you haven't changed much in the intervening sixteen years . . . still fussing." The aide knocks and enters, murmuring something about a meeting. Moving toward the door, Proctor Fonner says, "I trust that what I've shown you today will persuade you to at least stop fussing about finding your biological parents. Believe me, your energy and intellect are better spent elsewhere."

The words echo Dr. Ronan's and I wonder for an unnerving moment if they've discussed me.

He seems to take my compliance for granted, because he greets the people assembled in his vestibule and ushers them into the inner sanctum as I leave.

Proctor Fonner might accuse me of "fussing," but I've got another name for it: determination. Nothing is going to keep me from finding my parents. *Nothing.*

I hurry to the northeast tower, where the infants are housed. That's where Halla does her service, rather than in the dome. She's got a way with little ones and loves taking care of them. Give me a row of plants to prune or hoe or transplant any day—backbreaking physical labor—rather than a roomful of toddlers with snotty noses and dirty diapers. She says they make her feel needed.

The nursery wing is cheerier than the rest of the Kube, with yellow walls and softer lighting. A lullaby trickles from an open door and a baby crows with laughter. I'm peering into each room I pass, looking for Halla, when a proctor with black hair drawn back severely from her face stops me. "Apprentice, shouldn't you be doing your service? You don't serve here."

"I've got a message to deliver to AC Westin," I say, letting her think the message is from a proctor.

She sniffs and points to the next door down. "In there."

When she moves off I approach the door. The top half is glass and I can see Halla, seated on the floor, surrounded by eight or so three- and four-year-olds. She's reading a story while another AC readies snacks. The children are enthralled, and I almost hate to interrupt. What if Halla's still so mad or hurt she won't talk to me? Thank goodness she doesn't know I was going to betray her. I tap lightly on the window. Halla glances up and spots me. She starts to smile, but then her face freezes over. I beckon her to come. She hesitates, then hands the reader to the other apprentice, pushes awkwardly to her feet—I can see she's beginning to show—and comes to the door. She opens it a crack.

"What are you doing here? We'll get in trouble." Her voice is cool; she's still mad. She looks worn out, a gray undertone dulling her rich brown skin, her shoulders slumped. Realization lights her eyes. "What are your parents like?"

Even though she's mad at me and disappointed in me, she still wants to hear about what should have been the most momentous day in my life. That's why I love her. I say, "They didn't come. Long story." Before she can express the sympathy in her eyes, I grab her hand. "What we talked about Monday night—are you still planning to do it?"

She looks around to make sure no one can overhear. She nods. "Please don't try to talk me out of it again," she says wearily, tugging her hand away.

"I won't. In fact, if you'll let me, I want to come with you guys. I'm sorry about Monday night. I was a total chuffer. "

"What?" Her mouth falls open. "Oh, Ev, you don't have to—you can't—"

"I do and I can." I don't have time now to explain about Reunion Day, my conversation with Proctor Fonner or my realization that if I'm going to locate my parents, I need to leave Kube 9. So, I whisper that we should meet in the dome, in the small evergreen plot, as soon as service hours are over. "If we're leaving tonight, we've got a lot of planning to do. I'll tell Wyck."

A tentative smile creases her cheeks and I read forgiveness in it.

"Are you leaving, Appwentice Halla?" a voice pipes up. A little girl stands behind Halla, eyes big.

Halla scoops her up. "Not until dinner time, my little Hannah-banana." She lifts the girl's top and blows a raspberry on her stomach, and the child giggles. Over Hannah's head, she shoots me a warning look.

"Seven o'clock," I mouth at her.

As Halla closes the door and returns to her young charges, I hurry down the hall, making a mental list of everything we need to do if we're leaving tonight. I shiver involuntarily, both excited and scared by the prospect. I hadn't wrestled with the decision: the idea came to me in the elevator and I knew it was what I needed to do. No way am I staying at the Kube without my two best friends when the system I have trusted my whole life—and Proctor Fonner, in particular— have betrayed me, lied to me about my parents and how I came to be here. It makes me wonder what else they might be lying about. I feel a pang at the idea of leaving Dr. Ronan and my work, but hopefully, after I find my parents, I'll be able to return to my experiments, not at the Kube, obviously, but maybe with the Ministry for Science and Food Production. Or I can make my way west, to an outpost, and help establish a dome and reliable food production. I'll be able to contribute somewhere, I know.

CHAPTER SEVEN

Skulking past the cafeteria minutes before seven, I hear Proctor Mannisham's voice droning on about the responsibilities of citizenship. If the goal is to get apprentices to eat more quickly, the tradition of having proctors offer "improving" or "educational" comments during the evening meal is a great way to accomplish that. Safely past the cafeteria entrance, I trot down the long hall leading to the dome. It's empty. An iris scan gets me through the access doors. Tomorrow, when they discover we're gone, they'll be able to pull up the records and see that Halla, Wyck and I met in the dome, but by then it will be too late. Noticing that two scooters are missing from the docking station, I mount one and zip toward the evergreen orchard. The breeze I'm generating fans my hair. The fields are quiet, empty of workers, and I fancy I can hear the plants growing, inching their way through the loam to the surface, extending their leaves, soaking up the carefully calibrated light. It's peaceful.

If only my thoughts were equally peaceful. I glide straight to the far end of the dome where the copse is. The evergreen plot is densely planted with trees that are all over seven feet tall, and is a favorite spot of young lovers trying to find some privacy since the bushy limbs provide a fair amount of cover. They should be called "everpurples," though because we've genetically engineered them to produce deep purple needles that seem to deter the locusts. I wonder if this is where Halla and Loudon got together. Evicting that thought from my brain, I slow and maneuver the scooter between the trees. The light is dimmer here, a natural twilight. I breathe deeply of the pine scent that always relaxes me. It doesn't work this time. I dismount, prop the scooter against a trunk, and whisper, "Halla? Wyck?"

"Hey, Ev." Wyck emerges from between two conifers. His usual insouciance is missing; he's strung taut with tension.

Halla steps out from behind him. She hugs me without saying anything and I cling to her for a minute, relieved that we're okay.

We sink to our haunches and huddle together. I outline the plan I've been working on all afternoon. "Our first priorities are food and water," I say. "We'll also need maps, which I can get from the lab's computer; weapons, if we can find them, for hunting and protection; a tarp or something to use for shelter. We can't risk taking a train, so we'll be walking a lot. We can only take what we can carry. Even assuming we can cover twenty miles a day, it's going to take us three-plus weeks—if we're damn lucky—to get to Atlanta." The list seems pitiful, inadequate, naïve.

Not until this afternoon did I realize how little I know about what exists outside the Kube. Oh, I can label the cantons on a map, list the sites of the last major flu outbreaks and the location of the most recently discovered mass grave with more than six hundred thousand bodies in it, and pinpoint the battleground where the Maddow rebellion against the Pragmatists was put down, but I have only the haziest idea of the topography between here and Atlanta, and even less knowledge of what we're likely to encounter on our journey. There are outlaws, of course, but I have no idea how many or where. There is wildlife, some of it dangerous. If I had more time to plan I could collect information from the computer under the guise of lab research, but we're out of time. With Halla's physical looming tomorrow and discovery of her pregnancy certain, we have to leave tonight.

"I can get weapons," Wyck volunteers.

I don't ask him how or what. I just nod.

"I've already got some food squirreled away," Halla says, "and I can take more from the nursery once it's lights out."

"I'll go to the lab," I say. "I can get hydropure pills and maps"—I cross my fingers, hoping that's true—"and maybe some other stuff that will be useful. We'll need fire starters, for one, containers to drink from and cook in. We should each bring whatever might be helpful for getting food, protection, or shelter, but only what we can carry easily."

"We could take the scooters," Halla says.

"Unrecharged, they should have a range of a hundred to a hundred fifty miles," Wyck offers.

"Good thinking," I agree. "They might get us a third of the way there."

"We'll have to remove our locators," Wyck says.

I'd already realized this, and I nod. In unison, we look at our forearms. There is only one way to dislodge the locators, and it won't be pleasant. Still, we have no choice. If we don't cut them out, we'll be hunted down in hours.

We hash over our plan for two hours until Halla rubs her arms and whispers, "I've got to get back. It's my night to get the four-year-olds ready for bed. I'll be missed." She starts to rise and I grasp her hand to help. She holds tight to my hand, even after she's standing. After a moment, I reach for Wyck's hand and he takes Halla's other hand. We stand in a circle, silent, connected, committed.

"All for one and one for all," Wyck says jauntily, but with an undertone of seriousness.

The Three Musketeers. Buddies on an adventure. Of course Wyck would think of them. As Halla's hand tightens painfully around mine, I feel like we're bonded together, the three of us, our linked hands the shared electrons that form a covalent bond between atoms, virtually unbreakable. Peaceful resolve settles in me.

"Family," Halla whispers. She lets go of my hand to lay her hand on her abdomen.

Then Wyck pulls away and heads for the scooters. "See you at the docking station at midnight," he says.

Halla manages a smile and hugs me. "Thank you for coming with me," she says. "You're the best friend I'll ever have. Better than a sister."

A lump rises in my throat at the idea of us as sisters. Like Laura and Mary. Would that make Wyck our brother? I don't feel very sisterly toward him these days. None of us are really family, I remind myself. My time with the Ushers taught me that the only real family is your biological family. I say nothing, hugging my best friend tightly. There'll be time enough for talking once we put twenty miles between ourselves and the Kube.

CHAPTER EIGHT

Halla follows Wyck out of the dome, and I skim to the lab. The door *whoosh*es open at my iris scan and I walk in, merging with the hush. Refrigeration units hum, and a centrifuge clinks softly from the back. Familiar sounds. I walk the length of the lab to the computer room and sit facing a unit, placing my left thumb on the bioplate. It boots up with a whir and the display materializes in front of me. I'm uncomfortable abusing Dr. Ronan's trust like this—he may get in trouble for having assigned me my own access code—but needs must. My fingers flick the display. I don't have much experience with the computer and it takes me well over an hour to locate the maps we'll need. I download them to a portable data device and then print them out as well, to be sure. For good measure, I find the precise geocoords of Loudon's IPF base and the Ministry of Science and Food Production, which happens to hold the central DNA registry. Proctor Fonner might say the database didn't reveal my parents' identities, but he's lying. Everyone's DNA is in that database from birth.

I search the lab for other useful items, pocketing several chemical fire starters, two collapsible water-proof containers, a heat-proof beaker, sleeves of hydropure tablets, and, on impulse, some of the metal stakes we've been using to support the new pea hybrid. There's wire binding the vines to the stakes, and I take a roll of that, as well. I stash it all in one of the lightweight backpacks researchers carry when they're collecting soil, water and local area flora samples, first removing their instruments and sample containers. The researcher pack has a compass, and I take that, and then steal the compasses from two other researcher kits. I'd prefer the more advanced Navigizmos, but these will do.

I'm examining the maps when a muted *clink* jerks my head up. Dr. Ronan stands mere feet away, sipping Wexl from a lab beaker, eyes fixed on me. The glowing green liquid coats the glass as he lifts it to his lips. His incongruous blond hair is more mussed than usual and he's wearing a plaid robe and slippers, garb no apprentice would be allowed to own, much less wear. It's far too *individual*. I chew myself out for being so absorbed in my search that I didn't hear the lab door open or his footsteps. The tiny *clink* comes again as the beaker knocks against his teeth. He says nothing. His throat works as he swallows, stiff white hairs of unshaved beard vibrating as his Adam's apple moves. I don't realize I've reacted until the crinkle of paper tells me

I've crushed the maps. I whip my hand behind my back. Maybe he hasn't noticed what I'm holding. It's possible he's drunk enough Wexl not to notice much.

"Dr. Ronan! I wasn't . . . I was just—"

"You're leaving," he says, his words slightly slurred by the intoxicant.

"No! I mean, yes, I'm leaving the lab now. I needed to check on—"

He shakes his head back and forth in exaggerated slow motion. "No, no, no, Jax. Let's not part with lies. You're leaving the Kube, going in search of your parents." He throws back the rest of the Wexl and sets the beaker down with a sharp click. He takes a step toward me, swaying ever so slightly. He's close enough now I can smell the Wexl's chemical sweetness on his breath.

"I had a daughter once. Did you know that?" Not waiting for my startled negative, he continues. "Nothing like you. She wanted to be a ballet dancer of all things, back when we had time and resources to indulge in the arts. Can you believe the government used to fund painting and dance, opera and photography? She took her first class when she was three, and I can still see her in her pink leotard thingie and tights with a little puff of a tutu—that's a ballerina skirt made out of stiff netting," he explains at my puzzled look. "She had her hair up in a bun, like ballerinas wore, and the biggest smile I'd ever seen on her little face. To the day she died, she had that same smile every time she danced."

He clears his throat. "She seemed fragile as a dandelion puff, ethereal as a moonbeam when she danced, but she was all muscle and discipline. In that, she was like you—a hard worker, committed."

My chest tightens at the comparison.

"She could move people to tears. Early on, I tried to interest her in science, in botany or genetics, but dancing was fundamental to who she was. It would have been a crime against nature to try to make her be anything else. I didn't recognize that soon enough."

His eyes gleam wetly and he reaches for the empty beaker, stares into it blankly, and then sets it down again. "She died in the second wave of the flu pandemic. My wife died three months later." His jaw slides from side to side.

I whisper, "I'm sorry, sir," having trouble getting my head around the idea of Dr. Ronan with a family. He seems so self-contained, so focused on his work, so beyond needing people that I have trouble envisioning him falling in love, playing with a toddler.

"It is what it is, Jax. It is what it is." His gaze sharpens and falls on the backpack.

I stand helplessly as he pulls it toward him along the length of the lab table and rummages through it. I expect him to fling my survival items out, accuse me of theft, turn me in. I think about hitting him with a chair and tying him up or locking him in the storage room, but almost as soon as the thought materializes, I deny it. No way can I harm Dr. Ronan. I stand irresolute, trying to think of a way to warn Wyck and Halla, to keep Dr. Ronan occupied until they've realized I'm not going to show up at the docking station and leave without me. I pray they don't come here looking for me. I'm so caught up in my thoughts, I don't process Dr. Ronan's words at first.

"I said, you'll need medical supplies," he repeats impatiently. "There's a first aid kid in the storage room, top shelf, on your left. What are you waiting for? Go get it."

Almost in a trance, I obey, returning with the compact kit. I should have thought of it myself. "You're helping me," I state the obvious. "You're not mad that I'm leaving?"

"Might as well be mad at water for being wet," he grumbles, hitching his robe out of the way so he can organize the backpack more efficiently. "Compounds have to behave in keeping with their elemental make-up," he says. "Remember that."

When I stare at him blankly, confused and more than a little inclined to tell Wyck and Halla I can't go with them, Dr. Ronan straightens and glares at me from under the furry shelf of eyebrows. "Your going is pointless, but I don't expect you to understand that now. There's a lot of work left for you to do when you realize it, so don't get yourself killed."

"I won't," I promise, feeling half-comforted and half-foolish. "Thank you. You . . . you won't get in trouble for helping me?" I catch sight of the time: 2355. I've got to go.

"Pish." He flips his hand. "I haven't so much helped you as turned a blind eye. Besides"—he smiles almost impishly—"no one will know anything about it. You don't think I haven't figured out ways of entering my own lab without leaving a record of my presence, do you? There's no such thing as a security system that can't be penetrated with enough time and ingenuity. And I've got both, goddamnit."

I'm seized with the urge to hug him, but it feels like an impertinence, so I merely say, "Goodbye, and thank you. I'll miss you. Oh, and the new strain of wheat? You should call it *Triticum yuna.*" I sling the backpack over one shoulder, and head for the lab entrance, resisting the urge to catalog all the projects I won't see to completion, the data I'll never finish analyzing, the other lab apprentices and scientists I'll never see again. I'm close to tears.

I think I hear Dr. Ronan whisper, "Go with God," but it's drowned out by the sound of the cooler door sliding open and an irascible, "Where did that flask of Wexl get to?"

I step through the lab doors for what I'm sure is the last time, letting the gentle humidity of the dome caress my face, and start toward the docking station. Soon, I'm trotting, then running, the backpack thunking awkwardly between my shoulders, and my hair flying. It's midnight. It's time.

PART TWO

CHAPTER NINE

It's unbelievably dark four miles from the Kube. I can barely make out Halla and Wyck, even though Halla is an arm's length to my right and Wyck rides in front of us. Our scooters skim inches above the train tracks; it was Wyck's idea to simplify the first part of our journey by sticking to the tracks. We're heading for the central train transfer station on Jacksonville's west side. Adrenaline courses through my body and I'm hyper-alert, scalp tingling as the wind flaps my hair, ears attuned to the whisk of insect wings zipping by and rustlings deep in the kudzu, nose trying to categorize the many semi-familiar scents: creosote, rotting vegetation, smoke from someone's cooking fire, brine. The air is heavy with humidity and I'm damp all over by the time we see the strip of lighting around a tunnel entrance.

"This is as good a place as any," Wyck calls. "We can use the tunnel light."

I know what he means and I reluctantly bring my scooter to a stop. Keeping a healthy distance from the tracks, we crouch in a circle. Halla looks nervous but resolute.

"Let's get this over with," I say. I push up my jumpsuit sleeve, exposing my forearm. It seems unbearably white. "Do me first and then I'll do you," I tell Wyck.

Without speaking, he rummages in his backpack and withdraws a knife. The short blade gleams. "From the kitchen. I brought several. You never know when a knife will come in handy. Good for hunting, filleting, protection and the occasional minor surgery procedure."

It's nerves talking, I can tell. I grip my lips together and nod. I extend my arm. Halla holds my wrist while Wyck's thumb runs over the sensitive flesh of my inner arm until he can feel the locator, a grain of rice-sized lump beneath the skin.

"Hold her tight," he murmurs to Halla. "This might sting."

He pulls the skin taut between one thumb and forefinger, and then the knife slits my skin, a bright line of pain, and I'm gritting my teeth. A worm of blood oozes, black in the limited light. It makes me light-headed. Blood always affects me like that. Wyck wiggles the knife tip briefly and then it's over. The anticipation hurt more than the knife.

Wyck's holding the tiny locator up like a prospector with a multi-carat gem.

"You've got a future as a surgeon," I tell him, semi-mockingly. "You would've been wasted as a border sentry."

Wyck grins and punches my shoulder lightly. I can tell he's as relieved as I am that it wasn't worse.

"I've got sterile wipes and sealant," Halla says, pulling the items from her bag. Hers isn't a backpack like mine and Wyck's; she's brought a roomy diaper bag from the nursery. She blots the trickle of blood with a steri-wipe and seals the short incision with a thin strip of surgical sealant.

I do Wyck next and then he does Halla. We're surprised to see that only twenty minutes have passed since we hunkered down outside the tunnel. With our wounds safely covered by our sleeves, we're ready to move on.

Ten minutes later, Halla and I huddle behind a broken concrete block while Wyck uses the train ticket that was supposed to get him to his Border Security Service base to enter the train station and toss our locators onto a train bound for Dallas, the last stop on the line before the Cali-Mex frontier. Everyone will think we're headed for an outpost. When he gets back, we power up the scooters and head away from the depot, away from Jacksonville, away from everything I've known in my sixteen years. It's a weird feeling.

We skim west along the old interstate highway, I-10, for a couple of hours. The road is cratered in spots, bombed during the Between, undoubtedly, but navigable by ACV.

It's no wonder, though, that no one drives wheeled vehicles anymore. No one's about at this hour, and I can see nothing past the thin spear of my headlight. A soupy patchwork of darkness stretches on either side and makes me feel like I'll drop off the edge of the world if I steer a bit left or right, even though I know the landscape is probably a relatively level mix of abandoned buildings, kudzu, old parking lots, and sand. The small odometer says we've gone forty-three miles when the horizon lightens and a salmon-colored ribbon slits the seam between earth and sky, quickly expanding to a display of crimson, pink and gold that makes us all slow and finally stop to stare back the way we came in appreciation.

"It's an omen," Halla says when blue has reclaimed the sky. "Like the rainbow after the Great Flood."

I can hear how desperately she needs to believe that we are going to succeed.

"It's a sunrise," Wyck scoffs, igniting his scooter again. "We need to keep moving."

We glide on, past weathered and dangling signs that announce exits for towns long abandoned: Bryceville, Baldwin, Macclenny. The sun rises, beating down on us, and I'm grateful it's April and not the middle of the summer. My legs feel tired now, aching from standing on the scooter for so many hours. My shoulders hurt, too, from the backpack's weight, and my forearm burns from the incision. At least I'm not pregnant. Halla's shoulders are hunched forward, her head drooping.

"We need to stop," I call out. "Food."

Wyck, fifty yards ahead of Halla and me, circles back. Halla gives me a grateful smile and we pull to the roadside. A thicket of trees is nothing but gnarled branches bent west by the prevailing wind. The leaves are gone, courtesy of the locusts. Dust like fine powder poofs up with every step we take off the crumbling asphalt; if we have to leave the highway our ACVs will produce a dust cloud that even a brain-dead searcher could spot. The dust catches in my throat and I cough. Kudzu climbing over some of the branches makes a shady canopy and we head for the more sheltered spot and drop our bags.

"I've got to pee." Halla disappears into the brush.

"I'm stiffer than a board," Wyck proclaims, stretching his arms skyward.

"I'm dying of thirst." I find a water bladder and sip from the attached tube. It's warm and tastes like rubber. I could drink a gallon, but we have to conserve our water. Wyck and the returned Halla are likewise drinking and they tear themselves away reluctantly.

"We should take stock of what we've got," I suggest, emptying my backpack. The others do the same, although from the way Wyck manipulates his pack, I suspect he's hiding something. I don't challenge him on it. It might be something personal, like my feather and my *Little House* book, which I keep in the messenger bag slung across my chest, along with the maps. I'm sure Halla has her Bible tucked away in a corner of her bag. I catalog the supplies on the ground. Dozens of vegeprote bars in their edible wrappers cascade from each of our bags. A quick survey tells me we've got enough food to last a week, and water to last for three, maybe four days, if we're careful. After that, we'll need to find fresh water. Additionally, Wyck has brought four knives and a selection of hand tools, a couple of batteries, and a thermal imaging device which he must have stolen from an IPF soldier. Halla's bag contains intelli-textile blankets, a flashlight, an extra jumpsuit, and various small items like fasteners she must have filched from the nursery.

"We should each have a knife," Wyck says, handing me the longest blade and Halla a serrated one. He tucks a broad blade into the back of his belt. "And we should divide up the food, in case we get separated, or lose a pack."

We divvy up the food. I give them each a compass. In silent agreement, Wyck and I split the rest of the items so we are carrying the bulk of the weight, leaving Halla a lighter bag to contend with. When we're finished, we munch on high-calorie vegeprote bars. I slide an extra bar toward Halla. "You're eating for two."

After a brief hesitation, she nods and bites into it.

My "meal" only half satisfies the gnawing in my belly, but I ignore it. I know there's worse to come on this journey than hunger pangs.

On the thought, an eerie howling and yipping breaks the silence. It's not close by, but it's not too far, either. I hurriedly zip my backpack and sling it over my shoulder. Wyck does the same.

Halla jerks her head up. "What was that?"

"Dog pack," Wyck says.

Halla pales. We've all heard stories of people being mauled to death by the packs of feral dogs descended from pets left homeless when whole cities of people perished from the flu virtually overnight. The bounties on them have killed off the majority, but the government still issues warnings during Assembly sometimes. Two months ago, they showed video of a family that got overtaken by a pack. I had nightmares about it for a week. I reach down to help Halla up. As she grips my hand, she asks, "Do you think they know we're here?"

The wind is blowing softly toward the slightly louder barking. "Yep. Hurry."

We jog to the scooters. The air cushion pushes mine the usual foot off the ground and I wish it were six feet, out of reach of the dogs now crashing through the underbrush. One of them is baying, a chilling sound that sends goose bumps up my arms. Halla and Wyck head for the road. On impulse, I snatch up a fallen branch before following them

"Can a scooter outrun a dog?" Wyck calls over his shoulder. He's the first to hit the highway.

I lean forward, closing the gap between me and Halla as we veer onto the asphalt. The first dog lunges into the shady clearing. "I think we're about to find out."

CHAPTER TEN

The dogs waste brief moments snuffling around our picnic area for crumbs, giving us time to put precious distance between us and them. We're leaning forward, reducing our wind resistance, and the scooters are skimming at their top speed, a little more than twenty miles an hour. I'm beginning to hope the dogs might not think we're worth pursuing when a sharp bark makes me look back. The dogs stream out from under the trees, a small pack of eight or ten. The largest has a wolf-like snout and gray-black fur, and looks big enough, to my terrified eyes, to bring down a mastodon. Most of them, after decades of interbreeding, are a gray-brown lot, medium-sized, with scruffy coats. The one in the lead, though, is long and lean and comes at us like a missile, outpacing the rest of the pack. He's running twice as fast as the scooters, eating up our lead bound by scary bound.

We ride grimly in a line: Wyck in the lead, Halla in the middle, and me right behind her. The dogs are gaining. Halla looks over her shoulder, eyes wide with panic.

"Don't look back," I call to her. "Keep going, no matter what." I catch a movement in my peripheral vision and look down to see a narrow head drawing level with the back of the scooter, as high as my knee. Small, triangular ears are pressed against the bony skull, but it's the sharp teeth, revealed by drawn-back lips, that hold my attention. It snaps at my leg, missing by a hair.

I react instinctively, slashing downward with the branch. It catches the dog across the snout and it yelps. Lines of blood criss-cross its muzzle. The dog snarls and lunges. It snaps. A tug, a lance of pain in my shin, and part of my jumpsuit tears away. The attack pulls me slightly off balance and it costs me precious seconds to right the scooter. The pack has drawn closer. The lead dog spits out the fabric and comes toward me again as I regain speed.

"I'll try to draw them off," Wyck calls. He veers off the road, trilling "Yi, yi, yi," in an attempt to get the dogs' attention.

A couple of the dogs are slowing, giving up on the chase, but the one who has had a taste of my blood shows no sign of flagging. Spittle flecks his muzzle. *Slavering.* I don't know where the word comes from. If he so much as bumps into the scooter, I'll crash and they'll be on me. I'm desperate. Letting go of the handlebars, I hold the branch with both hands, and drive it into the dog's open mouth.

The dog makes a horrific gagging sound as the bough's forked end lodges halfway down its throat. He stumbles. His fall yanks the branch from my hands and I grab for the handlebars. The scooter slews wildly. The air cushion cuts out for a second. Fatal. I'm sure the leading edge of the scooter will catch on the road, I'll tumble off and the dogs will rip me to shreds. I frantically thumb the igniter which catches immediately.

Even so, I'm surprised the dogs haven't taken me down, and I risk a glance back. They're nosing at their wounded pack mate, and circling indecisively. One trots after me half-heartedly, but then gives up. I face forward, relief swamping me. Wyck glides to my side and asks, "Are you okay?"

"I think so." I'm alive. "Thanks." I push hair off my face with a trembling hand.

He shrugs. "It didn't work. Your leg is bleeding."

I look down and see a trickle of red where the dog's tooth sliced through my jumpsuit. I sway and look away. It doesn't hurt yet. "It's okay for now," I say, wanting to put more distance between us and the pack before we stop.

Wyck nods as if he understands and we continue on, side by side, catching up with Halla until we're riding three abreast. No one says anything for another hour. As the adrenaline slowly leaches out of me, I think. We need sleep and we need shelter. The highway, the entire landscape, is too open. Damn locusts. A proper forest would have come in very handy. By now, Proctor Fonner knows we're missing. I envision him in his office, thin-lipped, implacable when he hears the news. In all probability, he's had the IPF searching for us since shortly after six, when we would have been missed at breakfast. Assuming they were able to ping our locators and determine we were on the Dallas-bound train, by now they must have contacted the IPF somewhere along the train's route.

Worst case, the train has been searched already at one of its stops and they know we're not on it. That still leaves a lot of territory to cover, but Fonner's got resources, including microdrones. We need to find a town to hide in. We can't sleep in the open. We're too vulnerable. I share my thoughts with the others. "I'm not talking about a populated city," I say when Halla exclaims. "We need a small town, someplace deserted." Heaven knows, there are enough of those, towns where every citizen died off, or where small groups of survivors abandoned their homes to reunite with family members in areas less affected by the flu. Looters had a field day, at first, but as the flu spread, even criminals became reluctant to risk contact with infected items.

"A ghost town," Halla says.

I'd have thought she'd be spooked by the idea, but she seems fine with it.

"Right."

"Let's go," she says. "I'm so tired I'm going to fall off this scooter. And I have to pee again."

"I'll scout ahead," Wyck says, steering immediately off the highway. He swerves the scooter playfully in deep "S" turns and then takes off.

"We should stick together," I call after him, but he doesn't even acknowledge me. Halla and I look at each other and then turn our scooters to follow Wyck. We're going slower, conserving electricity—the readout on my dash is hovering perilously near the half-way mark—and pretty soon all we can see of Wyck is a dust cloud. Then, even that disappears. I frown. He can't be that far ahead. As we draw closer to where he disappeared, I spot something amazing. Green.

"Look," Halla breathes, pointing. "It's *grass*."

It is grass. Green, emerald green grass stretching as far as I can see. It's short, less than two inches tall, but it's so beautiful it makes me tingle. Clearly, the locusts haven't come this way in a month or so. On impulse, I stop and get off my scooter. I bend and begin to unstrap my boots.

Halla giggles when I scuff off the boots, shuck my socks, and stand, barefoot, in the grass. I walk slowly, letting the blades tickles my soles, then scrunch my toes into it. Something like peace settles over me. I sink down and run my splayed fingers over the grass.

"Me, too," Halla says. Removing her footwear, she comes to stand beside me. "Can you imagine?" she asks.

I know she's asking me to imagine the days before the birds died off and the insects rose up, when grass carpeted the earth, strewn with weeds and small flowering plants, when trees were crowned with leaves. I've seen pictures, but it's almost impossible to imagine. "No, not really." If I'd stayed at the Kube, I could have continued working with Dr. Ronan to find ways to eradicate the locusts and bring back the green. I thrust the thought away.

"I can't imagine Little Loudon growing up without ever seeing grass, and yet that's what might happen. I remember when I was little, living with my Nonna after my parents died, and she used to read the Bible to us, especially the Psalms. And one day she read the passage about 'the lilies in the field' and how 'even Solomon in all his glory was not arrayed like some of these.' I asked her what a lily was and she cried and cried. I don't want Little Loudon not to know what grass is." Her fingers wisp through the blades.

We're silent for a moment, and I think how lucky I was to grow up with the dome. Are there people alive now who have never seen grass?

"Come on," I say, dragging my socks and boots back on. "We'd better find Wyck."

We've barely mounted our scooters before we see Wyck heading back toward us. "I found us a place to spend the night," he crows, obviously pleased with himself. "Less than a mile ahead."

I wonder if he even notices the grass, but say nothing. We crest a small hill and a town lies below us. We pause. "Town" is too grand a word for the cluster of houses and what looks like one store and an old gas station. I don't have to ask Wyck if he's checked it out to make sure it's deserted; emptiness echoes from the buildings. The window glass is long gone and the openings are like zombie eyes: vacant and dead. I shiver.

"Great, huh?" Wyck says, setting his scooter in motion and gliding down the slope. Halla and I trail him. "There's even a well."

That's good news. A deep enough well might not be contaminated.

"I feel like I haven't slept in three days," Halla says.

Suddenly, weariness hits me, too. It feels like gravity is working with twice its usual force, pulling my limbs down. "Let's pick a house and get some rest."

Wyck leads us to the smallest house set a bit apart from the others, up against a band of dead trees. The house has weathered to a flaky gray so it blends with the tree trunks. The trees and house alike are half-smothered by chartreuse kudzu vines. "We should bring the scooters inside," he says.

The door creaks loudly as he nudges it open with the scooter. Inside, it's musty and dim, a single room with gaps and pipes to the right where a stove, sink and refrigerator used to be, and two doors on the left. One leads to a bedroom with nothing but an iron bed frame in it by way of furniture, and one leads to a hyfac—what would have been called a "bathroom" when this house was built, I suspect—coated in mildew so thick I can't distinguish the color of the tiles beneath it.

Halla and I gag and back out of the room hurriedly. "I guess the facilities are outside," I say. "Men's—first tree on the left, Women's—second tree on the right."

"Speaking of which . . ." Halla exits.

Wyck grins. "Wish you were back at the Kube?"

I straighten my back. Honestly, there's part of me that wishes I were working in the lab, looking forward to a hot dinner. But only a small part of me. "No. Do you?"

"Hell, no. Especially since I wouldn't be at the Kube— I'd be on my way to Base Kestrel." He looks around. "We need to have someone standing watch all night."

"You'd have made a great border sentry," I tease him.

Rolling his eyes, he says, "We should take care of your leg. Don't want it to get infected."

When he mentions it, I become conscious of the pain. I sit and push aside the torn fabric to inspect the bite. It's more of a shallow gash, four inches long, like one tooth glanced along my calf. Blood is crusted over it and it throbs, but I don't think it needs stitches. "It's not too bad."

"Here, let me." Wyck kneels to inspect the wound. Pulling out the first aid kit, he opens it and examines the contents. "We need to disinfect it."

He rips open a disinfectant packet with his teeth and swabs the gash. "Sorry," he says when I wince.

His head is bent and I'm staring into his brown curls. He smells not unpleasantly of sweat and fresh air and I'm absurdly conscious of his hand cupping my calf while he works to loosen the dried blood. He's got calluses on his palms that are somehow more arousing than soft hands would have been. I find myself wishing I'd shaved my legs yesterday and then half smile at the stupidity.

"What's funny?" He looks up and his hazel eyes, suspicious that I'm laughing at him, meet mine.

I shake my head and Wyck finishes by applying a sterile pad to the wound. Halla comes in as I'm re-sealing my jumpsuit.

"How are the facilities?" I ask.

"Um, rustic."

We all laugh.

"I'll take the first watch," Wyck says. "You and Halla sleep. I'll wake you in four hours, okay?"

"Yeah. Thanks."

I visit the facilities, and then we unpack the blankets Halla brought and arrange my backpack and her diaper bag as pillows. We each eat another vegeprote bar and Halla and I settle in the middle of the room, back to back, blankets wrapped around us. I slip *Little House* from my messenger bag and lay it close, where I can rest a hand on it. The floor is hard, unyielding under my shoulder. I'm bone-weary but sleep doesn't come. I sense Halla is still awake, too.

"Halla?" I whisper.

"Hm?"

"How did you know you were in love with Loudon? Enough to, you know, want to—?"

She gives a sleepy giggle. "Oh, Everly. We just knew. It wasn't like we weighed the pros and cons or gathered data. Being in love is not like a lab experiment." She giggles again at the idea, and the sound makes me smile. "We'd been friends for so long, and the love thing crept up on us. He knew before I did, I think. He said it first. As soon as he did, I knew I loved him, too, knew that I'd loved him one way or another for years. Making love was just the perfect way to express how we feel about each other. 'The two will become one flesh,' it says in the Bible. I miss him so much."

"And the baby?" I'm not sure what I'm asking—if she was happy about being pregnant from the start, if she's scared, something else.

She doesn't answer right away, and I think she's fallen asleep.

"When I first realized I was pregnant, I was scared, of course. Really, scared. I mean, Loudon was already gone by the time I knew, and well, I was just scared. But then . . . I'm not sure I can really explain it to you, to someone who's never been pregnant. You probably think of Little Loudon as a collection of genes and chromosomes, biological bits and pieces, but to me he's this beautiful little soul Loudon and I made together. He's a treasure, a gift. Giving him up would be like . . . like . . . .."

She apparently can't think of a comparison significant enough. "Ooh, he's kicking. Want to feel?"

I'm curious. I roll so my stomach is against her back and let her place my hand on her belly. It's rigid, with less give than I expect. The baby's kicks move my hand. "Feels strong," I say. He'll need to be. I expect her to answer, but a whiffly snore tells me she's asleep.

I ponder the joy in her voice more than her words and finally drop off, oddly comforted by the sight of Wyck silhouetted against the window opening by the setting sun.

Having stood the last watch, I shake Halla and Wyck awake at first light, anxious to put more miles between us and any searchers. They come fully awake quickly, as if the change in circumstances has changed something within, flipped a survival switch that knows a few seconds of lost alertness might be the difference between catching dinner and being dinner. We discuss our plan for the day.

"We should check the well for water—" I start.

"And see if we can find some clothes," Halla adds.

"And food," Wyck says, "although what are the chances it hasn't all been looted? You start with the houses, Halla"—Wyck points —"and I'll try the store."

With a mock salute, he shoulders his bag and heads out. Halla drifts toward the nearest house carrying her bag, and I go to inspect the well. It takes only seconds to figure out we won't be getting any water from it. When I drop a stone, it clatters when it hits the bottom. Dry. I head back to "our" house and meet Wyck returning, shaking his head.

"Not a crumb."

It's what I expected. "Okay. Let's check the map—"

A scream cuts through the still morning. Halla! Wyck and I exchange a glance and race out the door. Another scream pulls us to the largest house in the cluster. It has faded to gray, like the others, but has a wraparound porch and the remnants of gingerbread along the eaves. Wyck hurdles the steps to the verandah, and his foot cracks one of the boards. I ascend more gingerly, help him pull his foot free, and push the door open. Without thinking about it, Wyck and I enter back to back, each scanning for threats. A tatter of mulberry-colored velvet drapes a window opening and a shard of broken china rests in one corner. Other than that, there's nothing. This house is as empty as the one we slept in.

"Halla?"

"In here." Her voice quavers.

We follow her voice through a dining room to a laundry room. The washer-dryer is on its side, dented and clearly non-functional, door open, and Halla is scrunched on the floor behind it, clutching an armload of clothes.

"I saw someone," she whispers. "A man. I was in the kitchen"—she points—"and he looked in the window. He looked straight at me! He was horrible—bearded, hairy. I could *smell* him. I screamed and ran in here where there's no windows." She buries her face in the clothes.

"We need to get out of here," Wyck says crisply. "There might be more than one."

He and I each grab one of Halla's arms and haul her up. She stuffs the clothes she's holding into her bag. I put my hand on the knife tucked into my belt as we hurry from the house and jog back to where we spent the night. I see no one, but can't shake the feeling that we're being watched. From the other houses? I study them surreptitiously as we pass. From the trees? I use my peripheral vision to try and spot something new, something out of place. I try to dismiss the feeling as paranoia. In all likelihood, it was an animal of some kind that Halla saw—a raccoon or bear, maybe. She said it was hairy and stinky. I'm not sure why the idea of an animal is less terrifying than a human, but it is.

Reaching the house, we enter cautiously. My gaze flies to the scooters. One of them is gone.

CHAPTER ELEVEN

The missing scooter spooks us. Halla wasn't mistaken—there's someone here . . . or there was. I hope that only one missing scooter means he's alone. We're out of the house in seconds, plunging into the woods with the two remaining scooters. Halla and I share one; it's uncomfortable, slow, and means we're draining the charge faster than before. Wyck's got Halla's diaper bag with him on his scooter to lighten ours a bit. The scooters ride lower and maneuver sluggishly with the increased weight. Despite that, they're faster than walking, and we're desperate to put distance between us and the not-so-deserted town.

Forty-five minutes out, surrounded by dead trees, my shoulders relax and I feel safer. I mentally review my plan. The roads are unsafe now that there are undoubtedly searchers on our trail. There's a swamp between us and

Atlanta, the Okefenokee, and I think our best chance of making it to Atlanta lies in that swamp. For one thing, there'll be water.

We come to a break in the trees where we're able to ride abreast with Wyck and I explain my reasoning.

"Go through a swamp? Get real," Wyck says. "The roads are our best bet. We can make better time."

"We'll be caught on the roads, or anywhere there's dust. We need the cover of the swamp. The scooters won't send up dust plumes on wetter ground."

"What about snakes and alligators?" Halla asks.

"Immaterial because we're not stupid enough to go into the swamp," Wyck says.

I frown. "Seriously, Halla, there's going to be dangers of one kind or another—animal or human—no matter what route we take."

"Who died and left you in charge, Jax?" Wyck asks, real anger in his voice now. "You may have the highest test scores ever seen at the Kube and be a whoop-de-doo five percenter, but last I looked that didn't make you God. Halla and I had a fine plan before you horned in: get to Atlanta as quickly as possible. Going fast gets us there quicker so we won't need to find as much food on the way. And the fewer days we spend on the road, the less chance there is we'll run into trouble. Speed is the key ingredient here."

I'm stung by his attack, and cover my hurt with an acerbic response. "You're going to *speed* right into the IPF's arms. You won't get within a hundred miles of Atlanta." I tone it down. "Cover is more important than speed right now. In the swamp, we've got cover, we've got a chance. On the roads . . . we'll be back at the Kube, or somewhere worse, by nightfall. I'd rather take my chances with the swamp and animals than the IPF."

"Or that man back there." Halla shudders. "Okay, I vote swamp."

We look at Wyck.

He crosses his arms and glowers. Finally, he gives a tiny nod. "How's your leg?" he asks gruffly.

I recognize the olive branch and smile with relief. I don't like being at odds with him. "It's good, thanks," I say. "Due entirely to your doctoring skills. I'd probably have gangrene by now if you hadn't patched me up."

My lighter tone works. Wyck cracks a smile and says, "I'll play doctor with you any time."

His words jolt me, and I scan his face, but see no intent there except humor. The awkward moment passes when Halla says, "We should see if any of these clothes I got are useful. How many years do you think they sat in that washer-dryer?"

Looking at them, I'm guessing at least twenty. It strikes me as humorous that looters never thought to look inside the broken machine. The clothing consists of tunics and leggings made from some second or third generation intelli-textile, not nearly as figure conforming or temperature regulating as our jumpsuits. For a moment, I'm reluctant to abandon my more advanced clothing, but the jumpsuits are too distinctive and I accept the man's shirt and leggings Halla hands me without complaint. They're a dull brown that will allow me to blend in better, at least.

She hands Wyck a longer pair of black leggings and a tan shirt, and keeps a roomy tunic and flexi-waist pants for herself. By common consent, we semi-disappear behind the nearest trees and shuck our jumpsuits. I resist the urge to spy on Wyck, although I catch a glimpse of his tanned and muscular back by accident. I sniff at my underarm before donning my new clothes, hoping we get the opportunity to bathe before too long. If we have to go three weeks or more without a bath, searchers will be able to find us by the odor. With my belt, the shirt doesn't swallow me completely and I tuck the knife into the back again. Halla tosses me a pair of socks when I emerge.

"There are four and a half pairs of socks," she says, holding up a lone gray sock. "How does that happen?" She looks more pregnant, somehow, in the loose-fitting tunic.

Balling up the torn jumpsuit, I put it in my backpack, thinking that at the very least it will be useful as a pillow. Wyck returns in his new attire, smoothing down his curly hair, and we each eat a vegeprote bar and drink a little water before heading north into the Okefenokee.

The ground beneath us changes gradually and it's not until I hear a splash—frog or fish?—that I realize we're at the swamp's edge. It smells different here with a trace of sulfur in the air. Various forms of fungi sprout from the dead tree trunks, and Spanish moss drapes from the limbs, trailing almost to the ground in some places. It's misnamed, of course; it's really a rootless epiphyte from the pineapple family, not a moss, living on air which seems appropriate given its airy, tendrily appearance. Cypress trees rise spindly and tall, and the scrub oak we've been traveling through peters out. Dragonflies flit past, iridescent flashes of green, blue and red. Mosquitoes descend in a whining cloud and we're slapping at ourselves until we find repellant in the first aid kit and apply it liberally. The amber water on all sides fizzes like a carbonated beverage, small bubbles rising to the top with a barely audible but constant hiss. I eye it dubiously. What could—? Chemicals. Whatever chemicals are contaminating the water are breaking down the peat at the bottom, releasing carbon dioxide. I wish we had time to stop and test it, see what's causing that reaction.

The ACV scooters travel as easily over water and boggy patches as forest ground, so we're able to maintain our speed. "Our scooter is down to one-third charge," Halla says. She's been driving since we stopped for "lunch."

"Mine's just under half," Wyck says.

The hard part starts when the scooters die and we have to trudge the rest of the way. Atlanta is to the northwest and the scooters' compasses keep us headed in the right direction. About noon, Wyck gets bored and says he wants to scout ahead. Without waiting for me or Halla to reply, he skims away. I take advantage of his absence to tell Halla about my non-reunion Reunion Day and my conversation with Proctor Fonner.

"Your parents left you at the Kube?" she asks when I finish. "Abandoned you? The government didn't repossess you?"

"My parents or someone else," I say. "According to Proctor Fonner."

"Well," Halla says, "I'm sad that your parents didn't show up, but I'm glad that you're here with me. Is that horribly selfish of me?"

I shake my head. "I'm glad I'm here, too." Mostly.

We duck to avoid a low hanging branch, and skim across a wide stretch of tea-colored water, edged with algae and dotted with pale purple and yellow water lilies. I'm captivated by the flowers' beauty until I spot two alligators drifting log-like.

Halla asks, "How are you going to find your parents?"

I sigh. "I wish I knew. I need to get access to a DNA database and enter a sample."

Halla looks at me doubtfully.

"I know, easier said than done." I've had a day and a half to think about it, and I'm beginning to realize that gaining access to the kind of facility that houses a DNA database is going to be very hard now that I'm a runaway with no official affiliation. Maybe I can bribe someone to run my sample? With what? I have no electricity or food ration cards to offer. "I'll think of something," I say with fake confidence.

Halla nods and doesn't push. I think again that my problems aren't as big as hers. I may not know how to identify my parents, but at least I'm not pregnant and traveling toward a boyfriend who probably won't want to become an outlaw in order to be with me and our baby. I wonder what Halla will do if we can't find Loudon or if he's not willing to risk his freedom by deserting the IPF to be with her. She'll stay with me and Wyck, I decide. We'll all become pioneers. I deliberately don't think about what will happen when the baby comes or how hard it will be traveling with an illegal infant.

The shadows are lengthening, making it harder to discern boggy patches from solid ground. We should make camp for the night. It's still early, but there's no ghost town here in the swamp to provide shelter and we're going to have to rig something, possibly up a tree. As I'm looking about for a likely spot, Halla steers us out of the trees into a clearing. It's a stretch of open land with a small stream on the far side. Water! Moving water is good—less likely to be contaminated, or harbor prehistoric reptiles who could swallow us down in a single gulp.

As we move into the clearing, Wyck zips from the strip of trees on the far side, crowing, "I found clean water."

He sounds proud enough you'd think he combined the hydrogen and oxygen atoms himself. Halla and I exchange the kind of long-suffering looks that girls have to share sometimes when they're around boys.

He cuts the scooter back and forth across the stream, the air cushion spraying rooster tails of water behind him. Then, he leans deeply and starts toward us, going flat out across the stretch of ground between us.

"You should conserve your electricity," Halla calls. Her gentle face wears a disapproving look.

Wyck ignores her. "Watch this." He spins the scooter in a circle, laughing.

The ground beneath him ripples sluggishly away from the air current and I recognize the danger too late. "Wyck—!"

Pulling out of the spin, he leans forward a hair too much and the nose of his scooter strikes the ground. The air cushion cuts out and Wyck goes flying. The scooter falls, not with a metallic clatter, but with a hideous sucking sound. It begins to sink. Quicksand.

CHAPTER TWELVE

Wyck lands several feet from the scooter and tries to right himself. His lower half is trapped. He flails, bewildered, and sinks further. "Wha—?" His confusion turns to panic as he realizes he's caught. "It's quicksand," he yells. "I can't get out. Help me!"

Halla screams, "Wyck!" She starts to skim us toward him, but I stop her.

"It's not safe. We need something to probe the ground. We can't help Wyck if we get stuck, too."

She stops the scooter and we leap off, letting it fall. Halla frantically hunts for a branch or something to test the ground with. I rip into my pack, remembering the metal stakes from the lab. Finding one, I poke the ground three feet in front of me. Solid. I step forward. Wyck is thirty feet away.

His furious effort to swim, to propel himself toward solid ground, are only dragging him down faster. "Get rid of your backpack and be still. You have to be still," I tell him. "We'll get you out."

"Everly." His eyes plead with me as he shrugs out of his backpack. Mud streaks his face and weighs down his brown curls. His hazel eyes are haunted.

I move as quickly as I can, jabbing the stake at the ground before every step, until it sinks in. I'm still fifteen feet away. Too far. I stretch my arm out anyway, and Wyck reaches for me, but our fingers are still a body length apart. He's sunk to his armpits now.

"Here," Halla says.

She's come up behind me, breathing hard, and she hands me the dead tree limb. Hope lights Wyck's face. "Hold onto me," I tell Halla, grasping one end of the branch and extending it across the quicksand. Halla puts her arms around my waist as my foot moves perilously close to the quagmire. Wyck's left hand latches onto the limb and we all exhale with relief.

"Pull, pull," he says.

Taking a firm hold of the rough wood, I brace myself and pull. Wyck's torso begins to emerge from the muck. He grabs the branch with his other hand. There's a slurping sound as the quicksand releases him, and then a sharp *snap*. Wyck's mouth drops open as he stares at the fragment of splintered bough in his hand. He's still too far to reach. He sinks down to his neck and despair darkens his face.

My eyes fix on his and I swallow hard. He can't die. I can't let him die. I stand frozen for a split second and then

114

realize what I have to do. There isn't time to find another branch, and they'll all be rotten, anyway. The quicksand pulls Wyck down so it covers his mouth. His eyes remain fixed on mine and I think I see acceptance in them. No time. "Halla, grab my feet."

"Why?" She realizes. "Oh, no, Everly, you can't."

"Just do it!"

I strip off my clothes so I'm wearing only a bra and panties—less for the muck to grab onto. Then, I sink to my haunches and ease into the quicksand on my back, staying as flat as I can and distributing my weight over the largest surface by spread-eagling my limbs with Halla holding tight to one ankle. It's surprisingly cold. The muck clamps onto me, pulling me down an inch, and I fight panic.

"Don't let go, Halla."

"I won't."

I hear the steel in her voice and it helps me reach one arm over my head. It feels like moving through a soupy, bottomless bowl of grits. I'm partly on my side, fighting to hold my face out of the quicksand. Only the tips of Wyck's fingers are visible above the surface. He can't die. He can't die. *Don't die.* I grab for his hand. His fingers mesh with mine. He's alive. I'm pretty sure I'm crying. I put everything I have into my grip. Trying to lift him drags me deeper. "Halla, pull, pull!"

Her hands tighten around my ankle and I slide back a couple of inches. It's not fast enough. Wyck will drown. I manage to work my spread leg inward so she can grasp both my ankles. "Lift," I gasp, knowing that when she does so my head will slap into the muck and it will cover my face.

Wyck's fingers have loosened. *Don't die.* I clench my hand harder around his.

Halla hooks her arms under my knees and drags my legs to waist height, forcing my head under the quicksand. I'm ready for it, so I've taken a deep breath and closed my eyes and mouth, but the shock of it, of not being able to see or breathe still panics me. It's all I can do not to kick. I can feel myself moving backward, and I concentrate on holding onto Wyck whose hand has gone totally slack in mine. His weight makes my shoulder ache. It seems like hours, but is probably only twenty seconds, before my thighs scrape against solid ground. I scooch forward on my butt and sit up, and then Halla is grabbing onto Wyck's arm and we're pulling with all our might. I reach beneath the surface and feel for his hair, pulling him up by it until his head is free, then we're catching him under the armpits and hauling upwards. The quicksand releases him reluctantly, with a *thwuck*. His torso hits solid ground.

He lies still.

Frantically, I scrape the mud off his face. I reach into his mouth and clear it. "Water," I tell Halla. While she races to get one of the water bladders, I roll Wyck onto his side and pound his back. Murky water dribbles from his mouth. I turn him onto his back, straddle his waist, and begin to compress his lungs. "Breathe," I command with each push. "Breathe."

Halla returns and rinses his face and nose with some of our precious water. I keep pumping his chest. My arms are on fire. The quicksand caked on my face, arms and torso is drying. It itches.

Wyck coughs, gasps, rolls over and vomits a trickle of water, mud and bile.

I stand. Relief floods through me and my knees buckle. Halla is crying, patting Wyck's shoulder, and smiling all at the same time.

"You saved us," I tell her.

"I don't know where the strength came from," she admits. "I didn't know legs could be so heavy. I kept telling myself 'I can do all things in Him who strengthens me.' Then I'd take a step backwards, then another. My thighs hurt." She rubs them.

Wyck struggles to his knees and looks up at us. "Thank you," he tells Halla. His eyes lock on mine. "Thank you."

A lump rises in my throat, but then anger swamps my relief. He was showing off, wasting the scooter's electric charge, goofing around, and he almost died. *He almost died.* I fold my arms over my chest. "You lost the scooter and most of our supplies."

Turning my back on him, I march toward the burbling stream. I need a bath.

The cool, clear stream water is a huge relief. Algae- and alligator-free. Huge old cypress trees overhang it, with moss draping down like a curtain. It's only knee deep, so I remove my boots and wade in. I splash water over my torso and duck my head under. That reminds me too much of being in the quicksand and I jerk upright, my hair flinging water droplets. I gasp, then resume sluicing my upper body, removing my bra to rinse it out. When I'm clean, I wring out my bra and slip into my clothes, draping the wet bra over a branch to dry. I pull on my boots and rejoin the others. They've moved away from the quicksand to the far side of a cypress tree with a trunk big enough for all three of us to lean against. Our remaining scooter is parked on the right, forming a semi-barrier against anything approaching from that direction.

"My turn," Wyck says, not meeting my eyes. He walks toward the creek.

Halla is sunk down on a mossy hummock, resting, and I busy myself finding firewood, worrying about what the loss of our supplies will mean. It's catastrophic. By the time I return with an armload, Wyck is back from the stream, hair flattened, clothes dripping.

"There are fish in the stream," he says. "Big ones. I could probably catch one for dinner."

He hefts the metal stake I dropped; he's talking about spear fishing. "I'll make a fire." My tone is cool and he pauses for a moment, but then heads back to the stream without saying anything.

I've got a crackling fire going and have collected enough wood to last the night, and Halla is still asleep when he returns with a large catfish with yellow whiskers drooping from his makeshift spear. My tummy grumbles, but I say, "One fish can't replace everything you lost."

Without replying, he gets to work scaling and filleting the fish, cursing when his bare hands come in contact with the catfish's barbs. He wields the knife with dexterity, and

I'm caught up in how efficiently his hands move when Halla groans.

I turn my head to look at her. "You okay?"

"Cramps." She grimaces and presses a hand to her side.

"Wyck caught a fish."

"Excuse me." She stumbles past the fire, into the woods, far enough for privacy. I'm not worried about her getting lost because the fire will lead her back.

She's back five minutes later. "I'm bleeding."

"Did you cut yourself on some—"

"The baby." Her forehead scrunches with pain. "I don't want to lose my baby." Her distress makes her drawl more noticeable.

Oh, no. I have never felt so totally inadequate. I don't know what to say or do, how to stop the bleeding or deliver a pre-term baby. Any baby. "Are you . . . are you in labor?"

"I don't know."

She's on the verge of tears, so I get her to sit close to the fire and join her. "Is there a lot of blood, like gushing?"

She shakes her head. "No, just spots."

I relax a little. It doesn't seem like she's going to bleed to death immediately. Forgetting my animosity, I look at Wyck.

"I'll get a blanket," he says. He drapes it over Halla's shoulder and she leans against me. Wyck stands there for a moment, and then says, "I'll finish cooking the fish. Maybe you'll feel like eating in a bit."

Halla nods gamely, although I can tell food is the farthest thing from her mind. Soon, the aroma of broiling fish fills the air and my mouth waters. Even with no spices, it's the best thing I've ever eaten when Wyck hands me a slightly charred chunk. Halla gets a smaller piece which she nibbles at while Wyck and I wolf our portions down. At intervals, Halla winces or hunches forward slightly. I rub her shoulder; it's all I can do.

"Is it getting worse?" I whisper.

She thinks a moment. "No, I don't think so." She looks a little cheered by the realization, but then arcs forward with a low moan.

It's deep twilight by now and we need to decide what we're doing for the night. I had hoped to be able to find some way to sleep above ground, in a makeshift hammock, but the cypresses are too tall, their branches too high to reach. We're stuck on the ground.

"We should keep the fire going," I say, "and get rid of the fish remains. Who knows what their scent might attract?"

We're all thinking about the dog pack, I'm sure, even though we haven't seen any mammals all day. Wyck quickly gathers up the fish offal, walks a few yards, and flings it into the quicksand. "Nature's trash can," he says.

"I'll take first watch tonight," I say. I'm tired, but I'm not gray with exhaustion from near death like Wyck, or worried about miscarrying like Halla.

Wyck nods, says, "Wake me in four hours," rolls himself into a ball near the fire, and falls asleep. He doesn't have a blanket since his is buried in who knows how many feet of quicksand. The nighttime chorus of insects strikes up as the last vestiges of twilight fade to black, and I can hear the creek's burble and the squeaks of hunting bats. I strain to hear more ominous sounds. Almost as if I willed it, a grumbling bellow sounds and it takes me a moment to recognize it as an alligator's call. Fighting? Mating? Hunting? It's far enough off that I'm not too worried. I stay by Halla, stroking her hair.

I think she's asleep until she says in a low voice, "What if I lose my baby, Ev? This would all be for nothing. You, Wyck—all of us with nowhere to go, outlaws. I would have dragged you into this, put all our lives in danger, for *nothing*."

She sounds anguished and my only concern is to calm her. "First of all, you didn't 'drag' anybody away from the Kube. I came for my own reasons and Wyck came for his. Yeah, we wanted to help you find Loudon, but we're each here for our own reasons. I want to find out about my parents, remember? And Wyck's dodging sentry service. If"—I swallow hard—"if you lose the baby, we'll take care of you, and we'll get you to Loudon one way or the other. You'll still want to find Loudon, won't you?"

"Oh, yes," she says on a sob. "Everything will be okay then. Everything will be okay then."

I'm thinking that she's deluding herself, that finding Loudon will not even begin to solve all her problems—in fact, it will create new ones—when it dawns on me that I'm thinking the same way. I haven't looked past identifying my parents to what that *means*. Potentially nothing. I might not be able to find them once I know who they are. I make myself stop thinking about all the possible negatives by staring into the fire's flickering flames. They cast shadows over Wyck, twitching as if he might be dreaming. Nightmares about quicksand. They warm Halla's face and exaggerate the curve of her lashes where they rest on her cheeks. I ease away from her now that she's finally sleeping, albeit restlessly, and massage my stiff shoulder. Stretching my hands toward the fire, I'm unbearably grateful for its light and warmth in the middle of this vast, unfriendly swamp.

Without warning, the rain that's been threatening all day begins to fall. The fire fizzles. I endure it for four hours, wake Wyck, and wrap myself in my blanket, convinced I'll never sleep.

I wake to a hand clamped over my mouth and a body pressing down on me. My eyes pop open but I can't make out anything but a pale blur above me in the dark. Panic burns through me. I start to writhe and kick against the strong hold until Wyck breathes against my ear, "Soldier."

CHAPTER THIRTEEN

I still, and Wyck cautiously removes his hand from my mouth. I strain to listen and hear voices behind us, near the quicksand.

". . . got to be there . . . transponder . . ."

"It's a blasted bog—there's nothing here, for crap's sake."

I move cautiously to peer around the tree trunk. Wyck joins me. An IPF soldier, gray uniform ghostly in the first light of dawn, is scraping quicksand off his boot with a stick. He repeats, "The scooter's not here." His own ACV scooter stands at the clearing's edge.

I am overwhelmingly grateful for the rain I had cursed when it doused our fire hours ago. Almost simultaneously, I realize that the scooters must have transponders that communicated with micro-drones we never noticed, and that the soldier must be talking to a comrade via radio since there's only one man visible. He's fifty feet away, walking the edge of the quicksand, poking at it with his stick. He's headed away from us, but when he turns, he's going to find us. I wonder how far away his buddies are, and how many of them there are. I motion for Wyck to wake Halla, and pull my knife. My mind whirs with escape options. We've only got one scooter, Halla's ill . . . For a moment I despair. If we give ourselves up, will they go easy on us, maybe let us return to the Kube, serve a few zillion detention hours, and let things go back to the way they were?

Even as the defeatist thought crosses my brain, I remember Halla and her baby. I can't let them catch Halla. They'll take her baby away. My mind clears. I have the least to lose of our threesome. Halla will lose her baby if she goes back and Wyck will be tried as a deserter. They need to take the scooter and try to outrun the soldiers. I will have to make my escape on foot. We can attempt to meet up on the northwest edge of the swamp. It's not much of a plan and I don't have much hope that if we split up we'll be able to find each other again, but nothing better comes to me. The rain's patter hides the slight sounds I make as I crawl to where Wyck and the now-awake Halla are stuffing gear into her bag. I whisper my plan to them, emphasizing that they'll have to dump the scooter as soon as they get far enough away.

Halla doesn't argue; she sets her mouth in a grim line and begins to creep toward the scooter.

"You go with Halla," Wyck says. "I'll lead them—"

Before he can finish the thought, a shout sounds. "Hey, a brassiere. Hanging on a tree. Someone's here."

My bra! Damn.

Heavy footsteps thud toward us. Halla ignites the scooter and emerges from cover, bent low over the handlebars. The soldier whirls and reaches for the beamer strapped to his back. "Halt!"

Halla keeps going, zigzagging toward the trees. Before the soldier can react, I'm running to his scooter. I leap on it and barrel toward him, thinking of nothing but giving Halla time to get away. The soldier stares at me, eyes rounding as he realizes I'm not going to swerve. He yells something I can't hear over the blood pounding in my ears, and lowers the beamer to firing position. I'm only three feet from him when he fires.

The pulse strikes the scooter with a crackle and it flips end over end. Time slows. I go flying. The sky, then trees whirl by, and then I crash into the soldier who can't scramble out of the way fast enough. Smack. We go down in a tangle of limbs. The beamer skitters away. My head hits the ground, hard, and stars swirl. My legs are trapped under the soldier's torso. The soldier recovers first, shakes his head, and grabs my arm in his gloved hand. His face, behind the helmet's visor, is young. He's got sandy-red eyebrows and pale blue eyes. His expression changes from shaken to angry as I watch. He stands and jerks on my arm, hauling me to my feet. Pain rips through my shoulders and I cry out.

Before he can say anything, something tears his hand off me and he flies backwards, as if hit by a train.

Uncomprehending, I turn and see Wyck standing, legs braced, the soldier's beamer leveled. I look over my shoulder and see nothing but bubbles in the quicksand where the soldier landed with enough force to bury him immediately. I feel sick.

"He was already dead," Wyck says, understanding. "I blew a hole in him." The weapon he holds quivers.

I swallow hard a couple of time, and say, "There's another one."

Wyck nods. "He—or they—must have a bigger ACV. Think about it—if they found us, they'd need to transport us. It's too big to maneuver easily through the trees."

"When his buddy doesn't return, or answer the radio, they'll find a way to get here."

"We need to be gone. His scooter?"

Shaking my head, I say, "Too dangerous. That's how they found us—locators on the scooters. We should get rid of it to confuse the others."

Wyck runs to the scooter, ignites it, and rides it to the quicksand's edge. Dismounting without turning it off, he pushes it over the mire, repeating, "Nature's trash can." It skims easily over the quicksand, rippling the muck. When it is a good distance out, Wyck hits it with a single pulse from the rifle and it drops. The quicksand absorbs it with a phlegmy *glub, glub*.

Nature's graveyard, I think. I turn away before it's fully gone, retrieve the soggy bra that betrayed us, stuff the blanket into my backpack, and kick at the cold fire to scatter the evidence of our presence. I'm about to toss the charred bits into the quicksand and sink them when we hear the *whoosh* of an approaching ACV.

Wyck grabs my hand and drags me into the trees. We run.

At first we run blindly, stumbling over hummocks, letting the Okefenokee dictate our path by veering around expanses of water the scooters would have skimmed across without difficulty. The rain continues and I'm glad because it's washing away our tracks and drowning the sound of our headlong dash. I'm already so wet I can't get any wetter. Wyck, with his longer legs, is slightly in front of me most of the way. We don't spot our pursuers, but I think I hear voices once. Finally, he stops, pulling me under a moss-draped tree surrounded by dead brush on three sides; it's like a small cave. We breathe loudly, trying to catch our breath.

He gasps, "We can't just run. We need a plan."

"We can hide. Wait for them to give up. Then find Halla." I hope she is far from the IPF pursuers and that's she's okay.

Wyck shakes his head. "They're not going to give up. I killed one of them."

"They don't know that," I say quickly. "He could have had an accident, like yesterday's, and ended up in the quicksand."

Wyck gives me a look.

I squeeze water out of a hank of sodden hair, trying to think. "Right. Okay, well, we can't lead them to Halla. How many of them do you think there are?"

"Probably only one. Think about it: How many trained soldiers do you think Fonner would have sent to recover three kids?"

"But I heard voices." I answer my own objection. "The radio. So, even if there's only one now, reinforcements might be on the way."

We contemplate that depressing idea.

I'm wondering if we could fool the soldier by doubling back, when Wyck says, "We need to ambush him."

My initial response is negative, but as I think about it, I see how it could work. Wyck still has the other soldier's weapon. "I could scream," I muse aloud, "to draw him in. I'll be on the ground, gripping my leg like I'm injured. You'll be hiding. I'll tell him that when I twisted my ankle you kept running, leaving me to fend for myself. He'll get down from the ACV to take me prisoner, and you'll jump out and hold the weapon on him while I tie him up. I can use the wire."

"Then we can use the ACV to get out of this effing swamp. When we find Halla, we point the ACV to the east and let it go. With any luck, it'll be miles away from us by the time they locate it."

"With any luck," I echo. "I don't want the soldier to get hurt, though, not badly."

"They'll find him within a day, using his locator," Wyck says impatiently. "And as long as he does what we say, I won't have to fire. I didn't want to shoot the other one, but he had you and . . ." He peters out, looking haunted. "I killed . . . I killed that man. He's dead, really dead. He was a soldier, but I shouldn't—"

"You did what you had to do. You saved me," I say, and lean up to press a quick kiss on his lips.

He shrinks back instinctively, but then leans in and kisses me back. His lips are tentative against mine at first, but then the kiss deepens. We pull apart after a moment, and stand with our foreheads touching, eyes closed, fingers loosely entwined. After a long moment, I pull away and ask, "Where should we set up the ambush?"

"I saw a spot."

Wyck leads me past a stagnant pool alive with insect larvae to a slight depression on what looks like an old wildlife trail. "You lie here," Wyck says, pointing, "and I'll be hiding in there." He points to a stretch of shallow water where a cypress tree's "knees" stick up almost to waist height in spots. It's a good hiding place.

"We'd better check for alligators and snakes," I say.

Once sure that the hiding place is reptile free, Wyck wades in, crouches behind the knobby roots and disappears from sight. The rain has let up, but the ground is soggy as I arrange myself on the path, take a deep breath, and scream. I try to imagine the worst pain I could be in, and end up releasing my frustration over my parents, my fears for Halla, and my distress over the soldier's death in one long, trembling howl. "Help," I cry. "Please help me."

I stop and listen. Nothing. I try sobbing, interspersing my sobs with pleas for help. "I don't want to die out here. I'm afraid. Please, I'm sorry." Pretending to be afraid is making me afraid. I stiffen my shoulders and remind myself that I'm acting, that I'm tough, that Wyck is mere yards away. My throat is raw.

The clacking of dead reeds gives me a moment to hunch over and grab my ankle as if in mortal pain. I peek from behind my hair, expecting to see the soldier approaching in front of me. A footstep sounds behind me and I slew around to find myself facing a soldier, visor down, weapon leveled at me. From my vantage point, he looks ominously tall, burly and alert. He scans the area before focusing on me.

"AC Westin?" His voice is a bass rumble and he sounds older than the other soldier. His chin, which I can see below the visor, is square, his skin like ebony.

"Jax," I whisper. "Everly Jax. Halla took the scooter—she's long gone. Then Wyck left me when I got hurt. He left me alone, ran off and left me to die." I grab my ankle and find it's disturbingly easy to force out a few tears. "I don't want to die out here. I saw an alligator. I'm sorry I left the Kube. I want to go back." There's an undercurrent of truth in the words and they seem to convince the soldier.

He steps closer. "What happened to Corporal Heroux?"

I blank my face. "Who?"

"He found your camp! I can't find any trace of him or his scooter."

"I never saw him," I say. "We heard an ACV coming and we ran. Halla took the scooter and Wyck and I just ran."

"Get up." He motions with the particle beam rifle and frees a pair of cuffs from his belt with one hand.

"I can't."

"Try."

He's clearly not going to come closer, not going to give me a chance to pull a hidden weapon and attack him. I bite my lip, roll onto my hands and knees and make a show of shoving myself to a standing position. I balance on my "good" leg, holding my hands out to the side to show I'm unarmed. I put my other foot down gingerly, as if testing it to see if it will hold my weight, let out a shriek and crumple forward toward the soldier.

Taken off guard, he stumbles back a step, but I knock him off balance and latch onto the beamer's muzzle. Before he can recover, Wyck pops up from his hiding place, dripping, and points his weapon at the soldier's chest. "Freeze."

Realizing I'm between Wyck and the soldier, I drop and roll to my right before clambering to my feet.

"Drop your weapon and raise your hands," Wyck commands, "or I will shoot."

The soldier and I both hear the grim intent in his voice. Slowly, slowly, the soldier lowers his beamer and I grab it away. He raises his hands to shoulder height. "You don't want to make things worse for yourselves, kids," he says.

"Put the cuffs on him." Wyck's weapon never wavers.

"Hands behind your back," I tell the soldier.

Keeping a wary eye on Wyck, who has come closer, he complies. I figure out the magnet cuffs, loop them around his wrists, and activate them.

"Sit."

"You must be the deserter," the soldier says, facing Wyck. "Coward."

Wyck kicks his feet out from under him. Not able to use his hands to break his fall, he sits hard, letting out a pained *oof*. Pulling wire from my backpack, I bind his booted ankles. Wyck pulls off the soldier's helmet and communicator. He's bald, his head a shiny black dome. He glares at us. "You're being stupid. Running away was one thing, but now you've attacked an IPF soldier. Do you know what the penalties are for armed attack on a military member or facility? It's treason."

"Shut up." Wyck slugs him behind the ear with the rifle's butt.

The soldier slumps sideways.

"You didn't need to hit him."

"He's done worse."

"How do you know?" I kneel beside the soldier and check for a pulse. Still strong. Relieved, I stand.

"He's IPF. Like my dad."

Wyck stands rigid, beamer ready, like he'd appreciate another opportunity to clock the soldier, so I say, "We need to find his ACV and get away from here. "

"It can't be far." Wyck hunts to the left and I choose the right. The ACV is only a short distance away, an enclosed six-seater with IPF insignia on the armored hull. With its padded seats, it looks like the height of luxury after two days of slogging in the open air on the stand-up scooters. The guns mounted on either side remind me it's more than comfy transport. "Over here," I call to Wyck.

Wyck breaks into a smile when he sees it. "Twink." He leans into the driver's compartment and runs a hand over the seat. "I wish we could keep this. Ever driven one of these?"

"Nope."

"Me, neither." He climbs in, clearly prepared to give it a try. When he ignites it, a head's up display provides controls and firing mechanisms for the weapons. Wyck's hand lingers over them and I can tell he's itching to shoot something.

"Wait." I check the cooler unit tucked under the dashboard. There are several water bladders, food pods, and tangerines. My mouth waters at the site of the fruit. "I'm going to leave him some water."

Before Wyck can object, I take a bladder and carry it back to the soldier. He's conscious, and sitting up.

"Water," I tell him, placing the bladder on his lap so he can bend to reach the suction tube. "They'll find you before too long."

"We'll find *you*," he says, meeting my gaze without flinching. "Never doubt it."

Letting him have the last word—he was the one tied up and helpless in a swamp, after all—I hurry back to the ACV. Wyck barely waits until the door seals before skimming forward. Branches scrape the vehicle's sides until he gets used to compensating for its wider width. While he steers, I help myself to a tangerine. The fruit's brightness in my mouth is heaven. I close my eyes for a moment, savoring it, then offer a section to Wyck.

Barely chewing it, he swallows and says, "We should be there in a couple of hours, not long after Halla, assuming she doesn't run into any trouble."

Deliberately not thinking about the kinds of trouble Halla might have encountered, I begin to search the ACV for supplies that we can take with us when we abandon it. The back is configured with a storage locker running lengthwise between two rows of seats. I crawl into the rear and unlatch it, finding two beamers and an ESD, flashlights, twelve packets of dehydrated meals, a first aid kit, bio-chem gear, night vision binoculars, a pop-up intelli-textile shelter, and a duffel.

"Lots of good stuff here," I say, listing it for Wyck.

"Great. We can replace some of the stuff I lost."

We're both quiet, remembering the stupidity that led to the loss of most of our supplies.

"I've learned my lesson," Wyck says finally, shooting me a look. "I was an asshole. Irresponsible. Stupid. Selfish. All the things the proctors always called me. But not anymore. Not since yesterday. You risked your life to save me. I probably can't ever be worthy of that, but I want to be."

Tears prick my eyelids and I blink them back. The silence feels freighted with meaning, and I feel compelled to break it, to offer up my own faults. "Well, I can be too bossy, too controlling, too single-minded."

"Yeah you can."

He grins, and I grin back and the moment passes.

"Let's go find Halla," I say, relaxing against the seat.

CHAPTER FOURTEEN

We reach the Okefenokee's northwest corner without incident. Wyck even resists the temptation to put a few rounds into five alligators lazing on a mud bank. I'm very grateful for the ACV since getting through the swamp without it would have meant either long detours to avoid water, or taking our chances with the alligators. We see two lean-to huts camouflaged with moss and branches, not together, but no people, and I wonder if people live in the swamp or if the huts are long abandoned. Wyck wants to stop and check them out, but we've got enough supplies and I say it's not worth the risk. For the moment, he's willing to go along. I don't expect that to last much longer than it takes him to semi-forget the terror of the quicksand. I don't suppose he'll ever totally forget it. I certainly won't.

Gradually, the gleam of dark water beneath us gives way to firmer ground. Maple and oak trees, crowned with the neon kudzu but no leaves of their own, begin to replace the brooding cypress trees, and I can glimpse open space in the distance: brown and tan, lifeless, empty. Like so much of Amerada.

"Halla wouldn't be out there," Wyck says, echoing my thoughts. He slows the ACV. "She'd stay under cover."

"We need to get out. She's going to think we're the IPF in this thing." I pat my armrest.

"Wait." Wyck studies an icon on the display. "I think this might be a loudspeaker." He presses it and says, "Can you hear me?"

His voice booms out, tinny and distorted.

"I think they heard you in Atlanta."

He ignores me. "Halla. Halla Westin. It's me—Wyck. Everly's with me. Everything's okay. Come on out."

The way we're announcing our presence makes me vaguely uneasy. Maybe it's the memory of those lean-tos. We cruise back and forth on a north-south line with no reaction. I scan to either side, hoping to spot Halla, but see nothing.

"You try," Wyck says.

I lean toward the microphone. "Halla, please come out." When there's no response after another ten minutes, I say, "I'm getting worried. She should be around here somewhere by now, unless something's happened to her. Maybe the baby . . ." I have visions of her miscarrying in the swamp, of her bleeding to death, alone and helpless.

"We need to set this thing down and look for her. It's time to get rid of it anyway."

Reluctantly, Wyck cuts the power and the ACV settles on the ground, clear of the trees. We spend twenty minutes sorting through the supplies and fill an IPF rucksack with essentials. It's heavy, but Wyck insists on stuffing it as full as possible. I get the feeling he's trying to atone for losing our supplies in the quicksand.

"It's not going to help if you die of exhaustion," I point out.

"I've got this."

His tone makes me throw my hands up in a surrender gesture. "Fine."

Wyck leans into the driver's compartment, and fiddles with the gauges and controls to override safety protocols so it will continue pilotless on the course he sets. He ignites the ACV and backs out of the cockpit. "There. This puppy's headed for the beach."

I jump out of the way as it skims forward. I'm sad watching it go. Even though we only had it for a short time, it made me feel safe, like I was wrapped in an armored cocoon. With any luck, though, it will be a hundred miles away by the time the IPF intercepts it.

"A flare," Wyck suddenly says, excited. "We can send up a flare. Halla will see it." He pulls one from the rucksack.

"Other people might see it, too."

"Do you want to find Halla, or don't you?" Wyck asks.

"Of course—"

"Any better ideas?" Taking my "no" for granted, he sends the flare up before I even answer.

It whizzes skyward in near silence and bursts into an umbrella of orangey-red high above our heads. The intensity of the color is dazzling against the gray sky and the dun landscape. We tip our heads back and watch it for long seconds.

"C'mon," I finally say. "We can't stand here in the open. There's a tree over there we can climb. The branches are dense enough I don't think anyone will see us."

We melt among the trees and I point out the one I think will give us the best view. Stashing our packs under a nearby thicket we scramble up. I go first and work my way higher because I'm lighter. The view is exhilarating, although the branch I settle on shakes under my weight. I straddle it with my back against the trunk, my legs hanging down. Wyck settles below me, straddling a thicker limb, facing me. To the east, I can see into the swamp with the denser growth of trees and the occasional gleam of water. To the west, the ground is barren and almost flat. The featureless landscape offers few hiding places and my stomach clenches at the thought of traversing so much open country to reach Atlanta. Wyck and I talk in a desultory way for the first half-hour, but then he falls silent. I get the feeling he's thinking about shooting the soldier. To distract him, I ask, "If you could be anything, what would you be?"

He doesn't hesitate. "An astronaut."

I raise my brows. "Really? Why?"

"A universe that goes on for infinity . . . isn't that mind-blowing? In all that space, there's got to be another planet where we could live. I could discover it, colonize it. We—humanity—could have a do-over, not fuck it up so bad this time around." His tone lightens. "I'd invite you and Halla, a couple of others from the Kube, to come live on planet Wyckiter. What about you?" He cranes his neck to look up at me.

"I think I'd still want to be a bio-chemist," I say, semi-apologetically. I should want to be more than I am, shouldn't I? "Nothing fascinates me like genes and living things." I take his silence for disappointment in my lack of imagination and wriggle, trying to get comfortable on the narrow limb.

"How do you think we can find the Defiance after we drop Halla off with Loudon?" Wyck asks.

I stare down at him, puzzled, noticing a haze of whiskers on his chin and peeling sunburn on the bridge of his nose. "The Defiance? Why—?" I hadn't worked out the details in my mind, but I'd assumed we'd head for an outpost together, with or without Halla, depending, after I found a way to meet my parents—

He doesn't pick up on my confusion. "It's not like there'll be a sign pointing to their headquarters or anything. They've got to be careful, vet volunteers, make sure they're not taking in traitors. I overheard an IPF sergeant talking about the Defiance sabotaging manufacturing facilities near Auburn—"

"We're not joining the Defiance! That's treason."

Wyck's brow furrows. "The Defiance is fighting for individual rights, including yours. They're fighting to overturn the Prags, to win back our right to live where we want, do whatever kind of work we want to, have access to computers and communicate with anyone we want—maybe even in other countries, for everyone who wants to to have babies, regardless of their genes, for—"

"They're fighting. Great. Hasn't this country had enough fighting? The Resource Wars, the Between? We're just getting back on our feet. The quarantine and immigration laws have almost eliminated the flu. Everyone's got access to food under the Prags—no one's starving like before."

"Sure, if they toe the line and give up—"

"The Prags are going to find a way to eradicate the locusts. We're so close. Then we'll have more food, people can grow their own, and maybe the laws will change."

Wyck sneers. "People in power never willingly give it up. Even our own history tells us that. Look at the Revolutionary War, President Fredricks. If the locusts die off tomorrow, the Prags'll find other reasons to keep us under their thumb."

"That's not true." I take a deep breath and change tack. "We could go west, to an outpost. It'll be an adventure of sorts. The government isn't so influential out there; at least, that's how it seems on Assembly videos and from Proctor Mannisham's lectures. They need people—young, strong people like us. I can help with food production, and you can do your gadget thing—there must be dozens of processes you can automate at an outpost, things they do manually that you could invent a machine for, things that need fixing."

His corrugated brow tells me I'm not getting through. I bite my lip. I can't join the Defiance because their fighting and sabotage undermine Amerada's recovery, but I don't want to lose Wyck. I'm practically pleading with him. "I can't not use my bio-chem training, not after all the time I've put in, the money the government's invested in me. I have a responsibility—"

I think I see movement. I focus on the area, a couple of hundred yards into the swamp, and stare at it so hard it goes blurry. I blink twice, thinking I imagined the movement, and then a glint catches my eye.

"Wyck," I whisper. "The scooter." I point. Halla's weaving between the trees, obviously looking for something. Us. She's found a dark green jacket somewhere . . .

"Finally." He's about to yell to Halla when I kick his shoulder. "Hey, what the—"

"Ssh. I don't think it's Halla." The scooter is definitely the one we took from the Kube, but the bulky figure riding it doesn't look like Halla. A chill works its way up from my toes. What has happened to Halla? "Down, climb down," I say, as the scooter glides closer. "We've got to follow it."

We start down, the need for haste clashing with the need for quiet. Twigs snag my hair and gouge my skin. Perched on the bottom limb, we scan the area before jumping lightly to the ground. We can hear the *whoosh* of the ACV now and we duck behind the tree trunk as the scooter passes on the far side of the thicket. The driver, a man with a bushy beard scraggling half-way down his chest, is scanning from side to side. I bend forward instinctively to hide the white gleam of my face when the man looks in our direction. The scooter pauses, and I hold my breath, not daring to breathe, but then he continues on, picking up speed. Wyck and I grab our packs from their hiding places and take off after him. *Halla, we're coming.*

He's not traveling fast, but even so he's going faster than we can go on foot. We're trotting, dodging roots and fallen limbs and boggy spots, trying to keep the scooter in sight. It draws steadily further away, even though we pick up our pace until we're running as fast as we can. Wyck's face is red with the exertion of carrying his heavy pack and I'm gasping for breath. Intent on the scooter, I run full-tilt into a spider web strung between two trees.

"Oh!" The sound is involuntary, not loud enough to carry to the man on Halla's scooter, but Wyck frowns anyway. The web restrains me for a moment; it's made of the ultra-strong, ultra-sticky spider silk scientists genetically engineered in the '40s. They thought it would help the spiders to catch more locusts. Like so many of those initiatives, it was ineffective, if not an outright failure. Wyck pulls out his knife and slices through the web. I try to shake the sticky strands off as I run.

We can't see the scooter anymore, and we can barely hear its hum. "Left," I gasp, angling that way. I duck beneath some Spanish moss and find myself confronting a twenty foot wide strip of water. I'm about to plunge through it, suspecting it can't be more than waist deep, when Wyck grabs my arm. He gives me a little shake and points to the middle of the tarn. A snake oils its way across the surface, its thick body and triangular head a black stain on the amber-colored water. Cottonmouth. Poisonous and aggressive. I back away, sobbing with frustration at having to circumnavigate the pond. We reach the other side.

"Listen." I hold up a hand. I can't hear anything. I turn to Wyck, who looks as distressed as I feel. "I can't hear it. He's gone!"

"We'll find him. We'll find Halla. C'mon. We'll keep on this tack." He goes ahead of me now, and I follow.

We're less worried about making noise, and twigs crack under our boots. After half an hour, we take a quick break for water, but resume walking after a bare two minutes. For once, I'm grateful for the morning physical fitness sessions at the Kube. We check the compass frequently to stay on the scooter's last known path; it's all we can do. I'm determined to search for a week if we have to, but I'm so tired I can't squelch the words my mind is tossing out: futile, pointless, too late.

"Need a break." I drop to my knees and Wyck comes back to me.

He's bending to offer me a vegeprote bar when suddenly he straightens. He points up. "Look! Smoke."

The merest wisp of smoke snakes into the air behind me. A smile breaks over my face. "Let's go get her."

Hope gives us renewed energy and we make our way toward the smoke, using it like the magi used the Christmas star, in the Bible story Halla insists on reading aloud every December 25th. I wish we had a camel or two. Boy, I'm so tired I feel drunk, like the one time I tried Wexl, sneaking a taste from Dr. Ronan's stash. One sip was all it took to make me feel fuzzy. We move slowly now, placing our feet carefully to avoid twigs, and taking care not to brush against the crackly undergrowth or tree trunks.

I smell the camp before I see it. There's the fire, an earthy, slightly bitter aroma I guess is peat. They've dried and are burning peat dug from the depths of the swamp. Then there's a rancid, greasy smell that seems to leave an oily film on the roof of my mouth, and the sour smell of unwashed bodies. This is no overnight camping site; this is someone's—or multiple someones'—permanent home. I'm looking down to make sure I place my foot quietly when a dark glint warns me. I stop Wyck with a hand across his chest, and bend to get a better look at an early warning system consisting of a wire strung with utensils and cast-off bits of metal. If we'd tripped over it, the clanging would have given us away.

Easing back, we follow the wire to the right. It seems to circle the whole camp. I'm reluctant to risk stepping over it. I've about decided that's our only option when the wire ends at a stake, and a vile odor tells me we've reached the area set aside as a latrine. Makes sense: they don't want to trip over their own alarm system every time they need to pee. We're on the opposite side of the camp. The fire crackles with false welcome and the man we saw earlier putters around outside a lean-to constructed of branches and stretches of gray fabric that might have been sails or tarps. He's fussing with a contraption made of loops of copper tubing and glass vessels. It's filled with fumes that evaporate when heated to leave an orangey-pink sludge on the container's walls. Psyche, maybe? I've heard of the illegal hallucinogen during Assemblies, but never seen it. It's bad stuff and dangerous to make. Highly volatile. He carefully measures in crystals of some kind and adds water. Trying not to inhale through my nose, I watch for ten long minutes and almost decide he's a one man drug-making operation when he speaks.

"Tweren't nuthin, I tells ya. Nobbut the flare. Not the IPF nor no one else. Not no one lookin fer the breeder. You worrit too much." His voice is gravelly, his accent virtually unintelligible. I get the gist, though: he went to check on the flare at someone's behest and didn't find anything.

"Yer sure?" The voice is the crackle of a dried leaf. It belongs to a crone who hobbles out of the makeshift hut and stretches a hand to the fire. A braid of gray hair flops over her shoulder and she flings it back. "Didja find some of the mushrooms I sent yer fer? We're a-goin ta have ta feed the breeder fer another month, I'm thinkin, or the babe won't survive."

"We mun sell 'er now. We'll get a good price and not ave to feed another mouth," the man argues.

The breeder. They're talking about Halla, about selling her and her baby. We've got to rescue her. I back away slowly, motioning Wyck to come with me. When we're far enough away that I can no longer smell the latrine ditch, or hear the couple arguing, I whisper. "Halla must be in the hut."

"Who do you suppose they want to sell her to?"

"It doesn't matter." I brush the question aside. "We need to get her out of there. Tonight." I can't imagine how terrified she must be, especially if she knows their plans for her and the baby. "There's about two hours of light left. We need to get a look at the whole camp and be prepared to act anytime one of them leaves. It'll be easier to take on just one of them, preferably the woman." She looks tough and wiry, but she doesn't outweigh us by a hundred pounds like the man.

"I can shinny up a tree," Wyck says, "and scope out the compound."

He spent too much time listening to the Kube's IPFers. I mentally roll my eyes, but agree. "Good idea. I'll work my way all the way around the camp and see what's what. We'll meet back here."

His eyes shine and I know if Halla weren't in danger, he'd be enjoying this. Shifting the backpack on my shoulders, I creep back toward the camp, dropping to a crouch when I'm close. When I spot the wire, I follow it around. It takes me past the rear of the hut and I'm heartened to see that the back is no more than a flap of material. Maybe we can slice through it and spirit Halla out this way. *What if she's injured?* I think about that, wondering if the couple hurt her when they captured her. I give my head a little shake. I can't worry about it. She can't be too hurt, since the woman talked about keeping her for a month. I know the baby's not due for a couple of months, at least, and I try not to think about how they would induce birth so early.

We could buy Halla from them. The thought leaps into my head. I give it some thought. I have no idea what the couple expect to get for Halla. Would they accept our supplies as payment? We've got the tent, the NVGs and the weapons we took from the IPF ACV. They would make life a lot easier for people living off the land in this forsaken corner of the Okefenokee. Halla's captors might accept a trade, or they might try to kill or capture me and Wyck and steal our stuff. We can't risk it.

I'm far enough away that I rise to a half-crouch and immediately walk into a line of dangling, rubbery things. One drapes over my shoulder and I find myself eyeball to eyeball with a water moccasin. Its mouth yawns open, displaying the cottony inside and needle-sharp fangs. I bite back a scream and jump away. Another swings against my arm, cold and heavy. It takes everything I have not to run screaming. They're dead. *They're dead*, I tell myself again, fighting for calm. It's a line of snakes strung by their tails, six or eight of them, the longest about five feet and the shortest something under three feet. I recognize two cottonmouths, a rattlesnake, and a king snake. I ease myself away from the snakes and take three steps, shaking, before I can gather myself enough to keep going.

The couple are cooking something—snake, I'm guessing—and my tummy gurgles at the aroma of roast meat. I can hear them talking, but can't make out the words; I'm too far away. I'm almost to where we initially came up on the camp. A sudden gust of wind sets the utensils on the wire tinkling and I drop flat, pressing my face into the damp soil. The couple must be attuned to the alarm system's various sounds because they don't even pause their conversation. After long moments, I rise and make my way back to the rendezvous point and Wyck. My heart isn't pounding as fast as I would have expected, and I wonder if I'm getting used to living in fear. Thinking of the blithe way I promised Dr. Ronan I wouldn't die, I smile ruefully.

"They're eating alligator," Wyck announces enviously when I join him. "They've got a big gator carcass tacked head down against a big tree, slit down the middle."

"They must have weapons," I say, telling him about the snakes.

"And balls," Wyck adds, "if they're tackling fifteen-foot gators and poisonous snakes."

I tell him what I saw on my reconnaissance and suggest we sneak into the camp via the latrine to avoid the alarm, make our way around the back of the lean-to, and try to pull Halla out the back.

"We've got the beamers," he says. "Why not march in, show them we mean business, and take Halla?"

"Because we don't want to hurt them if we don't have to—"

"They kidnapped Halla!"

"—and because we don't want to give them a chance to hurt Halla, or use her as a shield," I add.

The light is almost gone. The swamp floor is dark, with a glimmer of light caught in the highest branches. Freeing one beamer from where it's strapped across the back of his rucksack, Wyck hands it to me, and pulls out the other one for himself.

"I've never fired one of these." The weapon is heavy and cold, but it quickly absorbs warmth from my hands and conforms to my grip.

"It's easy. Point and shoot."

Wyck leans over me to demonstrate, and his chest is pressed to my back for a moment, his cheek almost touching mine. His closeness is both comforting and distracting. I clear my throat. "Got it," I say, putting my finger on the trigger sensor pad. "We should go."

For a moment, I think we might kiss again, but Wyck pulls away, already intent on the mission. "Operation Halla Homecoming is a go," he says.

"This isn't a game."

"I know it's not a game, for God's sake." His face twists with frustration. "I just need—you wouldn't understand." He strides away from me, weapon held loosely at waist-height. He's making a lot of noise, but before I can caution him—and get another blast of his temper—he slows down and begins to move more carefully.

The fire is an easy-to-follow beacon and we stop shy of the makeshift alarm, to the left of the latrine. I'm hoping to see Halla, thinking she might have been brought out for dinner, but she's not visible. Neither is the man or woman. I wonder if they're all in the hut, retired for the night. If so, it's going to be harder to slit the rear flap and steal Halla away. Right then, the woman brushes through the scrap of fabric covering the opening, her hand clamped around Halla's arm.

"Gawdamn breeders, needin to piss twenny times a day," the woman grumbles, hauling Halla toward the latrine ditch, mere feet from where Wyck and I crouch. I feel him looking at me in the darkness and we freeze—no time to back away. Halla's hands are tied behind her and her feet are roped together, so she moves with an awkward shuffle. There's a scrape on her cheek, but otherwise she looks unhurt. She'll be able to run, I hope, once we cut her bonds. Her torn and muddied tunic falls mid-way down her thighs and her leggings are missing. With a lurch of my stomach I realize it's so she won't need to have her hands free to use the latrine.

The woman shoves Halla toward the ditch and stands there, arms akimbo. I don't see or hear the bearded man. Maybe this is our chance. Apparently, Wyck thinks the same thing because he surges forward, hurdling the alarm wire and the ditch where Halla crouches, sticking the beamer almost in the woman's face before she can react.

"Cut Halla loose," he calls to me.

The woman lets out a shriek. "Armyn!"

Swinging the beamer sideways with both hands, Wyck smacks her across the face and she falls. I dash to Halla. She's standing, confused, and looks at me like I'm a ghost.

"Everly?"

I draw her toward the fire so I can see well enough to slice through the ropes binding her wrists. "What? You thought we'd leave you?" I can't resist giving her a quick squeeze. "We need to get out of here before that man gets back."

A crash and a roar from behind us tell me it's too late. I press the knife into Halla's hands so she can cut her ankles free, and pick up my rifle. The man barrels forward, face a mask of confusion and rage behind the ginger beard, tossing aside the five-gallon container of water he's apparently hauled from a nearby source. It lands near the fire, sluicing it out, and the sudden darkness leave us disoriented. I hear Wyck's weapon go off and let loose a shot toward where the man was standing when the fire died. I don't know if it hits him.

Scufflings and grunts come from beside me and I think the bearded man is fighting Wyck. The meaty thwack of fist on flesh tells me someone's landed a punch. A heavy body thuds into me and I grab a sleeve instinctively. By the gamey smell, it's the man. He jabs his elbow back and it smashes into my nose. Searing pain fells me, still clutching a handful of his shirt. The man staggers. The shirt rips free. Wyck's on the man before he can regain his balance, the barrel of the beamer jabbed into his throat. I can just make out their silhouettes in the darkness.

"I gots her, I gots the breeder." The woman's voice rings out triumphantly. "Leggo my son!"

A horrible gurgle follows the last word. A cloying coppery odor bites at the back of my throat. I suck in a deep breath, fear turning me cold. "Halla?"

"Maw," the man bellows. He lunges forward, and Wyck fires. The man collapses, moaning. I can't see where he's hit.

It has all happened so fast, I'm momentarily disoriented. I can't breathe right; there's blood in my mouth from my broken nose. The man struggles to rise, a crippled mammoth. I bring my gun up. I hesitate. I can't make myself shoot him, not when there's any other option. "Run," I yell, heading to where I last saw Halla.

I trip over something and go sprawling. It's yielding and warm, with a ripe odor. My palm lands in a pool of slickness.

"Everly?"

It's Halla's voice, barely more than a whisper. I scramble up, and bump into Wyck who grabs my hand. We head toward her voice. Behind us, the man bumbles around and knocks into something that clangs. A moment later, there's a *whumpf* and a ball of pink fire boils up. The Psyche still. We can't help but pause to look. The gas hangs in the air like a weird pink fog, tendrils spreading toward us.

"Don't breathe it in," I tell the others, pushing at them to get them moving again. The pink fog disperses around us. I cough. "Run."

"Maw, Maw! Where are you? Talk to me, gawdammit, Maw."

He knows. I can hear the grief in his voice behind the rage, the dawning awareness of his aloneness. Great sobs, the bawling of a wounded animal, wrench at me as we run and run.

I plough into the snakes hanging from the tree. There's more of them, a curtain of sleek, scaled bodies patterned in mottled grays and blacks, in copper and geometric shapes, in red, black and yellow stripes. Pupils that are vertical slits regard me from beady eyes. They're still alive! They writhe and hiss, striking at me. I bat at them, terrified, and they swing toward me. One sinks its fangs into my arm and another latches onto my face. Their poison courses into me. I'm screaming and flailing my arms, trying to get away as they detach themselves from the tree and begin to twine around me.

"Everly, there are no snakes."

Someone is shaking me.

"No snakes. It's the Psyche. You've got to be quiet."

A hand covers my mouth, smothering me. It's not a hand—it's a snake, oozing into my mouth. I can't breathe. I buck.

"Please, Ev." The voice is desperate. "He'll hear you. Take my hand."

I do as directed, grabbing tight to an offered hand, and run. The snakes are still with me—we're not outrunning them—but ever so gradually they begin to fade as my system metabolizes the Psyche. I realize I'm holding Wyck's hand and let go. I've got a raging thirst, a product of the Psyche, but we don't stop. I'm not sure how long we run, bunched in a group, separating only to go around trees and other obstacles. We eventually slow to a walk for Halla's sake, and continue in silence until we reach the edge of the swamp. We stand within the tree line, drinking water, and contemplate the expanse of nothingness stretching before us. I want to keep going. The swamp provides more cover, but it gives me the willies.

"I am so done with this swamp." I dribble a little water into my hands and rub them, trying to get rid of the crone's dried blood. At least the snakes are gone. Hopefully, the

Psyche is well and truly out of my system. I've heard it can cause hallucinations months or even years after inhalation.

"What was it like?" Wyck asks.

"Horrible. I can't believe people give ration credits to experience that."

Halla fumbles awkwardly with her water bladder and the rising moon shows me that she's still clutching the gory knife. Horrified, I gently pry it from her hand. Without saying anything, she sucks greedily from the water bladder.

"We should keep going," Wyck says. "We don't know how badly hurt that guy is."

"Halla, are you able to keep on?" I ask.

In answer, she steps forward and strides into the open. Wyck and I follow.

The moon is full and the walking is easy, at least compared to the swamp. The moonlight gilds the occasional tree or rock and makes deep hollows of slight depressions in the landscape. The quality of sound is different in the open. In the Okefenokee, the insect chirrings and flappings and whinings were practically deafening, held in, perhaps, by the moisture and the denser vegetation. Out here, it's so quiet it's echo-y. I feel like a whisper would carry for miles, all the way to the stars blinking so high above. We walk until almost midnight and then, weary and hungry, stop for food and water.

"How'd they catch you, Halla?" Wyck asks, scooping up the nutrient-dense mush from one of the IPF food pods.

I've been carefully not intruding on Halla's silence, giving her some space, and I frown at Wyck. He doesn't notice because he's looking at Halla.

She starts to say something, but her voice doesn't work. She clears her throat. Her drawl is more noticeable than usual when she speaks. "When I first took off on the scooter, I was panicked. I think I skimmed around in circles before I finally thought to check my compass. Once I figured out which way to go, I didn't have any trouble at all, other than worrying about you. I got almost to the rendezvous point and stopped to rest. I was so worried about you, wondering if you'd manage to get away from the soldiers, hoping you weren't hurt, that I wasn't paying as much attention as I should have. That man snuck up behind me and picked me up, like I was a doll. I never even heard him coming. He carried me to their camp and handed me over to his mother like . . . like I was a special kind of mushroom, or tasty snake he'd found in the swamp.

"She knew right away that I was pregnant, and she was excited about it. She kept telling him how much money they could make selling me to Bulrush."

"Who's he?" I ask.

Halla shrugs. "No idea."

"Did they hurt you?" Wyck again, with the blunt questions.

"No. She even knew how to stop my bleeding. She said it happens that way sometimes, that pregnant women 'spot' a little, and that it was nothing to worry about. She told Armyn that because he didn't think it was worth feeding me. And then you guys came." She offers a trembling smile.

I suspect there was more that happened between her arrival at the camp and our appearance, but I don't call her on it. I lean over and hug her hard.

She pulls away after only a moment. "What happened with the soldiers?" she asks, wrapping her arms around her knees and resting her chin on them.

Wyck and I are quiet for a moment. I think we're trying to figure out how much of the truth to tell her.

"The scooters had transponders. That's how they found us," Wyck says. He pauses. "I shot one. He fell in the quicksand and disappeared. He was going to shoot Everly."

"She was going to take my baby."

I feel something happening between Wyck and Halla, a bond forging. They understand something about each other that I'm not privy to; at least, that's the way it seems to me. I'm the odd man out. The realization hurts me and knocks me a little off-kilter. Before, I was kind of our trio's common denominator; Halla and I were best friends, and Wyck was more my friend than Halla's. Now, the dynamic has changed. No one has said anything, but I know it. I itch at a mosquito bite and break into the silence to tell about ambushing the second IPFer.

I finish by enumerating the supplies we got from the six-seater ACV. "We're good for several days, even without your pack," I tell Halla. "Then, well . . ." The barren terrain doesn't hold out much hope for foraging success

"We should travel at night," Wyck says, "and hole up during the day. We're too easy to spot in all this"—he gestures widely—"emptiness."

Halla and I murmur agreement. Halla stands. "We should go."

Wyck scrambles up and joins her. I seal my backpack and follow, trailing them by two steps.

CHAPTER FIFTEEN

For almost a week, we travel by night and sleep by day, two of us in the camouflaged IPF shelter that alters color to blend with the environment, and one standing watch. We're all starting to smell a bit ripe, and it's most noticeable in the close space of the shelter. Wyck and I kiss again one night while Halla's standing watch, and his unshaven whiskers scruff my face. The feel of his tongue against mine makes my body pulse with warmth but Halla's there and we're tired, so Wyck draws away after fifteen heated minutes and we fall asleep holding hands. We see a small band of travelers once, on the horizon, what looks like parents with two small children, but they scurry away when they spot us. It's weird to think of anyone being afraid of us. We have to use the beamers to scare away a man who approaches our campsite near dusk one day;

Halla wants to offer him food, but Wyck and I don't like the look of him. The charge is getting low; we won't be able to count on the weapons much longer. We come across a creek on the second night and are able to top up our water bladders, adding hydropure pills to be safe. We bathe in the running water, relishing the opportunity to wash off the blood that lingers under our fingernails, in skin creases, and in Halla's case, stiffens the front of her tunic. In the dark, we scrub ourselves mere feet apart in the creek, afraid to separate. We continue on clean, not even minding the way our wet clothes chafe our thighs and underarms.

When we come across towns, we give them a wide berth even though, for the most part, they seem deserted. We catch a whiff of smoke one night and I think I hear voices. We hear an ACV not too far away another day. The countryside may seem lifeless, but there are people and animals out here, all of them as wary as we are, I think. I wonder about the people. Are they outlaws who committed some crime? Unlicensed parents who refused to let a Kube raise their children? Are they living apart because they're scared of the flu returning? Before I left the Kube, I lumped all the non-city dwellers into the "outlaw" category; now I see that people have lots of reasons for striking out on their own. Every now and then I get the feeling that we're being watched, but if so, it's probably only because everyone is wary.

On the sixth night, the terrain changes. It's hillier now, and there are more trees, most of them covered with a canopy of kudzu. We haven't crossed even a small road in hours, and I get the feeling that we're in a spot that would have been the middle of nowhere, even before the flu. Despite that, I feel uneasy and keep looking over my shoulder. With dawn approaching, we're looking for a place to sleep when Wyck stumbles.

"Ow." He bends to loosen the teeth of the concertina wire wrapping his ankle. He looks up. "Wow, what is this place?"

Wyck wears the NVGs most of the time, but I motion for them now. Spools of concertina wire trail from listing metal poles. There's an inner and an outer fence, both sagging, with two watchtowers on the north and south sides. What looks like a short runway stretches away from us on the far side of the compound, whatever it is. There are no structures except the towers. I suspect that before the locusts this facility would have been almost invisible, surrounded by forest and far from any form of civilization.

"Not a clue," I say, handing the NVGs to Halla.

"There's a sign," she says, pointing to a metal rectangle secured to the fence's metal links.

I put my face close to it, able to make it out as the first hint of light streaks the horizon. There are no words, just a stick figure getting zapped by electricity which tells me the fence used to be electrified. "Not much of a welcome mat." I look around. "I can't imagine what they wanted to protect—there's nothing here."

"Nothing we can see," Wyck says. His curiosity clearly aroused, he squeezes between a gap in the fence and begins to look around.

"We should keep going," Halla says uneasily. "It's getting light. We need somewhere to camp."

"This is as good a place as any," Wyck argues. "We can sleep up there." He gestures to one of the towers. "There's got to be something here. I'm gonna check it out." He moves further into the compound. After a moment's hesitation, I follow him. Halla lingers on the other side, but then wiggles through the fence to join us.

Wyck goes straight for the runway and walks its length, inspecting the cracked and frost-heaved pavement. "There used to be a hangar here," he said, sweeping his arm over an area where I can make out the marks of a rectangular foundation.

"Why? And why 'used to be?'"

"To build and supply something. And then to hide what they were doing," Wyck says enthusiastically, walking a grid pattern to the west of the runway.

"Who's 'they'?" Halla asks.

Wyck shrugs. "Depends on how old it is. Drug lords— this would have been a good place to grow marijuana in the old days. Well, it would have been before the locusts. Man, can you imagine a bunch of high locusts, buzzing around, bumping into each other?" He laughs. The sound ring outs, happy and almost carefree, and it makes Halla and me smile. "More likely, it was Psyche manufacturers and distributors, like that pair back there, but on a more commercial scale."

He is a ways away from us now and has to raise his voice. The ground slopes uphill slightly as I follow him.

Halla hangs back, "I don't want to find whatever it was," she says. "Let's keep going."

"In a minute," Wyck says absently. His foot knocks against something and he bends. He scrapes away a layer of dirt with one hand. "Look at this, Ev."

I hurry over. There's a grate inset into the ground, covering a two foot wide pipe. Wyck kneels and puts his eye to it. "That's why there's no foundation marks, except for the hangar," he says, tugging at the grate. It doesn't budge. "It's underground. This is probably an air ventilation shaft. There's got to be a door." He jumps up and renews his search.

I look up and scan the area. Other than the three of us, there's no sign of life, and yet I get the twingey feeling between my shoulder blades that we're being watched. *You're paranoid*, I tell myself. *We are in the middle of freaking nowhere—there's no one here.* I wiggle my shoulders to make the feeling go away.

"Aha!" Wyck's shout comes from a hundred yards away. With a glance at the disapproving Halla, I hurry over. His fingers curl into a barely visible crevice and he pulls. Nothing happens. "This has got to be the door," he says. He examines the surface again.

I look at the surface he's uncovered—what looks like a smooth steel plane—and notice something. "Wyck." I draw his attention to the bio hazard sign.

He doesn't respond. After a moment, he tugs on the apparent handle again, from the opposite direction, and a deep creaking sound issues as if from the bowels of the earth. I spring back. Wyck grins. "We're in."

"Not me," Halla says. She crosses her arms over her chest and puts on her mulish look. "I am not risking my baby's health by going down in some bio-hazard pit."

"Well, I'm going to see what's down here," Wyck says. "There might be supplies, weapons, something useful. We need food."

It's true. We're down to the last couple of vegeprote bars we took from the IPF vehicle. I look from Halla to Wyck. I sense that he needs to find food for us, that he's still feeling guilty about losing our supplies in the swamp. This place is so well hidden it's possible looters never found it, that there are provisions stored underground.

"Why don't you climb into one of the towers and wait for us?" I suggest to Halla. "You should be safe there."

"Good idea," Wyck seconds. "You can be our lookout and holler if you see anyone coming." He continues to pull on the door which is easily eighteen inches thick and opens via a pneumatic system that hisses as the door yawns wider. A staircase slopes into the ground. I can't see the bottom of it through the dark. Wyck is already three steps down.

"I don't like this," Halla says, moving toward the closest watch tower.

"We'll be back in ten minutes," I say. With only a brief hesitation, I put my foot on the first step.

The air is chilly and smells of—I take a deep sniff, trying to identify the faint but familiar odor—disinfectant. My unease ticks up a notch. The metal treads clang under our boots. It crosses my mind that they are a built in alarm system like the bootleggers' utensil-decked wire. The open door lights our way to the bottom, barely, where I find

Wyck waiting for me in a small tile-floored vestibule. Halls lead from it in three directions.

"Eeny, meeny, miney, mo." Wyck points to a hall and starts down it, clicking on a flashlight. "Here."

He tosses me one. Its beam is broad and bright and I feel a bit better. The hall we're moving down is nothing special: pale green walls with white tile floors. What look like old LED fixtures are attached to the ceiling. On impulse, Wyck reaches out and taps a light pad when we pass and the fixtures spring to life, bathing us in glare.

"Batteries not dead yet," Wyck says with satisfaction.

"How long could they last?"

He wags his head, considering. "With virtually no use—fifteen or twenty years."

I'm silent. How long has this place been here? How long ago—and why—was it abandoned? There's a door, half-open, on our left. We exchange a look and Wyck pushes it wider. It swings back silently. There's a narrow ante-room with an intercom grid, a red palm-sized button on the wall, and then another door. Like the airlocks at the Kube. We pass through the inner door and Wyck finds another light switch. It illuminates more white tile and little else; the room has been stripped of all fixtures.

Outlines suggest counters, and multiple outlets suggest equipment that required electricity. Plumbing rough-ins hint there were several sinks and even a shower. One small white basin remains. Two other doors, closed, are set into adjacent walls.

"It was a lab," I breathe, almost unconsciously recognizing the arrangement of counters and outlets. My mind fills in stainless steel, coolers, centrifuges. "That's an emergency eyewash station." I point to a dangling hose. "Well, it was." Thinking of the airlock and noting the openings in the ceiling that might have enabled air hoses, I add uneasily, "I think this might have been a Level 4 bio-containment facility."

"Twink," Wyck says, not one bit nervous. "Probably making drugs, don't you think?"

"I was thinking more along the lines of Ebola or anthrax," I admit, "but I suppose one might need similar facilities for manufacturing synthetic stimulants." I drift to the wall where half a piece of paper is still affixed. "'istry of Science and,'" I read aloud. "Not drugs," I say, considerably more nervous now. "The government. Look, there's nothing here. Nothing useful for us. Let's go. Halla will be getting worried."

A small scraping sound catches our attention.

"What was that?" Wyck whispers. He's moving toward the closest door and the sound.

I'm half-way to the hall door and escape. "Wyck!" I try to draw him toward me, but he keeps going. I quit breathing as he puts his palm against the door, hesitates a breath, and slams it back. So much for his promise that he's changed. Anger stirs beneath my nerves. I cross the room, intending to collar him and drag him back to the surface.

"Big furnace," he says. I look in on a huge blue incinerator with a control panel studded with red and green buttons and gauges, one of them with a temperature indicator that tops at 1100-degrees Celsius. Toasty. Wyck's moving to the next door before I reach him. I'm on his heels as he opens it. There's a built-in cupboard with labels I can't read from here. There's a cot covered with a rumpled intelli-textile blanket, with a rolling metal tray as a night stand of sorts. A mug sits on the tray, a wisp of steam rising from it. I'm fixated by the steam as it drifts up and dissipates. Someone is living here.

Before I can stop him, Wyck detaches the beamer from his pack, aims it at the cupboard door, and says, "We know you're in there." When there's no response, he says it louder, adding, "Come out now or I'll blast you."

The door eases open an inch. Wyck backs up until he's standing beside me. His knuckles gleam white as he grips the beamer. The door opens wider and a booted foot appears. The boot is slightly scuffed, not that old; whoever's in there has not been trapped here for decades. A hand curls around the door and I gasp. The hand is covered with boils and streaked with blood, flayed almost to the bone in spots. I'm suddenly sure this was a bad idea. A very bad, potentially fatal idea. If this person has something infectious . . . My brain runs through the options. The boils are small, like smallpox, some of them mounded atop others: boils on boils. The blood streaks . . . I don't know what infection would cause them.

"Don't shoot." The voice is soft, papery, male. A man emerges, hunched over as if trying to hide himself. One hand scratches at his arm through a thin jumpsuit. I imagine more boils beneath the fabric. He brings his hands to his shoulders so we can see he's unarmed. "I'm no danger to you." He raises his head.

I swallow hard at the sight of the boils crusting his face, neck and bald scalp. Bloody weals score them. From scratching. He has no eyebrows. His eyes are golden; he's geneborn. How did he end up here, in this condition? Boils bubble on his lips and inside his ears. From the way his tongue works at the roof of his mouth, I suspect they're also in there. His expression says he knows how horrible he looks.

"Who—who are you?" Wyck asks.

I can tell he's knocked off-balance by the man's hideous appearance. Pity is edging out our fear.

"Anton," he says, scratching hand moving to his neck. "Anton Karzov. I haven't introduced myself to anyone in a very long while."

"What happened to you?" Wyck asks bluntly. "What is this place?"

Anton eyes him warily and lowers himself to sit on the cot. Wyck watches his every move.

"This was a laboratory. A research lab. Run by the Ministry of Science and Food Production. I worked here."

"On what?" *Don't say "smallpox,"* I beg mentally.

"Vaccines."

"For?"

"Influenza, among other diseases. Mostly influenza. This was sixteen years ago—the third wave of the pandemic was still going strong. The Pragmatists had gained power a few years earlier. They wanted to create a vaccine that would show the population—what there was left of it—that they were capable of protecting them. As you can see"—he scratches his thigh—"the experiments were disastrous. They looked promising during rhesus trials, but when we moved to human subjects . . ."

"Who would volunteer to test a new vaccine that did, that had such"—I discard words like "horrific" and "hideous"—"painful side effects? And where did you find volunteers out here in the middle of nowhere?"

Anton doesn't answer. Only the sound of his scratching breaks the silence. My eyes widen. "Oh, my God. The Prags wouldn't do that."

Wyck looks at me, puzzled. "What?"

"They didn't use volunteers." I round on Anton. "Who were they?"

A gleam in his eyes applauds my analysis. "Prisoners. Criminals. Enemies of Amerada."

"They were still people!"

"We were working to save the human race," Anton says. "At the time, we were afraid the flu would wipe out every human on the planet. We did what we had to do. If the flu hadn't killed off so many, and if the insecticides hadn't left so many infertile . . ." He makes a moue, clearly telling us that it wasn't his fault, the forces of nature had forced him to participate in the vaccine study.

"So the vaccine didn't work and you gave up, abandoned your research?" I ask.

"On the contrary," Anton says. "The vaccine was effective at preventing avian flu infection. But the side effects . . . the blisters didn't show up until a couple of months after inoculation. They drove most of the test subjects insane. It turned most of them into animals. The howling—my God. The wards were supposedly sound-proofed, but even so." He closes his eyes and shivers.

"How did you . . ." I let the question trail off.

"One second's carelessness," he says bitterly. "I was disposing of a syringe we'd used to inoculate a test subject. It was the end of my shift. I'd already removed my PPE and was wearing only latex gloves. Someone had spilled water. I slipped, the needle pricked my pinky, and . . ."

And he was condemned to live in agony. I shudder, remembering the times in the lab when I was careless with safety procedures. I understand now why Dr. Ronan chewed us out and banned us from the lab when we didn't follow protocols to the letter.

"A couple months later the decision was made to abandon this site, take what we had learned, and resume modified experiments in another location." He scratches furiously at his scalp, and blood beads along the bare dome.

"Where did the test subjects end up?"

Anton ignores Wyck's question. "We were told to sanitize the entire site. We incinerated paper copies of our research and much of our equipment. Teams of IPF engineers came in to remove the computers, destroy the fixtures, and raze the hangar. There used to be flights from Atlanta, twice a month, with food and other supplies. Now, I scrounge and steal. I don't know what I'll do when the batteries die and the lights go out." He looks scared.

I can sympathize. I couldn't live in this underground warren to start with, but without lights it would be unendurable. Of course, his whole life is virtually unendurable.

"What happened to the test subjects when everyone left?" I repeat Wyck's question. I see the truth in Anton's face before he speaks.

"Euthanized. It was the only humane thing to do," he says. "Don't look so effing judgmental. You don't know what it's like. I do."

Wyck's brow wrinkles. "You killed them?"

"Not me. I was one of them by then. That damn bitch wanted me dead, too."

"Who?"

"The lab's head scientist. She didn't want any proof of her spectacular failure left around. And I'm pretty spectacular proof, aren't I?" His laugh is manic, and I shoot a look at Wyck.

"How did you escape?" Wyck asks.

Chewing at the boils on his lips, he says, "My wife helped me. Even after this happened"—he waves a hand in front of his face—"she still loved me. We'd applied for a procreation license, thinking that if *she* could gestate while working here, it would be okay. We were still waiting to hear when . . ." He exhales heavily. "She risked her job to hide me, and falsified the records saying I had been euthanized and cremated. Officially, I'm dead. I wish to God I really were, but Alaura can't stand it when I talk about killing myself. After what she risked for me, how could I leave her alone?" He steps toward us.

His use of the present tense raises the hairs on the back of my neck. His wife's here. I see the realization hit Wyck. "We're leaving now." He levels the beamer at Anton who has somehow gotten to within four feet of us. Madness glitters in his eyes.

"No, you're not." The voice, brittle and female, comes from behind us. We turn to see a blonde, as thin and brittle as her voice, leveling an old-fashioned automatic rifle at us. The weight of it makes the muscles and tendons of her forearm stand out. "Put the beamer down," she orders Wyck. When he doesn't comply immediately, her finger flexes on the trigger and six or eight bullets spit from the muzzle, chewing up the tile at our feet. Ceramic splinters jolt into the air and I close my eyes reflexively, expecting a bullet to plough into me any second. Wyck's beamer clatters to the floor.

"Alaura." Anton sounds almost wary. "Do you have to—"

"Yes. They'll tell. You know they'll tell. They're horrified by you. You disgust them." She glares at us. Her hair is slicked back, perfectly sleek. Her face is translucent porcelain, as white as her lab coat. Her eyes are geneborn gold and her thin lips virtually colorless. She looks like something has drained vibrancy out of her. Living in hiding. Scrounging for food. Loving the tortured Anton. "Throw us your packs." She gestures with the rifle.

Reluctantly, Wyck and I shrug out of our backpacks and slide them across the floor to the couple who have moved closer to the lab exit. When Alaura motions with the rifle, Anton grabs the packs' straps, wincing as they cut into the boils on his hands. He backs toward the door.

"That too," Alaura says, nodding to the messenger bag strung across my chest.

"No." I'm not giving up my feather and my book. I meet her gaze straightly.

I can see her decide it's not worth it. She joins Anton in the airlock. As the door whooshes shut, Wyck dives for the beamer and comes up shooting. The blasts thud harmlessly against the windows. Shatterproof. Fireproof. Alaura looks at us impassively. Anton carries our packs into the hall. Are they going to lock us in here to die of dehydration? I should be horrified at the thought, but we've got a chance if she doesn't shoot us. I'm guardedly hopeful. Maybe they only want to contain us long enough to get away.

Alaura's hand comes up and smashes against the button I noticed earlier.

An ominous hissing fizzes in my ears. I don't recognize it until almost too late.

"Halon!" I shout to Wyck. We'd had to activate the halon once at the Kube lab when a young AC ignited a fire by mixing the wrong chemicals. I'd watched, stunned, at how quickly the halon snuffed the fire. Already it's hard to breathe. I grab Wyck's hand and drag him into the incinerator room. The halon will suck all the oxygen out of the room in under two minutes. Our only hope is that the incinerator has an airtight seal. It must. We won't have a lot of oxygen, but we'll have some.

The incinerator takes up most of the small room. Its wide-mouthed door opens to the side by turning a wheel. Wyck clangs inside, and I jump in after him. We pull the door shut, which is hard to do from the inside. It seals with a reassuring *thwuck*. We're standing on a grate. I can barely touch the top of the chamber by standing on tiptoe and reaching my arms up. I take two steps to the side and reach a wall that feels like bricks or rough tiles. I run my hands down it and encounter metal tubes poking into the cavity; I suspect they're for gas. Wyck and I bump into each other. He puts his arms around me and I loop mine around his waist, leaning into him. I exhale, wondering as I do how quickly the two of us will deplete the oxygen inside. I estimate the oxygen volume at .2kg. Breathing as heavily as we are, we've got maybe an hour. I suspect Alaura and Anton are a bigger threat than running out of air.

"We need to get out of here," Wyck says, following my thoughts again. He looses me and moves a step away. I feel chilled. "Do you feel that?" he asks.

"What?"

"Air." It sounds like he's at the back of the incinerator. "This has got to have a vent." His voice sounds like he's speaking into a tube.

He rattles a piece of metal, pulls it loose and passes it to me; it's thin with hundreds of perforations. "Ta-da."

I put the filter down with a clang and come up beside him to look up the hole he's created. More blackness. I can't see a thing, but I can definitely feel moving air. Hope makes me giddy.

"It wouldn't surprise me if this leads to that grate I kicked up top," he says. "This is our way out."

"This?" The opening is two feet wide I ascertain by sticking my hands up and moving them sideways until I hit metal. The duct goes up into more darkness. "We won't fit."

"We'd better."

There's a humming from outside the incinerator. I listen intently and finally identify it. A fan. Alaura is clearing the halon from the lab. Within minutes, she'll be back inside, ready to shoot us, or worse.

"I'd better go first," Wyck says. "It may be hard to dislodge the grate at the top. With any luck it's screwed on, not welded..." I hear him maneuvering himself into the opening

"Hurry," I whisper.

I hear him place one foot against the duct's far wall and then jerk the other foot up with a clang. Scraping and shuffling tell me he's crabbing up the vent, pushing upward with one foot at a time.

"Everly?" His voice floats down, distorted by the metal.

"Yeah?"

"It's doable. Start climbing."

I brace my back against one side of the duct and put one foot against the other side. My knee almost touches my chest. I press back and swing the other foot up, so I'm suspended in the vent, held in place by my back and my feet. From the moment my second foot leaves the ground, the pressure on my back and knees is intense. Pressing down through my feet, I scooch up six inches. Encouraged, I maneuver one foot up, bumping my breasts with my knees, and push. My back scrapes along the duct wall and I move about a foot. I move my second foot alongside the first one and use my thigh muscles to power myself upward. Another foot. I try not to think about what might be filming the inside of the pipes, about whether or not the ash of one of the tragic test subjects is rubbing off on me. I tilt my head back but can't see or feel Wyck. I don't know how far it is to the top. The vent isn't quite vertical; there's a slight slope that makes it not impossible to support myself with knees and back. My arms are stretched overhead, almost useless. My fingers keep feeling the duct walls, but except for the occasional welded seam, there's nothing.

"Wyck?"

"I can see the top."

His voice, jubilant, floats down to me. I try to move faster and my foot slips. I slide down two feet and my knee twists awkwardly. It takes me a painful moment to right myself. I pause to breathe and hear a clang below. The incinerator door opening. I freeze.

"They must have gone in here," Alaura says. "There's nowhere else."

Anton mumbles something I can't make out.

Alaura answers, but it sounds like she's turned toward him and I only make out the last words, "—fire it up."

The rest of their conversation is largely lost on me, but I gather they are trying to figure out what combination of dials and buttons need to be engaged to fire up the incinerator. Alaura complains it takes too long to reach its maximum temperature and I give a brief prayer of thanks.

"They're going to ignite the incinerator," I call up to Wyck.

"I'm at the grate," he says, sounding much closer. "Not welded. Screws. Tight. Damn."

I continue to inch upward. Wyck must have shifted because suddenly I see bars of light. His body blocks most of the light, but the sight makes me want to sob. I stop, thighs trembling with fatigue, about four feet beneath Wyck. I can smell his sweat.

"I've got a multi-tool on my belt," he says, "But I can't get my arms down to it. Can you reach it and hand it up to me?"

I don't waste breath saying I'll try. I scooch my way up until I am underneath him, the top of my head pressed against his butt. Snaking a hand up, I feel around his waist. I unsnap the tool, tilt my head sideways, and gain another precious couple of inches until my cheek comes up against his butt. Practically dislocating my shoulder, I twist and wedge my hand between his hips and the duct wall, scraping off several inches of skin, and try to place the tool on his chest.

"Almost got it . . . Damn!" His foot slips and kicks my shin. I slide, grabbing at him instinctively. He braces himself sideways, crushing my arm. I cry out and a metal clanking tells me the tool has fallen.

"We're screwed, aren't we?" I say.

"Never say die," he says in a determinedly jaunty voice. He begins to bang against the grate and scream. "Help! I join him, screaming for Halla, screaming for help, praying, cursing. Putting all my weight on one leg, I use the other to kick at the duct wall, hoping the metallic echoes will reach farther than our voices.

I sniff. I catch a whiff of gas and then there is a roar. "They've got it started," I say. How long before the heat grows intense enough to turn us to ash? I remember the 1100 C on the temperature gauge. Will we burn, or die from smoke inhalation? The vent walls are already heating up, the thin metal conducting heat efficiently. Beads of sweat pop out on my forehead; my underarms grow damp.

"Oh, my God."

It's Halla's voice. Then Wyck's telling her to grab a tool from her pack and pass it to him. It grows hotter as he works, banging and cursing to loosen the bolts. Halla is murmuring encouraging words and Bible verses, telling him to hurry up, and crying the whole time. One bolt clinks past me, falling down the vent. Then another. Finally, the rattle of metal on stone tells me he's succeeded before he says, "Got it!"

He heaves the grate up and Halla drags it out of the way. Wyck kicks my face as he hooks his arms over the opening and pulls himself out, but I don't even care because he's reaching down to me, grabbing my hand, and pulling me toward safety. I get an elbow over the edge, see Halla's worried face, and know I'm going to be okay. We'll all be okay if we can hide before Alaura figures out we're gone and comes after us with her automatic rifle. We run. At the fence, we wiggle through and then thin branches are whipping at my face and I'm dodging tree trunks, my sides heaving for air, but in a good way, not in a there's-no-oxygen-because-of-halon way. It's a long while before we stop and take stock.

When we do, the picture is gloomy. We've lost two-thirds of our supplies again. We still have the shelter, the first aid kit and one blanket, because they're in Halla's backpack, but we've lost our weapons and Wyck's tools. The three of us stare at the two lonely vegeprote bars and the single remaining water bladder once we've pulled everything out of Halla's backpack. We went into the facility hoping to find more supplies; the irony almost crushes me. I reach for Wyck's hand where it lies on the ground between us. He pulls away, staring stonily ahead. Halla's crying, one hand massaging her belly. I get the feeling that if I don't do something, they'll sit here until Alaura and Anton show up, or worse. I can't think of worse at the moment, but I'm depressingly sure worse exists.

I get up, wincing from my assorted scrapes and bruises. "Let's get moving. We're probably only two weeks from Atlanta if we set a good pace."

CHAPTER SIXTEEN

Two weeks later, we're footsore, tired and hungry. Having to scrounge for food has slowed us considerably. I've been able to identify edible mushrooms and insects, and we've even stewed bark. Wyck caught a small fish, but that was a week back. We've all thinned down, but Halla's the thinnest, except for the baby bump which protrudes very noticeably now. The people we've seen since we left the lab—a husband and wife traveling together, and a mother and daughter who said their ACV malfunctioned—were all fixated on Halla's belly. The mother, drawing her teenage daughter close, rummaged in her bag and pulled out a shawl. "Here," she'd muttered. "This might hide it somewhat." Halla took it gratefully and draped it around herself; to my mind, it is like trying to hide an elephant under a tablecloth. I know her pregnancy makes us a target.

We've given up traveling at night because we need daylight to find food. I dislike being so visible, but there's no help for it. My tummy grumbles as we walk, but I try to ignore it. My boot sole has come loose at the toe and it flaps irritatingly with each step. Step, ka-flap, step, ka-flap. Wyck is quiet. He hasn't talked much since we left the lab. He walks with Halla during the day, helping her over obstacles, keeping her spirits up with an encouraging word or speculation about what Atlanta will be like. She tells him about her dreams for Little Loudon. He treats her like an older brother, and even though I don't feel sisterly toward him, I see the bond between them growing stronger and I feel left out.

At night, though, when Halla's standing watch, Wyck spoons up against me in the shelter, his arm draped over my waist, the one blanket covering us both. There's been no kissing, and I'm confused. Maybe Wyck's afraid it will lead to more; heaven knows one pregnancy among our trio is enough. Sometimes while he sleeps I lie there awake, appreciating the gentle puff of his breath against my neck or cheek, and the solidity of his body pressed against mine. We haven't spoken about what went on in the lab. I've had nightmares four times, where I've woken with a lurch, convinced the incinerator's flames are licking at my feet. From the way Wyck tosses and mumbles sometimes, I think he has nightmares too.

The terrain has changed, become hillier. It's hotter now that we're closer to summer and we're all darker. Streams and ponds are plentiful, so we've had no trouble filling our water bladder and we've still got the hydropure tablets. I'm grateful for that. Being hungry all the time is hard enough. We're on a two lane road that cuts through what used to be a peach orchard. Even now, probably a decade after they last bore fruit, I can smell the rich, sweet peach scent. Dusk is coming on, purpling the sky, and we're keeping an eye out for a place to pitch our tent.

"Over there looks ni—" Halla starts, only to be cut off by a net dropping atop her.

A man, his jumpsuit mottled to look like tree bark, twigs attached to a stocking cap that covers his head and most of his face, leaps down from the tree above her. Before Wyck and I can react, nets entrap us, as well. I struggle, but the fibers are sticky and elastic and seem to bind tighter the more I move. A spider silk blend. Two other men, camouflaged like the first one, drop from the trees. One tosses a rope over me and begins to bind me, net and all. He's big and hairy and his breath stinks of wild onions. Dye on the exposed portions of his face, around his bloodshot eyes, blends with the rest of his outfit. Except for the black hairs on the backs of his hands and fingers, he looks like a tree come to life. When he's got my arms pinned to my sides, he stuffs a ball of cloth in my mouth as a gag, and fondles my breast with his paw.

"Fine breeder, this one," he says. "I can always tell. We'll get top dollar."

I writhe in his grasp and he laughs, squeezes my breast hard enough that I grunt with pain, and lets go. The man holding Halla, identically tied and gagged, pats her belly. He's enough like the man in front of me to be his twin.

"This un's about ready to pop. Two fer the price of one. Tol' ya it was worth tracking 'em for a few days. We won' have to work for three months with what we'll get fer these two."

"What'll we do wi' him?" the third man, less bulky than the others, but clearly related, asks.

"Kill 'im," the first man says. "He's no use to us. Get the ACV."

I look at Wyck, but he's too busy glaring at our captors and struggling against his bonds to notice.

The outlaw who captured Halla jogs off through the orchard. It happened so quickly. We had no chance to fight back. I've still got my knife, but it's tucked into my boot and I can't reach it, not bound the way I am.

A hum heralds the return of the third brigand with a decrepit four-seater ACV. It lists slightly to one side because it's been retrofitted with a beamer mounted on the left. They load Halla first, two of them picking her up and bundling her into the ACV's storage compartment, folding her legs so she'll fit.

"This one can ride on my lap," my captor says with a big grin, wrapping one arm around my waist and lifting me, seemingly without effort. I kick, but he merely laughs. "Slit his throat," he tosses casually over his shoulder, "and bring the net and rope. Can't afford to replace 'em."

I crane my neck to see Wyck. In the gloomy light, the first outlaw approaches Wyck, drawing his knife. Wyck drops to the ground and rolls. The outlaw stops him by straddling him with his legs. "All the same to me if you're standin' or lyin'," he says. He shifts his grip on the knife and bends.

"No, no! Wyck!" I scream against the gag. My words are unintelligible. I strain toward him.

The man holding me tightens his grip. "Your lover, was he? No matter. They'll scrape his seed out of you at the RESCO and give you a better bun for your oven." He chuckles. "Get it over with," he calls to the man poised over Wyck who is bucking and kicking for all he's worth, keeping his chin scrunched down to protect his neck.

There's a thin whistling sound and the man with the knife keels over backwards, clutching the crossbow bolt protruding from his chest. His mouth is open in an almost comical "O" of surprise. My captor reacts by shoving me away and grabbing the automatic pistol holstered at his waist. I fall hard. As the man brings the gun up, I roll toward him, knocking into his shins. I don't know who the new attackers are—IPF?— but I'm on their side. He kicks me in the head and shards of light dance through my field of vision. Tangling his fingers in my hair he drags me toward the ACV which his brother is maneuvering so he can fire at the newcomers. My scalp is on fire.

There are three attackers, each riding a single-seat ACV. They're serpentining between the tree trunks, never slowing, making it impossible for my captor or the man trying to control the ACV to aim properly. They're not IPF; at least, their ACVs aren't marked. The kidnapper at the controls looses off a fusillade that caroms through the orchard. My captor has dragged me to the ACV and I writhe as he tries to lift me. I'm afraid that if he gets me inside, I'll never get away. I drive my knee into his groin.

He curses on an exhalation and crumples inward, not letting go of me. "Bitch," he growls. His fist comes toward me and then my head explodes.

I come to what can be only moments later, sprawled face down on the ACV floor. We're going fast and the ACV is rocking from side to side in a way that makes my stomach lurch. I fight down the nausea and use my abs to rise to my knees. I steady myself by leaning against the seat. I'm behind the driver; my captor has crawled into the right-hand seat and ducks each time a blast from our pursuers pulses past the ACV.

"I told you we needed a rear-mounted beamer," he says.

"Shut it, Kern," the driver says.

I turn to look out the back and can make out the three ACVs chasing us. They're dark as night and look like shadows. We skim over a pond and a curtain of water rises up to block my view.

"Just make it to the hollow," Kern says. "Then we're home free."

"What the hell do you think I'm tryin' to do?" the other man says grimly, leaning forward as if by doing so he could make the ACV go faster.

I'm suddenly afraid that our would-be rescuers will give up. I've got to do something. Neither man has noticed I'm awake. Kneeling, I reach for my boot and my fingertips graze the knife. I wiggle it free, almost losing it when the driver cuts hard left. I don't have the leverage to slice through the rope, and I don't have time for that anyway.

"Almost there," Kern says, jaw tight.

Grasping the knife's hilt so the blade faces forward at hip height, where my arms are pinned, I stand suddenly and throw myself against the back of the driver's seat. I know the blow won't be fatal—the blade's not long enough—but it's the only thing I can think of. The knife pierces the seat's thin frame and the driver screeches. "Holy mother of God!" He jerks and the ACV skids. He overcorrects and sends us hurtling toward a tree.

"Watch out—" Kern yelps.

He reaches for the controls, but it's too late. Saplings slap against the hull, slowing us slightly. Then, the ACV slams into the tree trunk with a tremendous crack. I try to brace myself against the seat, but I go flying. I flip over the seat. *Thud!* I collide with the windshield and fall with my head on my captor's knees and my legs across the driver. Kern's head rests at an angle and blood trickles from his temple; he's dead or out cold. The driver's not moving. I take stock and decide I'm not dead or mortally wounded. My ribcage hurts. My bonds have loosened enough for me to lower my face to my hand and pry the gag out with a finger.

"Halla?"

"Mmmhmpf."

She's alive! Thank God. I flop onto my back and sit up. Before I can decide how to get rid of the rope, the driver's side door unseals and hands reach in. They're pulling me out and I'm telling them where Halla is and then I hear

Wyck's voice. A knife slices through the ropes and net encircling me and they fall away. Relief floods through me and my knees buckle.

"Are you okay? Can you stand?" There's a crisp voice in my ear, and I murmur an affirmative, turning to catch a glimpse of golden hair and a tanned face before he leaves me to help pull Halla out of the storage compartment. She seems wobbly but okay.

"Everly?" She looks toward me.

I can't see her face clearly in the dark, but I hear the same mix of fear and relief and pain that I'm experiencing. "I'm good," I say. My voice sounds revoltingly trembly. I try again. "I'm fine."

"Quiet." It's a woman's voice, sharp as a blade in the now-still night.

"What do we do with these two?"

For a moment I think he's talking about me and Halla.

"Kern's dead," the woman says. She pauses. "Leave Fergus. Maybe this fiasco will teach him a lesson. I've got this one. Idris has gone ahead with the boy. You've got the blonde?"

That would be me. "I do," the golden-haired rescuer says, guiding me to his ACV scooter. He mounts in front of me and says, "Hold on."

Automatically, I wrap my arms around his waist and hold tight as we skim forward. I don't know who he is or where we're going, and I don't care.

We travel vaguely northwestward. The moon rises, showing me the outline of a slim, dark-haired woman riding with Halla. I don't know where Wyck is. We glide through trees and over hills, staying away from roads and the one town lit up in the distance. An odor like burning rubber tells me we're near a plastics manufacturing facility of some kind. I ask my escort where we're going, but he doesn't answer. I'm so tired and battered that I don't press the point.

"What's your name?" I ask.

"Saben." He doesn't ask my name.

Eventually, I rest my cheek on his back and half-doze.

We stop after more than an hour and I almost fall off the ACV. Before I come fully alert, Saben says, "Sorry," and flips a bag over my head.

Everything goes dark. I start to panic—Did we escape from one set of kidnappers only to fall victim to another?

He gives me a little shake and says, "It's okay. No one's going to hurt you. But you can't see where we're going. Security."

I calm down—mostly—and shift away from him on the ACV, occasionally balancing myself with a hand to his shoulders. We've been traveling a good twenty minutes, when we start to glide downhill.

"Duck."

I do. The ducking, plus something about the quality of sound, the way the air cushion echoes, makes me think we're in a tunnel. Old sewer pipe, maybe, by the smell. We turn several times, the sound and smell changing after the last turn, with the sound more muffled and the odor more loamy than metallic. We glide to a stop. Saben helps me off the scooter, leads me several steps, and hooks my hands over cold metal rungs.

"Ladies first. Climb."

Nervous and confused, I climb straight up. Memories of the incinerator vent intrude, but this isn't really like that. It's a short ladder and someone helps me up when I reach the top. I rip the hood off and look around. I take in cracked mirrors, shreds of red and gold brocade on sofas and chairs, a swath of velvet drapes, and a long bar. The windows are blacked out with a spray film that lets no light in or out. Light glimmers from a chandelier hanging crookedly above our heads. The place smells like lilies. Two staircases lead to either end of a gallery that runs the length of the room we're in. Wyck stands near a marble bust on a plinth.

"Where are we? What is this place?"

A man I haven't seen before—Idris?—speaks. He looks to be three or four years older than we are, with hair as black as the girl's, but longer, tied back in a ponytail. His irises are a light blue or gray, burning with intensity. "It was a brothel before the epidemic put Madame Lorraine out of business." He gestures to the sole portrait hanging in the gallery, of a woman in a long tunic and flowing pants from the 2020s, a fluffy little dog on her lap. "We're in Atlanta, never mind exactly where. You shouldn't have brought them here," he says to Saben, who followed me up the ladder.

I study him in the light. He's big—I knew that from holding onto him—with a deep chest and powerful-looking legs. I put his age at twenty or twenty-one. He's got an air of quiet confidence that Idris's belligerence doesn't ruffle. His blond hair falls over a broad forehead, but it's his eyes that startle me. They're golden—he's geneborn!

"They shouldn't be here," Idris says again.

"Not your call, is it?" Saben replies evenly.

"Only a matter of time," Idris says.

I don't try to follow the by-play. Atlanta! My eyes widen. We're here! I look around for Halla, to see if she heard. She's climbing up from the tunnel. I can tell by the smile lighting her face that she did. The dark-haired woman appears behind her, snaps the trap door down, and pushes a small cabinet over it. She's lithe, with short-cropped hair that sticks out around her oval face. A thin scar cuts through one winged eyebrow. She surveys us, arms crossed over her chest. She wears what looks like an IPF-issue camouflage jumpsuit of gray, tan, and brown, like Idris and Saben. There's a tough edge to her beauty, as if it's been refined by trials I can't even imagine. I put her at about twenty because of her commanding air, but she could easily be older or younger.

"Welcome to Bulrush," she says.

CHAPTER SEVENTEEN

Halla starts, Wyck whirls, and I stiffen at the word. Talk about out of the frying pan, into the fire. We're in the lair of the man the swamp couple was going to sell Halla to. I don't know who this Bulrush is, but I'm tired of being considered a commodity, tired of Halla having to worry that someone's going to steal her baby and sell him on the black market. I'm ready to have it out with him.

"Where is he?" I demand, stepping toward the dark girl.

Her brows slice down. "Who?"

"Bulrush."

She stares at me, dark eyes searching my face. "Bulrush isn't a 'who,'" she finally says. "It's an organization."

That gives me pause. I'm not giving up, though. "Fine. Then who's in charge?"

"You know," she says, "a thank-you wouldn't hurt."

"For what? Stealing us away from those other outlaws so you can sell Halla's baby instead? I'm not feeling the gratitude."

Idris starts forward. "Hey, that's not—"

The girl interrupts him. "You think Bulrush buys and sells women and babies, the way the Dravon brothers do? Did?" Her frown deepens.

Idris makes a disgusted sound. "Of all the—"

"Don't you?" I challenge her. "Halla got ambushed in the swamp and they said they were going to sell her to you, to Bulrush, so don't try to fool us. Look, let Halla go. She wants to find her boyfriend and raise the baby with him. Please." I try to sound conciliatory. "I'll stay. You can sell me, whatever you want. I'll work for you—earn enough money to pay what you would have gotten for Halla's baby."

"Everly, no!" Halla says.

"Me, too," Wyck says. "I'll work as long as it takes."

"You are as stupid as you look," the dark girl says coldly, eyeing me with disdain. "Look at you—too stupid to disguise yourself as a man, even though any idiot would know that a breeder age female is a target. Too vain to cut that sheet of platinum hair"—she flicks it with a knife that suddenly appears in her hand—"that amounts to a blond flag saying 'Over here, over here!' Too dense to recognize salvation when it's staring you in the face. Or be grateful for it."

She looks like she wants to spit on me, and I'm chagrined at how stupid I've been. She's right, but life in the Kube didn't prepare me for the real world—not even close.

A new voice comes from behind me. It's rich and smoky with an unmistakable drawl. "Bulrush doesn't sell young women or babies," he says. "We help them escape. Think of us as a late twenty-first century Underground Railroad."

I tilt my head back to stare into the gallery where a man stands looking down at us. He seems tall from this angle, almost willowy, with silver streaks in brown hair, sunken cheeks and a haze of stubble on his cheeks. His resemblance to the woman in the portrait is marked: same aquiline nose, high cheekbones, and deep-set eyes. He starts down the stairs, stumbles, and recovers. I can't tell if he's ill or intoxicated.

"And you're Harriet Tubman, I presume?"

He laughs. "Someone paid attention in history class. Not so stupid after all, eh, Fiere?" He's shorter up close, not much taller than I am.

"What about 'free air'?" Wyck asks in a low voice.

The girl's hearing must be acute because she snaps, "It's my name. Fee-AIR." She strides toward a closed door. "Some of us have work to do."

It could have sounded petulant, but it doesn't. I feel a sudden burning curiosity to know what kind of work Fiere—all of them—do. "Thank you," I call after her.

She acknowledges my thanks and implied apology with an uplifted hand, but doesn't turn.

Idris hesitates. "Don't tell them too much," he cautions the older man. "They might be working for the Prags."

"I've got this, Idris," the man says mildly. "Help Casanova prep our passenger for the mission tonight."

It's an order. Idris waits another beat, eyeing us distrustfully, then swings on his heel and leaves.

"Introductions, I think, hm?" the man says, crossing to where Wyck, Halla and I have drawn together. "I'm Alexander Ford. Let's sit."

Halla sinks into a love seat, Wyck leans against a sofa's rolled arm with the stuffing poking out of it, and I pull up an ottoman. Alexander sits in a wing chair and lets out a small, pained sigh. He's ill, I decide. When he's settled, he looks at Wyck expectantly.

"I'm Wyck." He points to me. "Everly. Halla."

He says nothing else and I applaud his discretion. Until we know more about Alexander and Bulrush, I don't want to share too much.

Alexander nods, studying each of us in turn. "I won't insult you by offering a history lesson. Let me just say that when the Pragmatists took over and it became clear that they were going to rebuild the population by deciding who could have children and who couldn't, by conscripting young women to be surrogates, there was a cadre of us who disagreed with that approach. It might have been the expedient thing, and I know some of them thought it was the only way to ensure our nation survived, but it wasn't ethical. The government shouldn't get to decide who has children. Bearing children is a God-given right, not one the government has any business regulating. I'll get off my soapbox now." He gives a self-deprecating smile.

"So. Those of us who split from the Pragmatists set out to help young women, couples, who wanted to bear their biological children and raise them themselves. We forged networks of people willing to help them move out of the eastern cantons to outposts. I'm the only one of that original group left, and I doubt I'll be around this time next year." He presses a hand to his side, wincing. "Sometimes we're able to rescue pregnant women taken by opportunists by outbidding other buyers, and we have agents who make contact with people like the pair who caught you, Halla. We've helped more than four hundred women, and some men, escape with their babies."

"That's where 'Bulrush' comes from," Halla says with the excitement of figuring out a puzzle. "From the Bible. From the story of baby Moses being left in a basket in the bulrushes on the Nile and getting rescued by the pharaoh's daughter."

"Exactly." Alexander smiles

Four hundred doesn't sound like a very big number to me, not over a period of many years. And even though Bulrush helped us and is going to help Halla, I can't approve of what they're doing. The government is working hard to re-build the population, and they know what talents and skills are needed to help us produce more food, re-engineer the nation's infrastructure, take care of our sick, and the like. They are carefully manipulating DNA from a centralized selection of eggs and sperm for the development of geneborn children who will have the abilities to pull Amerada out of crisis, and growing those babies to term in the not-plentiful-enough wombs. I look at Halla. She doesn't look perturbed; she's focused on Alexander.

"Can you help me?" she asks. "Me and Loudon?"

"And Loudon is . . .?"

"My boyfriend. He's in the IPF, at Base Falcon."

"Halla," Wyck warns.

Alexander shoots him an amused look. "It's all right, Wyck. I understand you don't trust us yet, but it's quite clear the three of you are from a Kube, probably Kube 9 since it's the closest. You're not geneborn and you're on your own—sans parents—so I don't think Halla was giving anything away when she mentioned the Kube. Tell me, is Proctor Fonner still in charge down there?"

Fonner's name sends an electric charge through me and I sit up straighter. "How do you know about Proctor Fonner?" I can't keep the suspicion out of my voice.

Alexander gives me the same gently amused smile he gave Wyck. "Oliver Fonner and I were at university together a lifetime ago. We started out in biology. I went into medicine and he left the sciences for a degree in public administration. I'm sure he's a fine Supervising Proctor." There's an edge to his voice. "We haven't talked in years. Decades." The last word is a little wistful.

"You're a doctor?" Halla asks. "Can you deliver my baby?"

"Lord willing and the volcano doesn't explode, as my aunt Lorraine used to say." He smiles.

I can tell Halla's ready to accept Alexander and Bulrush at face value for the opportunity to have a qualified doc present during Little Loudon's birth. I've got reservations, but I keep them to myself for the time being.

Saben's voice intrudes. "Fiere asked me to bring this up." He comes forward holding a glass half-full of a milky liquid.

"I hate that stuff," Alexander complains. He takes the glass and downs it with the air of a man drinking cyanide.

"I know, but it helps."

Saben turns to us and I get the full effect of his gold eyes. "You're geneborn," I blurt. "What are you doing here, with these—" No polite word comes to mind. Smugglers? Scofflaws? "—activists?"

Saben looks me over. His hair and eyes are almost the same shade of gold. "What's to say I can't be an activist?"

"But you're geneborn," I repeat. "Privileged. You were given to a good family, went to the best schools. Are you a doctor, too? An engineer?"

"No." He retrieves the empty glass from Alexander and leaves.

Alexander watches the interplay with interest. "All of us here have things we'd rather keep to ourselves."

It's a gentle rebuke and I flush.

Alexander struggles to rise and Wyck gives him a hand. "Thank you, Wyck. You must all be tired and you'd probably like a proper bath or shower."

"Oh, God, yes," Halla breathes. "With soap. Next time I run away, I'm packing soap first."

We all laugh, and Alexander says, "Aunt Lorraine put a cistern on the roof after Hurricane Melba, so there's running water. Don't be profligate with it or we'll have to do without until the next rain. Our electricity is supplied by solar panels installed almost forty years ago, so be conservative with that, too. You have the run of the house except for that wing." He tilts his head toward the hallway running to the right. "The men's dorm is upstairs to the left and the women sleep on the right. I'm afraid I haven't the energy right now to show you myself."

"We can find it," Wyck says.

We trudge up the stairs and I suddenly realize how tired I am. Someone tied cement blocks to my feet when I wasn't looking. Halla and I each hug Wyck at the top of the stairs before he disappears down the left hall. I watch him go with a feeling of loss, realizing this will be the first night we haven't slept curled up together in weeks. It's an odd feeling. I follow Halla to the right and offer her the first bath when the first room we look into is an old-fashioned hyfac with a claw-foot tub, chipped porcelain sink, and toilet that flushes with a lever and water. Strange. She immediately begins to strip.

I wander further down the hall to a large open room with seven mattresses arrayed on the floor. Only four of them have sheets; the others have bedding neatly folded beside them. I assume Fiere uses one of the beds and wonder about the others. There's a photo of two children, dark-eyed and dark-haired, on one pillow. I pick the mattress farthest away and flap the sheet over it. I lie down, intending to doze until Halla returns from her shower, and the next thing I know, I'm sound asleep.

I wake with a start. I know immediately I've slept for hours. It feels like early afternoon, although the windows of this room are darkened, too, so I can't use the sun as a guide. Halla is asleep on the next mattress, snoring softly. The other beds are empty. I tiptoe from the room to the hyfac, figure out the shower, and plunge under the stream. It's only lukewarm, but I don't care. There are soap, shampoo, and depilatory on a ledge and I use them all. Keeping in mind Alexander's warning, I'm out within three minutes, smelling like the lavender-scented shampoo. I suspect it's been here since the house was a brothel.

I wish I didn't have to put on the filthy, stinky shirt and leggings, but I have no other clothes. I wrinkle my nose as I pull them on, then return to the dormitory. Halla is sitting up, talking to Fiere. When she sees me, Fiere hands over the camouflaged jumpsuit she's holding. It's identical to hers.

"Here. Courtesy of the IPF. Next-gen intelli-textile construction. Auto-warming, -cooling, -wicking and camouflage shifting. It uses polarization to blend—see how it looks like fish scales? Un-rippable. "

"How did you get these?"

She smiles for the first time, revealing small, even teeth. "We have our ways. And our sympathizers. Halla,

Alexander is waiting to examine you. Everly, come on. Time to start your training."

I scramble into the jumpsuit which feels wonderfully crisp. Hopping on one foot as I pull on my boots, I follow Fiere. "Training?" I ask when I catch up to her.

"Alexander says we should train you and Wyck. He thinks you will be assets." Her tone says she disagrees.

"I don't think I even agree with what you're doing."

That nets me an assessing look. "That's honest, at least. Maybe Alexander's not as wrong as I thought. At any rate, you've got to have something to do while you're here, so you might as well train, learn self-defense a little so you can hold your own against thugs like the Dravon brothers." She leads the way downstairs, across the room we were in earlier, and through an archway. The room we enter is large, wood-floored, with high ceilings and deep crown-molding. Mattresses are laid end to end and side by side in the middle of the floor.

"Ballroom," Fiere announces. "Lots of spare mattresses in a bordello."

"What are they for?"

In answer, she sweeps my feet out from under me with her leg and I fall on my back on a mattress which wheezes dust.

"That," she says with satisfaction. Hands on hips, she looks down at me.

I scramble up, angry. "What the hell—?"

"Training. You've got to be able to protect yourself, Everly. Bulrush won't always be nearby to save your ass."

That brings a question to mind. "How did you know? About the ambush last night?" It's hard to believe they were merely passing by.

"We'd been looking for you for a couple of days, ever since the swamp rat Armyn talked to one of our agents about the pregnant breeder who got away from him and his mother in the swamp. He was swearing revenge for his mother's death. An accident, I guess?" Her tone is disparaging—she doesn't think any of us capable of doing what we did to escape the moonshiners' camp.

"Halla slit her throat."

Fiere's brows arch up a hair. "Well. Maybe I should be training Halla. We were about to approach you when the Dravon brothers made the first move." She kicks at my legs again, this time buckling my knees, and I fall forward, smacking the wooden floor in a gap between mattresses. My hair flops over my face. I push it back, and tie it into a low ponytail. I don't give her the satisfaction of complaining.

"Okay," I say. "Teach me something."

"Lesson one: be alert."

On the words, her leg comes up toward my face. I'm onto her tactics now, though, and I manage to duck away. I lunge for her, hoping to catch her off-balance, but she swivels and kicks my legs out from under me with her other foot. We both land on the mattress deck, but she springs up almost before she's down. I roll away, out of reach, before standing.

"Better."

We train for two hours. She teaches me how to break holds from attackers coming at me from the front or the rear. She teaches me to go for the throat, the nose, the groin, the solar plexus. My weapons, she says, are my palms, heels, knees and elbows. She demonstrates how to use each. She drops me every time I let my guard down, saying in a lilting voice, "Lesson one!" I'm dripping with sweat and I've added new bruises to my already colorful collection when she calls a halt. Fiere has remained calm, cool, and confident throughout. I don't think she even breaks a sweat.

"Where did you learn all this?" I ask, leaning over, hands on my knees, trying to catch my breath. My ponytail flops over my shoulder.

"Mostly Alexander. Some others who aren't with us now. They taught me how to be strong, how to fight back, how to protect myself. Now, I teach women like you. Two hundred each push-ups, sit-ups and squats. Then, be back here at five-fifteen for another lesson before dinner."

She moves with striking cobra speed and without knowing quite how I got there, I'm on the ground again and she's walking out of the ballroom. "Lesson one!"

I want another shower after I complete the exercises, but don't want to waste water. I climb the stairs and check the dorm for Halla, but she's not there. I descend again and wander through the old mansion, ending up in the kitchen, a cavernous space with an actual wood-burning brick fireplace against one wall. It's soot-stained, but long cold. This place must have been built at least two hundred years ago, in the late 1800s. I wish I could see the exterior. I spot a door that looks as if it leads to the outside and head for it. I turn the doorknob and tug, but the door doesn't budge.

"You can't go outside." Saben's voice is angry. I swing around to face him. "No one goes outside. As far as anyone knows, this house has been deserted for years, like most of the others in this neighborhood. That's why we come and go via the tunnels, why the windows are black-filmed, why there's never a fire in there." He points to the fireplace. "We can't have a drone spotting activity nearby or an informer telling the IPF that they saw someone outside this house. Think, will you?"

I'm embarrassed by my near-gaffe, but tired of being treated like a moron. "We're not all experts at skulking around and fighting and outlaw stuff," I say hotly. "If you'd just tell us a few things, instead of yelling at us when we screw up, we might not make so many mistakes."

"What would you like to know?"

"Where are we?"

Saben shakes his head. "Can't tell you. Our location has to remain secret. Hence, the blindfolds."

"You don't trust us. Me."

"About as much as you trust us."

Point taken. I think again. "Okay, how many people live here?"

"The ones you've already met, plus Casanova, Milo and Gunter on the men's side. Fiere is our only female agent, but we've got three passengers staying here now, waiting to move on. They're in the women's dorm. One of them's leaving tonight."

"Can you really help Loudon and Halla get away?"

"If he wants to go with her. Otherwise, we can move her and the baby on their own. It'll take a couple months, but we can get her to an outpost where she'll be safe. We'll build a new identity, make sure she has a procreation license and ration cards, give them both new names, a history."

"Can Wyck and I go with them?"

Saben shakes his head. "Nope. Too many of you together would make it easier to hunt you down."

"Fiere said something about Bulrush sympathizers in key places . . . do you have anyone at the central DNA registry?"

Saben gives me a curious look. "Why?"

I'm not ready to tell him; in fact, I feel a little foolish at the idea of telling this geneborn guy, who can no doubt trace his genes back several super-intelligent, motivated, carefully bred generations, that I don't even know who my parents were. Rather than answer him, I say, "Are we prisoners here, or can we leave?"

He hesitates. "You're not prisoners, but you can't leave, at least not without someone to get you through the tunnels and far enough away that you won't be able to ID the house. We can't put our passengers, the whole organization, at risk. Do you want to leave?"

I'm surprised to realize I don't. I'm tired of the road. A rest will do me good. "Not at the moment."

"Good." Saben smiles. He looks younger and disturbingly attractive. "Help me make dinner." He opens the door of an antique refrigerator with the name "Whirlpool" on the front, and pulls out lettuce, tomatoes, and an eggplant. All have the golden tinge that says they're genetically manipulated.

"You've got fresh vegetables." I'm astonished.

"Sympathizers in key places," he murmurs. "There are four domes in the Atlanta area, you know."

I didn't know. I have a burning desire to visit them, to see if their practices are the same as ours at Kube 9, to talk with their researchers. I know that's nothing but fantasy right now, but maybe someday. I rinse and tear the lettuce while Saben chops tomatoes. It reminds me of my younger days at the Kube, when I served in the kitchen like all the under-tens. Vegetable peelings go in a large compost bin. It's a comforting routine, although working alongside Saben makes me nervous. It's his eyes. The gold eyes so like Keegan's. He's careful to keep the kitchen knife for himself, setting me to tasks that don't require one. Our mutual distrust makes the large kitchen feel crowded.

We make stilted conversation about topics raised at the last Assembly until Saben asks, "Why'd you leave the Kube?"

"Why are you here, with Bulrush?"

Impasse. We stare at each other, neither willing to reveal anything remotely personal.

"You hold onto that like you're guarding a formula to make bread out of stones." He nods at the messenger bag slung across my chest. "What have you got in there?"

I hesitate. I'm not going to share my *Little House* book, but there's no reason not to show him the feather. I pull it out and explain what it is and where I got it.

"It's amazing," he says, the light in his eyes making me like him a bit better. "The gradations of color, the graceful curve of it, like a flowing line from a paintbrush. I'll have to find an albatross picture."

I'm wondering how he can research albatrosses when I hear a distant clock chime five times. "Oh, I'm supposed to meet Fiere for more training." I wipe my damp hands along the jumpsuit.

"Go." He waves me away.

I leave, feeling a bit unsatisfied with our interaction. I put it aside for now. I reach the ballroom ten minutes early, per my plan, and press myself up against the wall to the left of the arch through which Fiere will enter. She arrives minutes later and I use a move she taught me to sweep her legs out from under her as she comes through the arch. She takes me down with her, hard, but I get up with the satisfaction of knowing I got the drop on her.

"Lesson one," I can't resist saying.

She pops up, lips set in a grim line.

It's a long, painful session.

CHAPTER EIGHTEEN

After dinner, eaten family style on the floor of what used to be a dining room, I get a chance to talk to Wyck, whom I haven't laid eyes on all day. We find a small room off the front hall, what might have been called a "parlor" back in the day, and huddle together by an old piano. I guess looters couldn't move it. Leaning against one of the instrument's sturdy legs, I ask, "Where have you been today? I got self-defense training and served in the kitchen."

"I helped dig tunnels. We had to use actual shovels because excavators would be too loud." He holds his hands up, palms out, to show blisters at the base of every finger.

I touch one lightly. "Ow." I roll up my jumpsuit leg to show him some of my more lurid bruises. "Fiere. What are the tunnels for?"

He shrugs. "Cas and Milo wouldn't say. But I get the feeling that they've got a whole tunnel system running beneath Atlanta, tied into the old sewer pipes. We skimmed underground at least four or five miles before starting to dig. Oh, and we recharged the ACVs by tapping into an electric line right underneath the parliament building. They've got cables that they insert into the line that charge the ACVs much quicker than our docking stations. Cas says I can take one apart to see how it works, as long as I can put it together again."

He looks pleased at the prospect. Wyck and his gadgets. Halla's been seduced by having a doctor on site, and now Wyck's been co-opted by the opportunity to play with new technologies. Am I the only one of our trio not completely taken in by Bulrush?

Wyck leans forward and brushes my lips with his. "I missed you last night," he says in a low voice. "You don't snore like Cas. He sounds likes a locust swarm, I swear. Did you know he got involved with Bulrush when his sister and her husband were denied a procreation license? She got pregnant anyway, and Bulrush helped them escape to an outpost in the Rocky Mountain Canton. Cas had already done his border sentry service and was training to be a transportation engineer when he quit to help his sister." Wyck's tone is admiring.

My interest in Cas is minimal, at best. "I missed you, too," I say, although all my missing occurred before I fell onto the mattress. I lean forward and kiss him, but he turns his head after a brief moment. I draw back. I'm confused and hurt by the way he blows hot and cold, by the passion in his kiss in the swamp followed by weeks of nothing more than cuddling at night, like dogs seeking warmth. I'm on the verge of saying something about it when someone clears his throat in the doorway.

Alexander is standing there, holding onto the jamb, a twinkle in his eyes. "Come on. I want to brief everyone on what I learned at the IPF base today."

Wyck and I spring up and follow Alexander into the great room where the others are already gathered. There's more tension in the air than last night. Fiere sits forward in her chair, one foot tapping constantly. Saben is pacing. Alexander seats himself on the sofa. Idris stands behind him, almost like a bodyguard. Two other young men, one tall, one stocky, hover near the door; Wyck greets them as Casanova and Milo and goes to stand next to the tall, handsome one I guess is Cas. I choose a seat at Halla's feet and she leans forward to ask Alexander, "So, did you see Loudon? Is he okay? Did you talk to him?"

Alexander holds up a hand to stem the flow of questions. "I met with a contact from the base. He said Loudon's unit is doing training maneuvers north of Knoxville. They won't be back until the sixth."

"That's ten days." Halla's eyes widen with dismay.

"Yes. Unfortunate. Still, it could be worse. You don't want to travel at this point until after you deliver, and you're in a safe place with a qualified doctor on hand." He gives a slight bow. "We'll get in touch with Loudon as soon as his unit gets back in garrison—"

"How?" I ask.

"—and assess his willingness to go with you."

"He'll want to go with me and Little Loudon," Halla says fiercely. She rubs her stomach. "I know it."

"We'll start making plans and creating documents as if that were the case. Saben is a talented forger," Alexander says, his expression neither agreeing nor disagreeing with Halla.

The next seven days assume a pattern. Wyck extends the tunnels, mostly with Cas and Milo or Gunter, but sometimes with Saben, and receives training from them, as well. Halla puts on a little much-needed weight, her face filling out again on our better diet, which is to say we eat more often than every other day like on the road. We meet two women Bulrush is helping, although one of them departs the night we arrive. The other is four months pregnant but doesn't know who the baby's father is or where she was living before connecting with Bulrush.

"SMO. Specific memory obliteration," Fiere tells me, sadness in her eyes. "No way to know who did it or why. Maybe she was raped and the rapist wanted to obliterate her memory of the act. Trouble is, the technology isn't precise enough yet. You can wipe too much, or the wrong thing, or leave fragments of memories to torment someone."

The woman doesn't seem tormented to me, merely vague and very passive. Maybe she was like that before the SMO. "Can you get wiped memories back?" I ask.

"Sometimes yes, sometimes no. The brain is a tricky thing. It can rewire itself in astonishing ways. I've seen it happen. My brother—" She shuts down and I don't push.

I know there's another traveler in residence, Kareen, but her mattress and effects disappeared from the dorm and we never see her. I wonder at the secrecy. I train with Fiere, consistently getting beaten up, but reacting with ever increasing quickness. She drills me on what she calls lesson two, saying that my reactions need to become reflex.

"You won't have time to think in a fight," she says. "You need to count on muscle memory to react. Reflex."

We finish each session with strength and flexibility exercises. I can feel myself getting stronger even though I was so sore after the first few days that lifting my arms to wash my hair was a painful task. I would never tell Fiere, but I'm a little bit proud of how muscular I'm becoming.

Idris approaches me on our second day with Bulrush, and says, "Alexander says you need to know weapons." His expression makes it clear he disagrees, but he leads me up a flight of pull-down stairs off the men's dorm to an attic. It's hot and stuffy, and smells musty, like rodents nest under the wooden floorboards. Idris flicks a light switch and illuminates a long room that clearly runs the length of the house. The walls are a pale gray with a strange sheen to them. I stroke my hand down one. It feels almost metallic, but with a little give.

"The same armor the IPF uses on its transports and tanks," Idris says, "with muffling foam behind it. This room is sound-proof and weapon-proof. We can conduct executions with no one the wiser."

He moves toward me, pale gray eyes flat, and I jump back. He laughs. "Chill. It's for training, not killing. Usually."

I can see he's getting off on keeping me off-balance, so I smooth my expression and say, "We'd better get to it, then."

"So serious. That's good, because what Bulrush does is serious. Vital, even." He moves to a long table where a variety of weapons from ultra-modern beamers to ESDs, guns, a cross-bow and an actual sword are laid out. All the weapons look battered: pitted, bent, rusty. "We use what we can get," Idris says, watching my gaze move from weapon to weapon. "Sometimes silent is better," he adds as I run a finger down the sword's blade. I quickly pull my hand back.

"Let's start with a gun," he says, choosing an automatic pistol with a black finish marred by scratches. "Still effective and plentiful, despite the government's attempt years ago to outlaw them. Easier to conceal than a beamer. Hold it like this." He demonstrates. "Aim at center mass."

Before I can ask what that means, he straightens his arms at shoulder height and lets off four shots, not even telling me to move, but firing past me into the far wall where projected outlines of human figures have appeared. The bullets impact with a muted thud. "Center mass." He points to where red light bleeds through one outline's torso.

My ears are still ringing from the shots, but I refuse to give him the satisfaction of complaining. My science brain is wondering how the IPF armor is engineered to stop a bullet's momentum so completely that it simply falls to the ground on impact, rather than ricocheting.

"Come here." Handing me the gun, he shapes my fingers around the grip. His hands are cool, impersonal. Positioning my hips and shoulders with equal detachment, he steps back. "Try it."

I fire and my arms jerk up slightly with the force of the bullet leaving the barrel. I fire twice more, trying to keep my arms level and my stance steady. I look down range hopefully, but there's no red light poking through the silhouette I was aiming at.

Idris shakes his head, ponytail swishing. "This is a waste of ammunition. Again. Eyes open this time."

It becomes clear during that first week that Alexander is in command, with Fiere as his deputy. Saben and Idris, it seems to me, are jostling for the next rung in what is clearly a military-style hierarchy. They all come and go at odd intervals, conduct private meetings, and generally exclude us from everything. I explore whenever I get the chance and find myself growing fond of the old mansion with its elegant marquetry and crown molding, the graceful sweep of its banisters, and its perfectly proportioned rooms. Despite holes in the plaster, missing floor boards, and the lack of furniture, it still retains a certain tattered grandeur. I wish I could see it with natural light streaming through the windows. I muse about its comedown from family home to bordello to Bulrush headquarters. The house is like a grande dame forced to prostitute herself. I laugh at myself for the whimsical thought and poke around until I find two more tunnel entrances, one in the basement, and one leading from a small room near the back door I imagine led to a courtyard or carriage house when the home was built. I tell Wyck about them, and he reveals that he's doing his best to map the tunnels as he works in them.

I seize the first opportunity I get, of course, to sneak into the off-limits wing. It's five days after we move in. Picking a time when everyone seems to be out of the house, I slip down the forbidden hallway, armed with my EMP lock buster. The first door I come to is open and leads into a small room stuffed with cartons and racks filled with clothes and uniforms of all types and sizes, wigs, accessories and other gear. Disguises, or new gear for the "passengers," I decide. They probably have to leave behind everything they own when they run, like Wyck, Halla and I did. I don't waste time in here.

The next room is empty, except for a bed and a nightstand with a Bible on it. I wonder if Alexander sleeps here, since I can't imagine him sacked out on a mattress in the dorm with the other men. I reach for the nightstand drawer, but hesitate with my hand on the pull. I feel slimy invading Alexander's privacy. Backing away, I try the door of the room across the hall. Locked. *Aha!* Promising. I try the gadget but nothing happens. I feel stupid for not realizing earlier that these locks are antique, not magnetic locks that rely on electricity. Putting an eye to the door crack, it occurs to me that I can slide back the tongue if I can find something stiff yet flexible to wiggle around it.

Returning to the first room, I paw through the messenger bags and portable pockets lined up on a shelf until I score a used up ration card. It takes me two minutes to fiddle my way around the old fashioned iron doorknob with it. I push the door open, bracing for a squeal of stiff hinges, but they're well-oiled and silent. My gaze immediately falls on a computer. A model very like the one we have in the lab. So this is how Bulrush communicates with operatives, or gets information. I don't imagine Alexander can risk using it often or for more than a few minutes at a time. I make a note to ask Wyck what kind of equipment Bulrush would need to avoid detection and location. I'm tempted to turn it on and see if I can figure out what the last search or communication was.

"You shouldn't be here." Saben stands in the doorway, an expression of mingled disappointment and anger on his face. "What are you looking for?"

"Nothing! I was . . . I didn't—"

He lets me flounder, not saying anything. His gaze makes me feel small, like I've let him down, and I fight the feeling. Like it or not, I'm trapped in the Bulrush headquarters; I've got a right to understand the operation, don't I? Knowing more means Wyck, Halla and I have a better chance of protecting ourselves.

"Saben, where's—"

It's Idris. He cuts off the question when he spots me in the office. "Damn it, Saben, you shouldn't have brought her here. We can't trust her. You damn geneborn think you know better than everyone else. Alexander should never have given you access. I told him he shouldn't trust you, shouldn't trust anyone geneborn, but his illness is affecting his decision-making."

"Alexander in his grave could still out-think you," Saben responds, fists clenched at his sides. "Don't think that if Alexander, when he—You'll never take over Bulrush. How anyone who's been with Alexander for so long can possibly still be so rash is beyond me. Leading Bulrush is about more than conducting missions. It takes discretion and maturity and you've got neither."

"I suppose you think you do?"

"I don't want to command Bulrush."

"No, you want to destroy it. You've been looking for an opportunity ever since Alexander took you in and now you've got her to help you, or to blame—I'm not sure which. You're patient, I'll give you that." Idris shoulders past Saben and gets between me and the computer.

"You're the one who wants to destroy it, by joining with the Defiance and abandoning Bulrush's mission."

Hostility shimmers between them. I get the feeling this confrontation has been simmering for a long time, that my unauthorized presence in the computer room is only the catalyst.

"He didn't bring me. I was"—there's no nice word for it—"snooping. I'm sorry."

Idris grabs my wrist and twists it painfully. "You'll be sorry."

"Let her go," Saben says, stepping forward. "This is between you and me. You haven't trusted me since day one. Well, I think you're a danger to Bulrush. You act like you're on board with Alexander's vision, but I know you've been talking to the station masters on your own. Alexander doesn't know that, does he? And don't think I don't know who's sneaking weapons from the armory. I haven't told Alexander because I don't want to upset him, but I know you're plotting something more than the usual missions, something Alexander hasn't authorized."

Taking advantage of Idris's distraction, I use a move Fiere taught me. Twisting my arm sharply up and over, I'm free. I put the desk between me and Idris, but he doesn't react; he's focused on Saben.

"Bulrush has been moving women to the outposts for fourteen years," Idris says. "We've got the organization and the training to do more, to hit the Prags where it really hurts. It's time we aligned with the Defiance. We've got the knowledge and contacts they need to operate effectively in this region, and they've got the experience and weapons." Ignoring me, he stalks to the door, coming within half an inch of Saben but not bumping the larger man. "Get her the hell out of here," he snaps as he stomps away.

"The Defiance?" I ask, forgetting my tenuous position. "You'd work with the Defiance?"

Saben skewers me with a look. "Get back to the great room, Everly. Now."

Recognizing implacability in his tone, I go. I expect Alexander to confront me about my trespassing, but he doesn't. I don't know if it's because neither Saben nor Idris ratted me out—hard to believe—or because he's playing some game I don't quite get. I should be relieved, but it leaves me uneasy.

I tell Halla about the encounter that night in our room before Fiere comes up to bed. We're lying side by side on our mattresses, staring up at the ceiling. Two-thirds of a chipped plaster medallion cups an opening where a light fixture once descended.

"It *is* hard to understand why Saben's here," Halla says when I finish the story. "But we don't really know why any of them are doing this. Why do you distrust him in particular? Because he's geneborn?"

"Exactly." Memories flash through my mind, disjointed, out of sequence: a woman's hug, tousled auburn hair, the water, the water . . . can't breathe, Keegan's smile. I stifle a gasp and concentrate on breathing slowly and deeply. There's plenty of air.

"Is it because that boy made his parents bring you back to the Kube after they'd fosted you?"

On her first night at the Kube, Halla, five, had heard me crying, awakened by the recurring nightmare I'd suffered since being with the Ushers. She'd left her bed to cuddle with me in mine, patting my arm and saying, "Be okay, be okay."

Even so, I've never told her or anyone everything that happened when I lived with the Ushers, so I say guardedly, "That might be part of it. Mostly, it's because it doesn't make sense for a geneborn to be part of this, to risk death to undermine the government by smuggling women and babies."

"People don't always do what makes sense," Halla says with a rueful chuckle. "We can't all be logic-driven Everly Jaxes. Look at me."

I can't see her, but I know she's rubbing her baby bump.

"It didn't make sense for me to fall in love with Loudon or get pregnant or decide I want to keep the baby, but I did. And I'm glad."

"I'm glad you're glad." I drift off to sleep wondering how she can possibly be glad in the current circumstances. No answer comes to me in my dreams.

CHAPTER NINETEEN

I'm getting a serious case of cabin fever by the eighth evening. As we finish eating, Alexander meets Fiere's eyes. "You should be going."

With a nod, she rises and leaves the room. I watch curiously. Going where? I know better than to ask.

"This should be my mission," Idris says angrily.

Saben rises, too. "We'll give you a report when we get back," he tells Alexander.

"I wish I were still up to it," Alexander says. He grimaces. "Makes me feel like an old man to watch you go off on this mission without me. Time was . . ."

Saben grips his shoulder. "Can't risk the general on the front lines."

Alexander covers Saben's hand with his own. "Godspeed."

Idris watches this byplay and his face hardens. Without a word, he stalks out of the room.

Saben nods and leaves. I look at Wyck and Halla to see what they make of it all, but they look as clueless as I am. I guess that the mission has something to do with moving the invisible Kareen, but I don't understand why they're all so tense. Surely it's become routine by now, shuttling women to the next stop on their Underground Railroad, wherever that is? Despite my disapproval of Bulrush's goals, I find myself interested in how they move people to the west, and their logistics. In a subdued mood, we all go up to bed early.

Saben and Alexander are eating breakfast, IPF-issue field rations, when Halla, Wyck and I come downstairs. Their expressions are tense. Saben's saying, "It was like the IPF was waiting for us. As soon as we approached the rendezvous point, they opened fire." He notices us and breaks off, greeting us with forced cheer. The three of us help ourselves to the flash-dried rations and sit.

"Didn't go well last night?" I ask.

Saben looks at Alexander, who nods.

"No. I had to bring Kareen back here. Fiere and Cas led our pursuers away."

"They're not back yet," Alexander says tightly. His face is white, his mouth set in a thin line. His hand presses into his side and I wonder again what's wrong with him.

"They'll be back any minute," Saben says.

"God willing and the volcano don't explode," Alexander says. The words are almost prayer-like.

"We'll have to try again tonight," Saben says. Perhaps to forestall further questions, he turns to me. "I can train you."

Wyck looks from Saben to me, glowers, and goes off toward the kitchen. More shoveling on tap for the day, I guess. I don't blame him for looking disgruntled.

"Can I watch?" Halla asks Saben. "I can't fight like this"—she indicates her belly—"but I might learn something."

"Absolutely."

The three of us traipse to the mattress-cushioned ballroom. I immediately leap aside and Saben looks at me curiously. "Sorry," I say, feeling foolish. "Fiere usually puts me on the floor within a nanosecond of stepping through the door."

"She's intense," he says. "She has reason to be."

"What reason?" Halla asks.

Saben hesitates. "If she wants to tell you, she will."

We spar with Halla cross-legged on the floor watching our every move closely. Saben is impressed with my progress.

"Are you sure you've never fought before?" he asks. "You're a natural. Fiere better watch out."

I smile and wonder if either of my parents is agile or strong. With more practice, I might be able to defend myself effectively against the likes of Armyn or the Dravon brothers. Part of me looks forward to the opportunity to try. Part of me is appalled at the idea, wanting to return to the lab where Dr. Ronan might chastise me for sloppy procedures or sloppy thinking, but where I won't end up winded on the floor with someone's knee in my back.

Saben gets off my back and reaches down to help me up. We're both breathing hard, both sweaty, and his callused hand grips mine firmly. "Enough?" he asks with a cocked eyebrow.

"For now."

He laughs and I'm glad I made him laugh. Halla and I watch him leave the ballroom. "If I weren't totally in love with Loudon," Halla says, "I'd say that's one fine looking man."

I have to admit—but only to myself—that Saben's rear view in the fitted jumpsuit is impressive. "I haven't thought about it," I tell Halla.

She gives me a sly smile. "It's not a matter of thinking," she says.

"You should know."

She gasps, but then breaks into laughter, the snuffly chortles I haven't heard from her since before she told me she was pregnant. The sound brings me such happiness I grin widely. Cas comes running in.

"Fiere's hurt. Alexander needs Saben."

"He just left," Halla says. "I'll find him."

Cas and I run to the tunnel and climb down. I let go of the ladder and my feet thud on the dirt. It's damp. The tunnel is shored up by mismatched ribs of lumber that look like they've come from dozens of old houses like the one we're living in. It is ill-lit by bioluminescent pods fixed at intervals along the walls. It smells earthy. I run after Cas until we reach a spot where the tunnel forks. Alexander is there, kneeling beside Fiere who is groaning. He gently palpates her abdomen and she yips like a wild dog.

"Is she okay?" I ask.

She opens her eyes at the sound of my voice. They're almost black against her skin's pallor. "I'm fine," she grits out. "A graze. Cas and I led them on a wild goose chase, Alexander. They didn't get within five miles of here. I got hit early on; I guess I didn't realize I'd lost quite so much blood. Sorry." Her head droops forward; she's lost consciousness.

I don't see any blood.

White lines bracket Alexander's mouth. He smoothes a hand over her sweat-damp brow. "You did fine, my dear." To Saben and Cas he says, "We need to get her upstairs. Stat. I'm afraid she's got internal bleeding. Her abdomen is stiff."

They bend and lift her as gently as possible. Maneuvering her up the short ladder is difficult, but they manage. Halla and Wyck hover anxiously at the top. Alexander snaps at me, "I need boiling water right now, and clean cloths." I don't ask how or where; I head for the kitchen, figure out the stove, and put water in a pot to boil. While it's heating, I find a linen closet and appropriate a stack of pillow cases and towels. The flowered pillow cases have the lingering scent of lilies that seems to pervade this house and I wonder about all the heads that have lain on them as I slice them into wide strips with a butcher knife.

Tossing the cloths over my shoulder, I lift the heavy water pot and stagger out of the kitchen. Realizing I have no idea where they've taken Fiere, I pause in the hallway. The murmur of voices comes from my left and I head that way. I find Alexander, Saben, Wyck, and a woman who must be Kareen gathered around Fiere in a small room that might have been a butler's pantry or still room for preparing herbs or flowers. The room smells of alcohol and the men are rubbing their damp hands. Fiere's unconscious on a narrow table. The black-film has been stripped from the room's windows so light pours in. I know she must be in desperate shape for them to breach security like this.

Kareen is efficiently slicing Fiere's jumpsuit off with a razor tool. She's about my height, but with extra padding. She looks soft until I watch her steady hands on the blade and notice her expression of total concentration. Her face is shadowed by the silk scarf that drapes her head and neck. As if sensing my gaze, she looks up and meets my eyes. Hers are brown with slightly droopy under lids that expose a rim of red. Her skin is the color of toasted almonds and the crow's feet tell me she's older than I thought. I'd been expecting a pregnant girl, or someone likely to conceive, but she's past that. She nods acknowledgment of my presence and says to Alexander, "She's brought the water. Sterilize your instruments." Her voice is low-pitched and musical.

Alexander unfolds a leather pouch that contains a startling array of old-fashioned surgical implements. There's alcohol and syringes and various other medicines and bottles already lined up on the windowsill. He gestures for me to pour boiling water into a bowl into which he puts the surgical instruments. He wipes them thoroughly with alcohol and lays them on a clean towel. Fiere is naked now and I can see her abdomen is distended and bruised blue-black. There's an old scar low down, a hair above her pubic bone and about four inches long. It's clearly surgical. It could be a hysterectomy scar. That's a death penalty offense.

The enormity of that barely dawns on me before Alexander motions for the men to hold down Fiere's shoulder and legs. I draw a quick breath. There's no anesthesia. I pray that Fiere remains unconscious as Alexander takes up a scalpel. His hand shakes.

"I should do it," Kareen says, holding out her hand. When he hesitates, she says calmly, "You're ill, my friend, and too close to the girl. Do you doubt my skill after training me?"

He still hesitates, then slaps the scalpel into her palm. Looking at me, he says, "More boiling water. Keep it coming." He positions himself by Kareen's side as she places the tip of the scalpel so it indents the skin of Fiere's abdomen, and then draws it down with one steady movement. Blood gushes and I feel woozy. "Water," Alexander says sharply, staunching the blood, and I leave.

The surgery takes two hours. I boil water and haul it to them, removing the bowls of bloody water that accumulate near the makeshift operating table. Once, I bear away a bowl with a small, pinkish red organ in it. It turns my stomach and I avert my head. I don't know what to do with it and end up burying it in the compost bin. When I return to the room the last time, Fiere is gone and Halla is helping Cas re-film the windows.

"They've taken her upstairs," she answers my unspoken question. "They had to take out her spleen, but they think they got the bleeding stopped. She should be okay, Alexander says, if she doesn't get an infection. Do you think I could be a doctor?"

Saben appeared in the doorway. "Everly." He jerks his head.

Curiosity consuming me, I follow him to the main room where Kareen, Alexander, and Cas are assembled. Alexander's looking slightly better and he gives me a small smile when we come in. "Fiere should be okay," he tells us all. "She had an excellent doctor—"

"Trained by the best," Kareen murmurs.

"Kareen had to take out her spleen, but it looks like we stopped the internal bleeding, which is the main thing." He rests his palms on his thighs. "We've got to talk about how to get Kareen out of here. Last night's mission went awry; it looks like the IPF was waiting for them at Station Delta. Now, it might be a coincidence—the patrols have been stepped up since Kareen went missing."

The others nod as if they know why. I don't have a clue.

"But, there's also the possibility that one of our station masters has been turned, has betrayed us. The only possibilities are at Station Delta itself, or at Station Foxtrot which was to be her next stop. I've known Janssen at Delta for thirty years; I can't believe it's him. At any rate, Cas and Kareen will leave at dusk and head for Station Lima, circumventing the usual route. It'll take you two days," he tells Cas, "but it can't be helped."

Cas nods. Kareen tries to maintain her serene expression, but worry lurks in her eyes.

"However, we can't operate with a traitor on the railroad, so we need to sniff him or her out. Additionally, as we planned, it's by far the best if the IPF and her husband think Kareen's dead. Otherwise, they'll never stop searching for her. So, Saben, I need you to head for Station Foxtrot tonight, as would be the usual protocol. With Fiere out of commission, Everly needs to go along as the decoy."

"What?" All eyes turn to me.

"I can't ask her to do that," Kareen says. "She's a child, untrained."

"I'm asking. She's smart, resourceful and about your height," he says in an uncompromising voice. "Your scarf can hide her hair. Saben will be with her. What do you say, Everly?"

"Of course I'll do it." I have no idea what "it" is, but I want to get out of this house. Also, some part of me wants to please Alexander; I'm not sure why.

"Good girl. Saben, as the mission commander, you work out the details. You know the parameters: identify and neutralize the traitor and convince the IPF that Kareen's dead. Oh, and bring Everly back safely." His gaze fixes on me. "You can't tell Wyck or Halla. Operational details are on a need to know basis; frankly, I'd prefer not having to use you, but needs must. Understood?" His uncompromising tone hints at severe consequences.

I nod.

He sags against the couch, clearly exhausted. "Right. Get to it, then."

Kareen goes to Alexander as Saben leads me out of the room. "What's wrong with him?" I ask.

Saben answers in a low voice. "He was helping move disabled patients from a rehabilitation center when it was hit with a chemical weapon during the Between. He doesn't know for sure what the agent was—a synthetic compound of some kind—but it's been eating away at his organ tissue for years. If he'd gotten a full blast, his organs would have more or less disintegrated on the spot. He got just a whiff, but even that . . . The medicine he takes slows it, but he's weakening.I think sheer stubbornness keeps him going."

It nauseates me to think that a chemist would turn his or her skills to such an evil end.

Saben spends the rest of the afternoon outlining his plan and getting me outfitted. We stain my hands and face with a nut dye to approximate Kareen's skin tone, and pull a close-fitting black cap over my hair, tucking the blond tresses up inside. It doesn't work; my hair's too thick. With an exclamation of impatience, I pull out my knife, bunch my hair in my fist, and begin to saw through it at jaw level.

After an initial exclamation, Saben leaves and returns with scissors. He finishes the job of cutting off my hair, stroking his hand down it gently when he's done. I'm amazed by how light my head feels, but I take care not to look in a mirror. The black cap fits fine now.

We leave the house shortly after dark. I'm wearing two layers of clothes—so I'll match Kareen's plumpness—over what Saben assures me is a projectile-stopping IPF jumpsuit two sizes too big. "The only one we've managed to get," he says, "so don't lose it."

Yeah, right. Like anyone could lose a jumpsuit. It weighs more than a normal jumpsuit and the tight weave of the intelli-fabric is almost oily under my fingers. Kareen's silk scarf conceals my face. I'm wearing a backpack that supposedly contains the clothes and necessities Kareen would be taking to start a new life wherever. My knife goes in a sheath strapped to my thigh. A bladder filled with three pints of Kareen's blood, collected over several weeks, I'm told, is taped to my torso. If things go as planned, the blood's DNA will tell the IPF they shot Kareen, and the quantity will tell them she's dead, even though, hopefully, they won't have a body. If they have a body, it'll be mine, and that will screw everything up, as Saben keeps reminding me. Like I need reminding.

Once in the tunnel, Saben slips a hood over my head. "Sorry."

"You trust me to be a decoy and risk my life for some woman I don't know, but you don't trust me to know where your headquarters is?" I'm miffed.

"Sorry," he says again, taking my hand and leading me to an ACV. We skim through the tunnels, banking several times and making a hard right once, and then I can feel that we're in the open. When we've gone what feels like two or three miles, Saben stops and removes the hood. We're outside Atlanta, although I can see lights glowing in the city, and the shape of a large dome lit up on the horizon. It makes me homesick. A breeze blows the scent of water from the Chattahoochee River.

We're early and Saben glides the ACV to a bluff so we can watch the bridge where the rendezvous is supposed to take place. The plan is for us to approach the old drawbridge and for Saben to give the code. If the response is correct, I'm to walk onto the bridge to meet the station master, like Kareen would have. He doesn't know Kareen's name or what she looks like, so I only have to look like her from a distance to fool any watchers. He'll take me to the next station down the line and Saben will pick me up there, ready with a story for that station master. If this guy is the traitor, Saben expects the men hoping to reclaim Kareen to open fire on me. I'm to spill Kareen's blood and take shelter in the bridge keeper's hut until Saben comes. I suspect Saben has more in mind than he's told me; still, I can count at least forty-two holes in his plan.

"Why is Kareen so important?" I ask as we wait in the ACV parked behind a clump of dead bushes. "She looks like she's past child-bearing—why is Bulrush helping her?"

Saben's profile is pale in the wash of moonlight. "She was one of Alexander's med students, and a Bulrush founder. He had to leave the city, go underground, but she was well-placed to both feed us information about what the government knew about Bulrush, and help women and girls who needed relocation make contact with us. Her husband is a government minister. He began watching her, having her followed, and she suspects he intercepted one of our communications. It was only a matter of time before he had her arrested, or, more likely, had her tortured and killed once she gave up everything she knows about Bulrush. She had to leave her children behind."

I remember the photo I saw near her mattress. "How horrible."

"She'll probably never see them again. He'll tell them she deserted them and they'll grow up despising her. She's a strong, brave woman. She's sure her husband won't want many people to know he was married to a traitor, so only a few of his most trusted bodyguards are likely to be here tonight. She thinks two or three. That's all there were last night, and I took one of them down. It's only bad luck that Fiere got hit. They surprised us—that won't happen again."

"IPF?"

"No, private security."

It crosses my mind that maybe the traitor isn't one of the station masters. Maybe it's someone at headquarters. What if it's Kareen herself?

"It must be incredibly difficult, virtually impossible, for a mother to leave her children," I say, trying to sound offhand.

Saben slants a look at me. "It's not Kareen. Alexander swears it's not. I trust his judgment."

I see movement by the bridge and Saben raises night-vision binoculars. "I think that's Federico," he says. "You ready?"

Butterflies swarm my stomach. I nod, unable to speak. He grips my hand tightly for a moment and then ignites the ACV. I surreptitiously scan Saben's profile. Can I trust him? What if he's the traitor? I've never understood why he—a geneborn—is with Bulrush. Not a good time to ask. We skim down the slope and approach the bridge. It's pale stone, ghostly in the moonlight, with a graceful metal arch spanning its length. Pretty. I'm not in the mood to appreciate pretty, though, with every muscle tensed and my brain running over my instructions again and again. We walk onto the bridge. The surface is pot-holed asphalt at first, but changes to a metal grid as we reach the middle. A figure wrapped in a bulky coat steps out of the drawbridge operator's hut as we near.

Saben steps forward to meet him. I lag behind, keeping my head bowed. They exchange a few muttered words and I guess Federico got the code right because Saben motions me forward. "She's all yours," he says. "Keep her safe. This one's special."

The man grunts a reply and starts off toward the far end of the bridge. He's stockily built, and walks with a slight limp. With one last look at Saben, I hurry after him, playing my part. Every moment I expect to feel the thud of a particle beam on my back, tearing through my supposedly projectile-proof jumpsuit to shred my innards. I force myself to take long, slow breaths. The farther we get, the more I relax. Maybe Federico is okay. We reach an ACV he's got hidden behind the stone parapet. The passenger side is closest and he reaches for the door. As he does, the scarf slips, revealing a slice of my face.

"Hey," he says. "You're not her."

He's not supposed to know about Kareen. He grabs for me. Reacting on reflex alone, I pull my knife and, in one smooth movement, plunge it into his throat, just as he yells, "It's not—"

The blade chokes off the words. He makes a horrible gargling sound and claps both hands to his neck as I withdraw the knife. Blood leaks around his fingers. The coppery smell nauseates me, but I don't have time for that. *They've got to think Kareen's dead.* Under his starting eyes, I open the front of my jumpsuit and slit the bladder taped to my abdomen. Blood gushes out. Sickening. I breathe shallowly through my mouth. I'm surprised not to hear any voices, any blasts. Who was Federico calling to, if not Kareen's husband's bodyguards? Where is Saben? Federico sags against the ACV, croaking. I step away from him to spill the blood over a wider area as quickly as possible. As I do, there's tremendous *whumpf* and the ACV explodes.

The force knocks me flat. I lie winded for a moment, until the heat from the blaze forces me to crawl forward. Now I know why the bodyguards didn't shoot; they were willing to sacrifice their mole to ensure Kareen's death. I hear voices. *They can't find me.* I drag myself a few more inches and then manage to push to my feet. The burning ACV lights up the night. I glance up and see a man sliding down a rope attached to the bridge's superstructure. Ah, clever. Footsteps pound on the bridge. One or two men, like Saben guessed. *They can't find me.* I'm too wobbly to run far. They'll be on me in a moment. There's only one option. I stagger to the river bank. The water flows quickly, dark, deep and dangerous.

I'll drown. I can't. My throat closes up at the mere thought.

A nearby rock explodes, hit by a beamer blast. The fragments pepper me.

I have no choice. I can't die here where they'd find my body. They've got to think Kareen is dead. Taking a deep breath, I throw myself into the river. It would be nice if I knew how to swim.

CHAPTER TWENTY

The water closes over my head, chilly and dark. I can't see anything. No gold eyes, no bubbles, no water-blurred face smiling down at me. I sink like a stone. The jumpsuit! Its weight is pulling me down. Holding my breath, I frantically rip my way out of the layers of clothes atop the jumpsuit and tug at the seal. It holds for a moment but then gives. I pull my arms out of it and push it down. It snags on my boots. I scuff them off, shuck the jumpsuit, and finally kick it away with one foot. It continues down. *Saben will be pissed.* Seeing dark spots, I kick for the surface.

I can't help myself, I stick my head out and gasp for air.

"There she is," a man's voice says.

Beamer blasts streak the dark and plough through the water near me. Sucking in the deepest breath I can manage, I duck underneath the surface. This time, I keep my eyes open, but it doesn't help much. The water is murky with God knows what and I hope I'm not swallowing enough chemicals to make me glow. I become aware that the current is carrying me downstream, away from the bridge. At first I'm relieved, but then I realize it might sweep me so far that Saben can't find me. The need for air drives me to the surface again. This time, I'm more in control and manage to expose only a sliver of my face as I gulp another breath. Then I'm down again. A minute later, I rise for more air. The bridge is barely in sight behind me. There's no pursuit. *Saben.* He took them down.

My fierce exultation in our success fades as I try to make my way to the bank. It seems impossibly far away, and my uncoordinated flailings and kickings aren't moving me closer. I'm tiring quickly. The cold is sapping my energy. It's getting harder and harder to work my way to the surface for air when the current sucks me down. Something knocks into me, spinning me 180-degrees, and I gasp. My first thought is *alligator*, but it's a tree, roots and all. I grab onto a branch which breaks. I grab another and work my way along it to the trunk. Throwing one arm across it, I give thanks and rest for a moment. I'm losing feeling in my hands and feet.

My toe scrapes the bottom. I'm still in the middle of the river, so this must be a sandbar. I don't know how big it is, or how deep the water is. Hold onto the log or take my chances on the sandbar? The log is pulling me along . . . I only have seconds to decide. I let go. The log scrapes past me, keeping me off balance as I try to gain a foothold on the sandbar. I manage to steady myself in waist deep water.

I'm jubilant for a moment, but then find myself taking a step backward. Another one. The current is pushing me. I can't maintain my position. I should have stayed with the log.

Fear washes over me. I don't want to drown. Another step back. The water is past my waist now. I'm running out of sandbar.

I hear something over the river's gurgles. An ACV. It's got to be Saben. I risk calling out. "Here! I'm here."

A dark shape detaches from the riverbank and angles toward me. The pilot doesn't speak. I think I've made a horrible mistake and am about to let the river take me again, when an arm reaches down. "Grab on and I'll drag you to the bank," Saben says. Moonlight glints off his hair.

I grab for his hand and his fingers lock around my wrist. In less than thirty seconds, he's towed me to the shallows. He lets go of me to set the ACV down a safe distance away. Barely able to stand from exhaustion, I splash through the knee-deep water to the shore and collapse onto the muddy bank. I might be crying. Then Saben's beside me, lifting me, wrapping me in a blanket.

"Are you okay?" he asks over and over again.

I don't have the energy to answer, but force out one word. "Fine." *I didn't drown.*

He chafes my bare hands and feet, working his way up my calves. Warmth returns to my extremities. I'm naked except for thin panties and camisole. I don't care. A gentle hand pushes the sodden hair off my face and he wipes the mud off with a corner of the blanket.

"We have to teach you to swim," he says.

That makes me choke on a laugh which warms me faster than the blanket. Saben helps me to sit up and holds a flask to my lips. "Drink."

I take an incautious swallow. The fiery fluid burns its way across my tongue and down my throat, pooling in my stomach and warming me from the inside out. Wexl. I smile fuzzily, understanding why Dr. Ronan likes it. "I didn't drown."

"No, you didn't drown. Were you expecting to?" There's whimsy in his voice, but it breaks something free inside of me, or maybe the Wexl does, and I find myself telling him about Keegan, spilling the whole story. I wrap my arms under my thighs and stare at my feet so I don't have to watch his face while I talk.

"When I was little, four, I think, the government started an experimental program where they fosted out children from the Kubes—natural borns, of course—to specially approved families who were willing to take them. It's because the Kubes were getting crowded and there weren't enough geneborn babies to go around. I went to a family called Usher. They already had a geneborn son, Keegan"—I can't say the name without shuddering—"but they desperately wanted a little girl. They got me for four months."

"What happened?" Saben's voice is darker with no hint of humor now. He knows something went badly wrong.

"The son—they wanted me to think of him as my brother—hated me. He was pathologically jealous, I think, looking back on it. He pinched me and hit me and pulled my hair whenever he could do it without getting caught. I was afraid of him."

"How old was he?"

"Eleven. Seven years older than me." My feet are long and pale, toes water-wrinkled, against the muddy bank. "His parents caught him slapping me once and punished him, and that made it worse. He tried to push me off a train platform, but a bystander caught me before I went over the edge. Keegan got away with it by saying he'd stumbled. Then, one day when his parents were at Assembly, he tried to drown me. In the tub." I cough, like I'm gagging up water, even though my throat is clear. Taking another swallow of Wexl, I continue. "His mother felt unwell and came home early and saved my life. I don't remember that part clearly—just my chest aching for several days after they took me back to the Kube and my throat being sore. I think she did chest compressions to get me breathing again."

"He's still in prison, I hope?" Saben's voice is cold, but his arm is warm as he puts it over my shoulders and pulls me close.

"They hushed it up. He was geneborn. I've been scared of water ever since. I could never make myself swim in the ocean, go deeper in than my knees, even though I wanted to." I smile wryly and dig my big toe into the warm, oozy mud. "I should be over it by now, right?"

"I think you're very brave."

I'm embarrassed and speak quickly to cover it. "I grew up thinking that I'd done something wrong because the Ushers gave me back, that I wasn't good enough to be part of a family. Then, for a while, I thought it didn't work because they weren't my biological family. No real brother would have done that. Then I figured out that Wyck's dad, his biological father, beat him, and I didn't know what to think."

"Your ideas about family got all mixed up. No wonder. You were only four." He tugs on a hank of my short, wet hair. "That's okay. You can be part of the Bulrush family now. You okay to start back?"

I nod, preparing to stand, but Saben scoops me up and carries me to the ACV. The strength in his arms, the solidity of his chest, and his distinctive earthy scent make me feel strange. It's the Wexl, I tell myself. I'm feeling rosy-warm all over. He slides me into the passenger compartment and I pull the blanket tighter around me. As he ignites the ACV and we rise, I ask, "The soldiers at the bridge?"

"Dead. It'll look like Kareen managed to shoot them before the ACV exploded, mortally injuring her. Investigators will see she almost bled out before falling into the river. No way she could have survived after that much blood loss. The scene will play out exactly the way we wanted it to. You did fantastic."

On the way back, I wait for him to stop and pull the hood over my head, but he doesn't.

Federico floats toward me, his hair billowing in the current, blood spurting from the hole my knife tore in his neck. His mouth opens and closes like he's saying something, but no words come out. I'm trying to swim away from his grasping hands, but they're reaching for me, reaching for me . . .

I sit bolt upright on my mattress, breathing ragged. It was a nightmare, I tell myself. A dream. I look around the dormitory, focusing on now familiar objects. Fiere's mattress, empty. Halla on the mattress beside me, sleeping on her back with her rounded belly sticking up. The wooden chair in the corner. The torn travel poster tacked to the back of the door. "—sit exotic Bangkok" the text below a golden Buddha figure begs.

I lie back. It must be almost morning. It was after midnight when we got back, although I felt like we'd been gone for days. Alexander was waiting for us, skin waxy with pain and tension. Saben gave him a brief sketch of what happened, playing up my role. Alexander kissed me on both cheeks, gave me a draught he said would counteract most of the chemicals I might have swallowed in the river, thanked me, and sent me to bed. I know he and Saben talked for a while longer because their voices, words indistinguishable, drifted up to me.

I lie back down, but sleep eludes me. All I can think now is, I killed a man. I *killed* a man. I killed a *man*. The words loop through my head. I'm not sure how I feel about it. Bad. I roll that idea around. I'm not even sure I feel bad. I ought to. Killing is wrong. Amerada needs all of its citizens to rebuild and repopulate. It happened so fast. Reflex, muscle memory, just like Fiere talked about. In that split second, I knew it was keep Federico from warning the others, or die. I didn't want to die. I didn't want Saben to die. It was us or Federico. That justified it, right? It was combat, not murder. Federico betrayed us thinking he was betraying Kareen; he deserved to die. I can't quite convince myself of that. I lie awake, wrestling with it, until a lightening beyond the filmed windows tells me the sun is up.

"Oh, my goodness! What happened to you?" Halla is awake, facing me, eyes wide. "Your hair. And why are there brown streaks on your face?"

I scrunch my fingers through my shorter hair. "I, uh, got tired of it, thought it would be easier to take care of this way," I lie.

She gives me a look that says she knows I'm lying. Best friends can say all sorts of things without opening their mouths.

"I helped Bulrush with something, okay? I can't talk about it."

"As long as you're okay." She rolls out of bed and stretches. "I am so ready to have this baby. Loudon's unit should get back today. I can't believe I'll see him tomorrow. By the way, I think your hair's cute like that." She disappears into the hall.

When it's my turn in the hyfac, I scrub my face until it's red, trying to get rid of the dye. There's nothing I can do about my hair which seems to have developed a wave now that it's shorter. I cock my head and assess it in the sliver of mirror hanging over the sink. It's not hideous.

Apparently, Wyck thinks otherwise. "Why'd you cut off your hair? Where'd you disappear to last night?"

I'm too tired to lie. "I can't talk about it." I try to move past him, eager for breakfast—starved, in fact— but he blocks my way.

"Saben was gone, too." There's accusation in his voice.

"So?"

"Were you with him?"

"I can't talk about it."

"Were you with him?"

The look of frustration and jealousy on his face makes me say, "Not in any romantic way."

Before I can guess what he's going to do, he grabs me by my upper arms and kisses me. He mashes my lips against my teeth. It hurts. I wrench away. "What the hell, Wyck?"

He runs his hands through his brown curls. "I'm sorry. I didn't mean to hurt you. I just—You can't trust him, Ev. He's geneborn. What's he doing here anyway?"

I wasn't about to discuss Saben with Wyck this morning, despite having some of the same reservations. I was too emotionally and physically battered. "I can't do this," I say, and brush past him.

Halla is already in the dining room with Alexander, Saben, and surprisingly, Fiere. Halla's standing, staring down at Alexander who is sitting with a dish on his lap. "What do you mean the house is on 'lockdown?'"

"One of the ministers' wives was murdered last night," he says calmly without glancing at me or Saben. "The city is in an uproar, with IPF everywhere. We can't risk going out for a day or two. I know you're eager to see Loudon, my dear, but you're going to have to be patient a day or two longer."

"I'm having his baby any day now. I need to see him," she pleads.

"You will," Alexander says. "Just not today. And probably not tomorrow."

Halla runs out of the room, tears in her eyes. Emotions are running high with everyone, I note. I glance at Fiere who is ghost-pale but composed. No one would guess she had surgery yesterday. "How are you?"

She gives a wry smile. "Better than you'd think. Kareen's a miracle worker, despite her sub-par training." She shoots a mischievous look at Alexander who manages a smile.

"I'm the one who'll be changing your dressing later this morning, so be careful," he says. It's a hollow threat. He's so pleased she's doing well that he looks twice as energized as yesterday.

"There's no sign of infection," she tells him. "I peeked."

"I'll be the judge of that."

"Would I be this perky if there were?"

"Perky" is not a word I'd have associated with Fiere.

"You'd probably still be annoying if you had gangrene, the flu and cholera," Saben teases.

Fiere actually sticks out her tongue at him. I watch in mild astonishment. Alexander looks on with a smile, a benevolent father watching his children spar. For a moment, I want more than anything to be part of this family. Then I remember that they're not really a family and that if they were, they regard me as the third cousin twice removed who has to be tolerated for a while, but not really included. I remember that I've got plans of my own—finding my real parents—and that Bulrush is not part of those plans. Wyck concentrates on his breakfast of mushrooms, potatoes and dried fish and leaves as soon as he scoops up the last bite.

As soon as he's gone, Fiere leans forward, then winces and straightens again. "I hear you did well last night."

I don't know what to say.

She doesn't seem to expect a response. She says, "Must be the excellent training you received."

Saben jeers, Alexander smiles, and I can't help laughing. "Must be," I agree.

I help Fiere to her temporary room on this floor so Alexander can examine her. I suspect she has overexerted herself because she leans heavily against me. I steady her as she sits on a bed that's actually up on a frame. She starts to untie the loose robe wrapped around her, but then stops.

"I already saw the scar," I say neutrally. "You had a hysterectomy, didn't you?"

With a decidedly less friendly glance than earlier, she says, "I suppose you think you have something on me now."

"No. I don't want 'something on you.'" Who would I tell anyway? It's not like I'm in a position to trot to the IPF with the information, no matter how condescending she is sometimes. I wouldn't anyway; I don't want Fiere put to death for having her womb cut out.

"Then I suppose you think I owe you an explanation."

"You don't owe me anything. Give it a rest, why don't you?"

I'm on my way out the door when she says, "I've borne two children."

I turn slowly, not sure how I feel about receiving her confidence, but not feeling like I can reject it and walk out, either. "You were a surrogate?"

She nods. "Against my will."

"How can that be? What do you mean?"

"Four years ago. I got careless. Doesn't matter how. Bounty hunters snatched me and sold me to a RESCO. They inseminated me."

"What's a RESCO?"

Fiere looks like she can't believe I don't know the term. She hesitates, as if she regrets starting this conversation. "Reproduction Support Community. Hah! It's a euphemism for hell, for baby-bearing slavery."

"My God." I imagine people like Armyn and his mother, or the Dravon brothers, running these baby factories. "What happened?"

"I had a baby. I don't even know if it was a boy or a girl. They took it away and inseminated me again two weeks later. I had no opportunity to get away, no way to contact Alexander. I thought about killing myself. But I didn't," she spits. "There were dozens of us there. Some of the women had had six or seven babies in as many years. They treated us well as long as we didn't cause trouble. The food was good and plentiful, the medical care the best in Amerada. They kept telling us how privileged we were to be bearing Amerada's future leaders." Her snarl says what she thinks of their rhetoric. "I made a contact. One of the midwives. She smuggled a note to Alexander for me. He got me out after I had the second baby. I begged him for a hysterectomy." Her fingers pluck at the robe. "In the early part of the century, they outlawed what they called 'puppy mills,' which was the same concept, only with dogs. They treat women like dogs, worse than dogs."

"It can't be legal," I breathe.

She gives me that disbelieving stare. "Legal? The RESCOs are government-run. Don't you know anything about the real world?"

I stand abruptly. "That can't be true! Sure, the government encourages women to be surrogates, but they don't force them. I've had friends from the Kube volunteer for surrogacy. They have a baby and then they move on, go to school or move to an outpost."

"Have you ever talked to one of those women again?" Fiere asks with a knowing smile. "They volunteer to have one baby, but then they find they're virtually prisoners, forced to have baby after baby until they're worn out. The government usually lets them go after eight or nine, I understand."

"Then how come the whole country doesn't know about this? How do they keep these women from telling everyone what happened to them?" I'm sure she's wrong.

"Memory wipe," Fiere says soberly. "SMO."

"That technology's still experimental," I say. "It doesn't always work. Sometimes it wipes out too many memories."

"I know."

I take a hasty turn around the small room. "I don't believe you."

Fiere seems too tired to argue with me. She lies back against the pillow. "Whether you believe it or not doesn't change the facts. That's where the Dravon brothers would have taken you and Halla if Bulrush hadn't kicked their asses."

I know the government is concerned about growing the population, but what Fiere's suggesting is gross, repulsive, horrifying. She must be wrong. The Pragmatists can't sanction this, can't employ thugs like the Dravons. Maybe these RESCOs exist and Fiere got caught in one, but they can't be government institutions. They can't be. They must be run by individuals, criminal organizations who are selling the babies on the black market. I know there are lots of people who want children who can't have any themselves and who have been on the government waiting list for a geneborn child for years. Some of them, I've heard, will pay for a baby and forged procreation license.

"You can tell Halla," Fiere says. "Not about me, but about . . . about RESCOs. She should know. She needs to be careful."

"Thanks, Fiere." She's in pain, only a day out of surgery; I'm not going to argue with her.

"This doesn't make us best friends or anything," she says as I walk to the door. "I just thought you should know."

"Got it, Fiere. Not best friends. Ships that pass in the night. Two people who happen to be putting up at the same brothel, sharing a wall, passing in the halls, one of them occasionally throwing a roundhouse kick at the other . . . nothing more. Got it."

Alexander's in the hall, about to come in, so I leave the door open as I stalk away. "What's bothering Everly?" I hear him ask before I move out of earshot.

What *is* bothering Everly, I ask myself as I run down the hall. I desperately want my beach. I need the pounding waves, the scouring wind, the briny scent. Being cooped up in this house is driving me crazy. Never mind that I was out of it last night and almost got shot and drowned; I need out *now*. There's nowhere to go. I suspect Halla's upstairs, crying about not getting to see Loudon, and I can't cope with her pregnancy-addled emotions right now. Idris is probably doing something Bulrush-ish somewhere, maybe on the illicit computer. Wyck . . . I can help Wyck dig tunnels.

I don't know exactly where I'm going, so I'm forced to ask Saben. I find him in the kitchen. He shoves aside a sheet of paper when I come in. Probably secret Bulrush plans. I'm tired of all the secrecy. He gives me a curious look, but tells me how to find the new tunnel excavation. "Want me to show you?" he asks.

"I can find it." I hurry down the ladder, wincing as abused muscles complain, and borrow one of the scooters

Saben said would be hidden in a declivity not far away. I zip through the dimly lit tunnel, feeling like a mole. I remember the story of Thumbelina, forcibly wed to a mole, and I shudder. When I get within a few hundred yards of the excavation site, I hear the rhythmic sound of a shovel hitting dirt and then tossing it. *Clang, scrrrape, plup. Clang, scrrrape, plup.* I come around a corner and see Wyck, shirtless, shoveling with a fury that suggests he, too, is working through something.

"I've come to help," I say when he looks up.

"Grab a shovel." He nods to where three shovels are leaning against the tunnel wall with a stack of old flooring for braces.

We shovel side by side for half an hour, dumping the dirt into a cart. "What do they do with all that?" I ask, leaning on my shovel for a breather. My palms are blistered.

"Take it up top and spread it around at night." Wyck keeps shoveling, doesn't look at me.

"Look, I'm sorry about this morning. It's not that I don't want to tell you, but I promised."

"It's okay. I understand."

Even if he understands, it's clear he's not okay with it. "Where shall we go after Bulrush moves Halla and Loudon and the baby to wherever?"

This makes him pause and look at me. Sweat drips into his eyes. It's not hot down here, but it's muggy. "You still want to go?"

"Of course. You didn't think I wanted to hang on here, did you, become part of the Bulrush underground railroad?"

I can tell that's exactly what he thought.

"I'm not a . . . not a that kind of person." Not a rebel, not particularly brave, not a risk taker. "I'm a scientist. I need a lab, plants, the opportunity to help a community, maybe an outpost, grow food. I know cloning vectors and gene expression, not ambushes and fighting and super-secret code words."

The old grin lights Wyck's face. "I am definitely not a shoveler. So, when Halla's safe, we're going to go west, find an outpost and do our thing?"

I nod. "Sounds like a plan."

He reaches out a callused hand and I put mine into it, moving closer so he can kiss me. This kiss is gentle and sweet. I smile up at him.

"Cas was talking about coming with us," Wyck says, releasing me. "That would be okay, wouldn't it? I mean, three of us would be safer than just us two, right? He's got military training, after all, and knows all the Bulrush stations en route to the outposts."

I'm taken aback. Cas and I haven't conversed much beyond "good morning" and details of the Kareen mission. "I suppose," I say slowly. "I didn't know you had discussed us—our plans—with anyone else."

"Cas is a good listener," Wyck says, not meeting my eyes.

Puzzled, I study his face. "I need to get back and check on Halla. She was really upset about the lockdown."

"I'll go with you. I've had enough of this shoveling crap to last a lifetime."

It takes only a few minutes to skim back to the ladder below the brothel. Wyck leads the way confidently, having traveled the route daily for more than a week. We part with a quick hug. I head upstairs to find Halla, steeling myself for the inevitable outpourings of tears, frustration, and worry.

She's not in our room. Hm. I check the hyfac. Empty. I trot down the stairs. She's not in the main room, the ballroom or the kitchen where Gunter and Saben are cleaning a bag of vegetables that a sympathizer has dropped off. I peek into Fiere's room, thinking Halla might be keeping her company. Fiere's asleep and Halla's not there. I'm beginning to get worried. I return to the kitchen. "Have you guys seen Halla?"

"Not since breakfast," Saben says. He puts down the clump of radishes he's cleaning. "Want us to help look?"

I nod. The three of us fan out and search. We meet back in the main room five minutes later. Alexander joins us, having been alerted by Saben. "Halla's gone," I announce.

Alexander frowns. "Where could she—"

"Loudon." I'm suddenly sure of it. "She's gone to find Loudon."

"How could she?" Saben asks. "She doesn't know where the base is."

Cold steals through me. Without a word, I dash upstairs and grab my messenger bag. Book, feather, other detritus. . . The map I printed out at the Kube is gone, the one with the geocoords for Loudon's base. I return to the others. "She's got a map," I say. I explain.

"Damn the girl," Alexander says, worry etching his face. "Even if she gets to the base, she'll never get access to Loudon. She'll be arrested."

"Or worse," Saben says.

With Fiere's tale of RESCOs fresh in my thoughts, I blanch. "We've got to find her."

"I'll go," Saben says. "She can't have left more than— at most—an hour ago, right? With any luck, I can catch her before she gets to the base."

"I'm going with you." Wyck flings a challenging look at Alexander, but no one says anything about not letting him out of the house.

"Everly and I will take the other ACV," Alexander says. He shuts down the objection Saben's about to make with a look.

"What about Fiere?" I venture.

"She'll be fine for a couple of hours," Alexander says. "It's Halla we've got to worry about right now. With the extra patrols out because of Kareen—" He doesn't finish the thought. "Saben, put out an alert. Get the network to keep an eye out."

I wonder briefly how many people there are in the network and how they contact them. Saben takes off and Alexander beckons for me and Wyck to follow him. He heads for the kitchen. I think he's getting food to take with us when he enters the pantry and I'm impatient with the delay, but he holds his eye to a hidden iris scanner on the back wall and the wall slides back to reveal a weapons cache. The armory Saben mentioned. He tosses a beamer to Wyck who catches it one handed, and another to me. He selects a crossbow for himself. "Okay, let's go."

CHAPTER TWENTY ONE

In silence we meet up with Saben and descend into the tunnel. I'm jittery, much more so than last night. Halla . . . nothing can happen to Halla. Alexander and I claim the nearest ACV while Saben and Wyck run down the tunnel to where another one is hidden. "Scooter's missing," Alexander says tersely as he ignites our two-seater.

We zip through the tunnels. I'm expecting to come out at the car wash, but we emerge into a cavernous warehouse. Checking to ensure that no one observes our exit, Alexander zooms the ACV through the garage-style door and out into the middle of Atlanta. It's the first time I've seen the city during daylight and I'm amazed by how busy it is. At least two dozen ACVs of every size skim over the buckled streets and sidewalks. Several of them have IPF markings. There are still more derelict, deserted houses and buildings than occupied ones, but the city feels more *alive* than Jacksonville. Some of the houses have flowers growing in planters under glass. It seems frivolous to grow flowers instead of food, but I have to admit the sight of happy yellow marigolds makes me smile. I wonder where all of these people serve, what they *do*. A gilded dome rises in the city center, the gilt peeling in spots, but still magnificent with the sun sparking off it.

"The Capitol," Alexander says, observing the direction of my gaze.

I want to ask about the Ministry for Science and Food Production, but I don't. This trip is about Halla, not about finding access to the DNA registry to identify my parents.

Soon we're out of the populated city center and skimming past long-abandoned shopping malls with roofs caved in, schools, listing skyscrapers, and heaps of brick, wood and twisted metal no longer identifiable as particular buildings. I notice it all on some level, but pay attention to none of it. After twenty-five minutes, we top a rise and Alexander slows, keeping the ACV in the shadow of an old magnolia grove. Below, a fence-encircled compound sprawls. Low tan buildings. Lightly armored ACVs and heavier tracked vehicles. Sentries. The IPF base. I gape at it in dismay. Halla's quest was pointless from the word go; she had no chance of finding Loudon. The place is huge and soldiers are everywhere. They all look alike in camouflaged jumpsuits like the ones Alexander and I are wearing. "She could be anywhere," I breathe.

The hum of an ACV signals Saben and Wyck's arrival. They hover beside us. "Seen her?" Saben asks.

Alexander shakes his head. "Hopefully, she'll see how impossible it is and turn around. Position yourselves so you can watch the southern access route."

Saben nods and he and Wyck whiz down a gentle slope and are soon out of sight. Alexander scans three hundred sixty degrees with binoculars. A slight tremor in his hands makes me wonder how long he'll hold up.

"There." Alexander points to a scooter below us. Without ceremony, I grab the binoculars and peer through them. Halla. Her curly black hair bounces as the ACV stutters over uneven terrain. She's a quarter mile from the base entrance and seems to be slowing. Hallelujah. She's seen the futility. She's going to turn around. "Let's go get her," I urge, lowering the binoculars.

Alexander's mouth sets in a grim line. "Trouble."

I follow his pointing finger and see two two-seater ACVs detach themselves from points near the sentry-manned gate and head toward Halla.

"Her ACV isn't squawking the right IFF code," Alexander says.

A voice in my head screams that we need to zoom down the hill, attack the ACVs, and rescue Halla. Reality is staring me in the face, however, in the form of too many soldiers and weapons to count, all within shouting distance. Rushing to Halla would be suicide. We can only watch it play out from our vantage point. Halla's scooter speeds up and I can feel her fear from here. The ACVs give chase like wild dogs galvanized by prey running from them. Within thirty seconds they've overtaken her. One ACV slides in front of her scooter and the other pulls up behind it.

"No, no, no."

I don't realize I'm talking aloud until Alexander says, "There's nothing we can do right now."

Two armed soldiers approach the scooter and haul Halla off it. I can't see clearly, but suddenly she's crumpled on the ground, as if she's been struck. I cry out.

"We can't help her now, not here," Alexander says, swooping the ACV around.

"We can't leave her!" I'm turning in the seat, trying to see what's happening to Halla.

"We must. She's pregnant; they'll take her to the RESCO. We have a chance of rescuing her from there. Here, we'd all die for nothing."

He's implacable and I subside, knowing that his assessment is probably accurate, but torn apart by having to leave Halla behind. It's like opposing forces have hold of each of my arms and are pulling so my tendons and joints pop and rip from the force, so my skin splits open. Alexander reaches over to grip my forearm. His grip is stronger than I expect and I wonder how and why he made the transition from surgeon to rebel leader. Now is not the time to ask.

We gather in Fiere's room so she can be part of our discussion. She, after all, has greater knowledge of the RESCO than any of us. She goes stony-faced when we tell her what Halla's done and what has happened, and then says, "That poor girl." I wonder if I would have caught the undertone of fear in her voice if I didn't know her history. She joins Saben, Idris and Alexander in discussing how many Bulrush sympathizers they might be able to gather.

Idris urges an immediate frontal assault. "We've got the manpower, the weapons. This is our opportunity to show that Bulrush is more than a baby-smuggling service." His eyes are alight.

Alexander listens quietly for a few minutes and then says, "It can't be done."

All eyes turn to Alexander. He focuses on Idris. "You know it can't be done. How many women and babies would die in the kind of action you're talking about? Bulrush would be exposed, unable to operate in future. We'd lose people. We can't put the whole operation at risk for the sake of one woman. The best we can do is get word to Pharaoh's Daughter and hope she can find a way for us to extract Halla."

"It's time for us to—" Idris starts.

"We're not attacking," Alexander says with finality.

Idris goes rigid with fury.

"You can't leave her there. We have to get her out now," Wyck says hotly.

"Alexander's right," Fiere says reluctantly. I can see what it costs her. "There's too much at stake."

"He wouldn't say that if it was you," Wyck yells.

"I did say exactly that," Alexander says.

There's silence.

Wyck looks from Alexander to Fiere to me, confused. Alexander pinches the bridge of his nose between his thumb and forefinger, and then looks up. From his expression, he considers the discussion over. "I will set about contacting Pharaoh's Daughter. It may take a day or two to get word to her."

"You have lost your nerve," Idris says. His face is pale, with a muscle jumping beside his mouth. "You are too old and too sick to be in command." He locks eyes with Alexander and waits for a response.

Fiere springs forward, clearly planning to deck Idris. When Alexander merely motions her back without breaking eye contact with his challenger, Idris makes a disgusted noise, turns on his heel, and walks out.

I speak into the silence. "There might be another way."

They all look at me, Wyck hopefully, Saben warily, Fiere with skepticism, and Alexander wearily.

"I can go in."

CHAPTER TWENTY TWO

There's hubbub and objections and an hour of ranting and trying to talk me out of it, but my mind's made up. I've thought it through and they eventually cave to my logic, although no one likes the plan. That's only reasonable; I don't like it much either. I'd rather tramp through the swamp again, dodging alligators, mosquitoes and moonshiners, than voluntarily turn myself over to a RESCO, but it's Halla.

"I can tell the RESCO I want to volunteer to be a surrogate," I say. "Once I'm inside, I can find Halla and get in touch with this Pharaoh's Daughter." Why couldn't they give her a simpler code name? Agent 10, for instance? "She can help me and Halla get to a prearranged location where you will be waiting to extract us at a set time. Easy." I say it breezily, knowing it will be anything but easy. A potential problem occurs to me. "Unless you think they'd know who I am and notify the IPF rather than let me in?"

"Unlikely." Alexander shakes his head. "It's not like the IPF would have had reason to alert RESCOs about three runaways. There's no reason your name should raise alarms."

"They'll inseminate you, you know," Fiere says. She's busy sketching the layout of the RESCO as she remembers it. There are four buildings labeled "dormitories," "medical center," "staff quarters," and "administration." The medical center is the largest, a U-shaped building with one arm labeled "exam rooms/insemination suites," the cross bar marked "nursery," and the other side of the U tagged "birthing center."

I give a tiny nod. I know it's a risk, although I'm hoping to be in and out so quickly that they don't have the opportunity. "Maybe."

"We can make sure you don't get pregnant," Fiere says. "There's a pill. You can't get caught with it, though; it's a death penalty offense."

I can imagine.

"Take it immediately after the procedure." She hands me the map. "Memorize this. You can't take it in with you. And above all else, remember that they are watching you and listening to you at all times, except in the hyfacs. There is no privacy. None."

Alexander says, "We'll have a team waiting here"—he marks the map—"starting day after tomorrow at 0400 hours for three days. You'll know the spot because there's a huge oak that was split by lightning right outside the fence.

There's an electrified area extending from the fence to approximately fifty feet into the compound. We will deactivate it when we see you coming. You'll have three minutes to cross it. If you and Halla can't make it by the third day . . ."

I nod my understanding. We'll be on our own.

"God willing and the volcano don't explode, it won't come to that." Alexander says.

"I should go," I say. There's no point in waiting. Nothing will prepare me for what I'm about to experience. I won't be able to sneak in weapons or locators. I'll have my wits, my pill, the RESCO's layout in my head, and my ten days of defense training with Fiere and Saben. It doesn't seem like much.

"Now?" Wyck objects. "I thought tomorrow morning—"

I shake my head. "Halla's due any minute. We need to get her back before the baby comes; otherwise they'll take it from her, won't they?" I look to Alexander for confirmation.

"She's right." He leaves the room.

"I'll take you," Saben says.

Wyck's about to argue, but realizes that would be foolish. He comes over and hugs me hard. I tear up, but blink rapidly to keep the tears from falling. We hold onto each other for long minutes.

"Finish up that tunnel while I'm gone, okay?" My voice is shaky.

"See you in a couple days," Fiere says with an attempt at casualness. "Don't get too out of shape at the RESCO. I don't want to have to start your training over at the beginning."

Alexander returns and takes my hand in both of his. "You're resourceful and strong," he says, looking into my eyes. "I'll be waiting for you at the lightning tree. Halla's lucky." When he lets go of my hand, I'm holding a tiny yellow pill no bigger than a poppy seed.

"Right. Don't give away my mattress while I'm gone." I walk out, head held high, determined to act like I know I'll be back in a matter of days. I will be. With Halla.

I don't even go upstairs for my messenger bag with the feather and my book; Fiere said they're liable to take anything I have in my possession when I arrive and I can't risk losing them. "They'll strip you and get rid of your clothes, and search you, too," she told me, "so be careful where you hide that pill."

Saben catches up to me and we walk toward the tunnel entrance. "Wait a sec," he says, and disappears into the kitchen. He reappears in a minute and gestures to the ladder. "Ladies first."

We climb down and get into an ACV.

"Ready?"

"As I'll ever be."

It's an hour's ride to the RESCO northeast of Atlanta. If I weren't so tense, I'd have been interested in seeing more of the city, including a couple of manufacturing plants that

Saben says only started production last year. As it is, I'm too busy studying Fiere's RESCO drawing to even look out the windows. I've got the layout memorized and am staring dead ahead, clasping and unclasping my hands in my lap, when Saben says, "I'm an artist."

This is so far from anything in my head, that he might as well have said, "I'm an alien." "What?"

"It's the reason I'm with Bulrush. You wanted to know why I left my family to become part of Bulrush. Well, that's why: I'm an artist. I paint and draw."

I try to read his expression, but I can only see his profile.

"By all rights, I should be a physicist—the gametes implanted in my mother were chosen to yield a great physicist. But I have no interest in physics or science of any kind—none—and not much aptitude, either. From as early as I can remember, I've drawn. Any piece of paper that came to hand, I doodled on it, sketched pictures of my parents, my brother and sister, my teachers and schoolmates. At first, no one minded. But as I grew older and it became clear that I wasn't developing into much of a scientist, they called it a 'distraction.' They took to tying my right hand behind my back so I couldn't use it. I had to learn to write and compute with my left hand. It didn't help though—I was still a disaster in a lab and with computations. I even got so I could draw with my left hand; in some ways, it made me a better artist, opened up a new well of creativity inside me. The punishments for being caught drawing got more severe."

His nostrils go pinched and white at the memory. I don't know what to say. No one calls themselves an artist. Amerada needs scientists and builders, leaders and soldiers—not artists and musicians and writers. The Kube proctor who'd tried to get music added to the curriculum was gone within a week.

"I know," Saben says of my silence. "You don't have to say anything. No one understands. I don't understand; I just know I've got to draw. Genes are not destiny. I left when it became clear I was putting my family at risk. There was some discussion at the ministry level that my sister should be removed from my parents' care and placed in a Kube because they'd failed with me. The committee blamed them, you see."

"That's awful. Where did you go?"

"I wandered much like you and Halla and Wyck did, although I had food and electricity ration cards and an ACV, so I didn't have such a tough time of it. Eventually, I bumped into two women who were looking for Bulrush; I helped them find Bulrush. Alexander convinced me to stay. I've discovered I have something of an aptitude for leadership and planning. Who knew, right?" He looks at me and smiles. "Like your aptitude for fighting. I'll bet you didn't know you'd be as good at fighting as you are at dissecting locusts."

The ACV settles near a culvert on a dirt road. A sludge of algae-scummed water trickles from the corrugated metal tube. The doors unseal. A breeze wafts in; that's why I get a sudden chill, I'm sure. We get out and Saben comes around to my side of the vehicle, standing close.

I guess he senses my confusion because he continues, "I'm telling you this because I've sometimes felt that you're wary of me. You don't trust me. I get that. I'm geneborn. Bulrush is the last place I should be. I thought maybe if you understood why I was with Bulrush, you'd trust me more. You need to trust me—all of us. That trust is all you'll have to hang onto once you're in the RESCO. You can trust that I—we—will be waiting for you at the lightning tree every day. We will get you out of there."

I swallow hard. "Thanks," I whisper. I ask the question that's been tugging at me. "Did your parents want you to leave?"

"No."

"Do you miss them?"

"Of course! They're my mom and dad, my sister. I love them. They love me. They felt like they failed me. In the best of all possible worlds, parents help you become more *you*—they don't mold you into someone you're not. Good parents don't, anyway. My parents understood that. But this isn't the best of all possible worlds and they couldn't do that, not without putting all of us at risk—that's why they let me go."

He had what I've wanted always, and he tossed it aside. Before I can stop myself, I say, "I don't know how you could give that up, just to be an artist."

"I wouldn't expect you to."

"You're no better off now."

"My family's better off. The women I create new identity documents for—they're better off. Are you better off, Everly, since you left the Kube, I mean?"

I think. "I don't know. I still don't know who my parents are—I don't know who I'm supposed to be."

"Oh, Everly." He snorts gently. "You don't need to know who your parents are to know who you are." He presses a hand over my heart. "Who you are comes from in here. You are already exactly who you are meant to be: strong, passionate, courageous, smart."

I can't do anything but stare up at him, not recognizing myself in his word picture. His hand is heavy above my left breast, and I can feel the weight of it all the way down to my groin. He looks into my eyes, his gold eyes half-searching, half-determined.

His fingertips graze my clavicle, and then his hand is behind my neck, cupping my head. I tilt my face up and lean forward to meet him. His mouth comes down hard on mine and his body presses me back against the ACV. His fingers thread through my hair and hold my head still. My mouth opens under his and his tongue against mine sends a shudder through me. I want more.

My blood thrums, liquid lava, and I need to feel his skin. My hand works its way under his jumpsuit and he gasps as my palm slides across his bare chest, heat on heat. Our kiss deepens, lips, tongues, teeth grazing, probing, yielding. I'm drugged, mindless, all sparking nerve endings. We're both breathing heavily when Saben suddenly pulls away and our lips part with a silly little *pop.*

I've never felt like this. Wyck's kisses never left me breathless and on fire. I'm confused and a little embarrassed. With obvious effort, Saben steps back so we're no longer touching. I feel momentarily chilled, bereft.

"This is as far as I can take you," he says. "I shouldn't have—The RESCO is a mile down the road. It's not too late to back out and come back with me. No one will think badly of you."

"I will. Halla needs me." I want to go with him. I find it hard to tear myself away from the look in his gold eyes. "I—You—See you in a few days."

"Wait." He reaches into an inner pocket and withdraws a folded sheet of paper. "I drew this for you."

Wonderingly, I unfold it and find myself looking at an albatross, wings spread, every feather finely detailed and alive with motion, eye gleaming. "How did you know? This is lovely."

"After you showed us your feather, I looked it up. I thought you might like this."

He seems uncertain and I recognize that his drawing gift has been disdained and vilified for so long that he's not sure how I'll react. Part of me knows right then that his ability is as essential as my scientific talents. "It's amazing. Truly. Thank you. Won't they take it from me?"

"If they do, I'll draw you another."

Carefully refolding my albatross, I tuck it inside my bra. Saben presses a quick, hard kiss on my lips and returns to the ACV's cockpit. He seals the doors but doesn't leave, just keeps watching me. Somehow, his gaze is giving me strength. I lift my hand in a tiny wave, turn, and start down the road to the RESCO. After a moment, the ACV hums away. I don't look back.

PART THREE

CHAPTER TWENTY THREE

The Reproduction Support Community looks innocuous, even peaceful. It's surrounded by a tall stone wall, gleaming creamy-white under a benevolent sun. Even the jagged shards of glass topping the wall look pretty in the sunlight, glittering green and dark brown and amber. One of the glass scraps, a curvy one, has red lettering that spells out "Coca-Co." Four buildings, made of the same stone as the wall, are barely visible behind a screen of gnarled magnolia trunks and branches. A flash of blue suggests there's a small lake. Several women walk in the grounds; they're not in shackles, at least. There don't seem to be any gates in the wall and I'm wondering how I'll get in when an IPF ACV swoops up, probably alerted by the micro drones buzzing around the perimeter. Problem solved.

I tell the IPF sentries and then several other sets of guards, administrators and doctors my story: I ran away from my Kube, saw the error of my ways, and decided to become a surrogate. I manage a few tears, and leave them with the impression that starvation and fear drove me to the RESCO. I'm searched several times. First, by the sentries before they bring me into the compound, then by more senior guards, and finally by medical people who make me strip and examine every cranny. They miss the tiny pill tucked under my big toenail, however, and I feel mildly triumphant, even though the thoroughness and invasiveness of the search are humiliating.

I expected a government institution of stainless steel and white, but the RESCO's interior walls are a soft pink and the examination room has a padded chair upholstered in a floral pattern. I'm sitting in it, wearing a robe, because they took every stitch of my clothing. They left me the drawing, however, after some discussion amongst themselves and a fingertip exam of the surface. I'm curious as to whether the décor is because there is scientific evidence proving that women are more susceptible to successful implantation when they're relaxed, or because the administrators are trying to keep the surrogates happy in their pink/floral/padded prison. Maybe both. I'm analyzing this to distract myself from my nervousness. It's not working.

A woman appears in the doorway. She's as tall as Saben, better than six feet, and her skin is several shades darker than Halla's. Heavy-lidded gold eyes observe me. "I'm Dr. Malabar," she says. "Welcome to the RESCO. We all celebrate your willingness to help grow our great nation's population. It's the most critical work a woman can undertake."

"It will be my privilege," I say, keeping my eyes downcast.

She seems to approve of my meekness and launches into an explanation of the fertilization procedure and the RESCO's routines. "For tonight," she says, "you'll be housed with the non-gravid women. There are only a handful, mostly mothers resting between giving birth and undertaking a new pregnancy. We rejoice that so many are willing to be surrogates multiple times."

Hm. I'm skeptical about her definition of "willing."

A siren suddenly erupts, its piercing shriek hurting my ears. "What's that?" The exam room door slides shut and a lock clicks.

Dr. Malabar frowns. "The nursery alarm. It goes off when someone tries to remove a baby from the nursery. Sometimes, it gets triggered when a carer even gets close to an exit with a tattooed baby. It locks down the complex until security resolves the situation."

"Tattooed?" The alarm cuts off, thankfully. A moment later, the door clicks open.

She nods. "Indeed. Every infant delivered here is immediately imprinted with a special magnetized tattoo to make it impossible to sneak it out of the nursery. The tattoo can only be deactivated by a coded scanner issued to the parents who have been approved to raise the child. They bring it when they come to take the baby home with them."

"That's twink," I say.

"Brilliant, indeed, and unfortunately necessary. You don't know the lengths some people will go to to get a baby."

I don't contradict her.

"Once you undergo the procedure, you'll be moved to the dormitory with the other expectant surrogates."

"I can't wait," I say truthfully. I can't wait to find Halla, who must be in that second dorm, and get the two of us the hell out of here.

"Let's do some tests."

For the next ninety minutes, she pokes and prods me, measures every vital function possible, draws blood, and takes a complete medical history. She frowns when I confess that I don't know who my parents are. "Unusual," she observes, "but our DNA database will tell us. You're a little on the thin side, but we'll make sure your diet contains an extra quota of vitamins and calories to bring your weight up to norms for your height and build. Assuming we don't get any bad news from the tests, we should be able to arrange your IVF procedure for tomorrow afternoon."

They have a DNA database! Of course they do; they're in the business of mixing and matching ova and spermatozoa for best effect. I wonder where it is and how hard it would be to access. She's looking at me, expecting a response, and I stutter, "Th-that's great. I can't wait. I really feel this is the right path for me."

"Great. I'll see you tomorrow. Here's Bronnie to show you to your sleeping quarters."

The door opens and a slight, red-headed woman comes in. Her face is a mass of freckles and she's got a sizable baby bump. Not as big as Halla's—a month behind, I estimate. She's wearing a pink tunic over matching drawstring pants and our first stop is to get me an identical outfit. It doesn't take me long to realize that everyone is color-coded; doctors wear white, technicians wear blue, non-medical staff wear yellow, and surrogates wear pink.

"Jumpsuits don't work well when you're pregnant and have to pee all the time," Bronnie confides.

She takes me on a tour that includes a dining facility, a gathering area where pink-clad women are playing games, reading, or talking in groups of twos and threes. It looks deadly dull. A couple of them look up and smile when I approach. Everyone looks happy. Happy and a little vacant. A dark-haired woman looks vaguely familiar. With a start, I recognize Ping from Kube 9. She left three years ago—or was it four?—to volunteer as a surrogate. She was planning for a career as an engineer in the Ministry of Transportation and Infrastructure after she delivered. Her presence here, at least two years after she should have left, gives me the chills. Any lingering doubts I had about Bulrush's assessment of the RESCO die a shivery death. I keep an eye out, but don't spot Halla.

I trail Bronnie upstairs to the dormitory. Again, very like the Kube. The sleeping quarters are as serene as the rest of the RESCO, with pale blue walls and head high dividers separating the beds and affording a little privacy. Frankly, all this designed peacefulness is getting a bit cloying. There are four beds in the room she leads me to, and an attached hyfac with two stalls and two showers. "Lovely," I say.

"You won't be here long," Bronnie says. "Dr. Malabar mentioned you'd be joining us in the expectant mothers wing tomorrow or the next day."

"When is your baby due?"

"'Fetus,' not 'baby,'" she corrects me. "Six weeks. It's my third."

"Boy or girl?"

With a frown, Bronnie says, "We never know. They don't want us to get attached. It's 'the fetus.'"

"You don't mind giving them up?"

Bronnie looks unsure. "I'm sad for a few days after the delivery, but then I feel better. It's the shots; they help."

The hairs on the back of my neck prickle. I want to probe her for more information about the shots, but I sense I'm treading on sensitive territory. Besides, she probably doesn't know. "I'm starving," I say instead. "When's dinner?"

Halla is seated two tables away from me at dinner. I'm sitting with my dorm mates and I'm sure she's with hers. This place is run a lot like the Kube where we were segregated by year when we ate. Bureaucratic minds think alike. I want to make contact with her, but in such a way that she doesn't give the game away by making it obvious that she knows me. Dinner is amazing—I can see where the food alone would tempt some girls to become surrogates. I'm eagerly forking up fresh tilapia with pale orange flesh, obviously treated some way to make it resistant to the chemicals in the lake water, I assume, and enjoying crisp Brussels sprouts when the clatter of dropped utensils makes me turn. Halla has risen and is staring at me like she's seen a ghost. My eyes beg her not to give us away.

There is mingled hope and fear in her eyes.

"What's wrong, Halla?" a girl at her table asks.

"Um, uh . . . a contraction. I think I had a contraction." She doubles over convincingly and I breathe a sigh of relief.

"Maybe you're in labor," her tablemate says. "Let's get you to the clinic." She leads Halla away.

I return to eating, realizing that talking to Halla is going to be a challenge. With Fiere's warning in mind, I have to find a natural way to bump into her. I can't go sneaking through the halls at night, like we would at the Kube, to have a conversation in her room. I might have to wait until I'm assigned to her dorm to tell her the escape plan. Making an effort to talk to my tablemates, I finish the meal without coming up with a better plan than "seize any opportunity that arises." As plans go, it seems inadequate.

I dream again of killing the station master, of the crunching sound his windpipe made when my knife perforated it. I hadn't noticed the sound at the time, but it crunches in my nightmares, waking me in a sweat. I sit up. It takes me a moment to remember where I am, to look around at the other sleeping women, visible by the blue glow of a bio-luminescent night light. One is tossing and turning, muttering in her sleep, and I wonder what her particular nightmare is. I lie back down, but stay awake until dawn, holding the albatross drawing and studying every pencil stroke and every permutation of light and shading.

I don't see Halla at breakfast and am a little worried. Maybe she is having an exam, or something, I speculate. No one comes for me, so I drift outside after the meal, getting a feel for the grounds. The surveillance micro-drones are everywhere and I can see soldiers patrolling outside the fence. This place takes its security seriously and I wonder if they're more interested in keeping surrogates in or would-be rescuers or outlaws out. I'm sure the abundant food is a huge temptation for outlaws. Synthetic grass sweeps down to the lake, creating a pretty picture, and I stroll to the water's edge. It's an acid blue that doesn't look natural up close, and signs warn against entering the water.

Having established that I'm merely drifting around harmlessly, trying to get a feel for my new home, I leave the lake and head back to the main building. My target all along has been the DNA database. It's almost got to be in the building Fiere labeled "administration" on her map. Cutting through the lounge area where expectant surrogates engage in innocuous pursuits, I exit on the far side of the building and amble down a walkway that leads to the administration building, a square, one-story structure. The door opens as I approach and a lab assistant pushing a cart loaded with vials in racks emerges. I politely hold the door for her, earning a "thank you," and slip inside before it closes.

The interior is a marked contrast to the birthing clinic. It's stainless steel, tile, and white. Walls that are glass from ceiling to waist height reveal scientists at work on either side of me, hunched over microscopes, studying data on computer displays, and pipetting liquids into test tubes. It feels like home. I don't know if it's the hum and chirp of lab equipment and coolers, the mixed scent of chemicals and recirculated air, or the sense I get of people focused on their tasks, but a wave of homesickness for Dr. Ronan and my lab washes over me.

I pass the labs slowly. No one pays attention to me. There's a closed door at the end of the hall, with an iris scanner mounted at eye height. I'm sure this is where I'll find the DNA database. How to get in? Before I even reach the door, a sharp voice calls, "Who are you and what are you doing in here?"

I turn. It's a lab coated woman with wide set eyes behind thick-lensed glasses. I'm willing to bet she runs the labs. I decide on a version of the truth. "I'm Everly Jax. I worked in the labs at Kube 9 and wanted to see what the set-up was here. I miss my work."

Her eyes are distorted behind the thick lenses, giving her what I'm sure is an illusory air of vagueness. "What were you working on?"

It's a test question. I give her a lengthy explanation of our how I was working to create a virus to wipe out the locusts. I explain the difficulty of infecting all the locusts so isolated pockets of the locust population don't avoid infection and survive to reproduce and repopulate after the majority are killed off. When I pause for breath, she says, "Interesting approach. Why are you a surrogate? Surely you've been offered the opportunity to pursue your education and research?"

"I think it's every female citizen's duty to bear a child for the state," I say.

"Commendable." She says it like she means, "Stupid." "Come in and see what you think of our latest approach to reducing miscarriage. I'd be interested in your take on our efforts to avoid the trisomy that can accompany our mitochondrial-transferred embryos."

I'm burning to enter the lab, but the building door opens and a blue-coated technician appears. "Everly Jax? I've been searching for you for twenty minutes," she says testily. "This area is off limits, as I'm sure Dr. Wendt has explained. It's time."

For what? Then I know. Time for the procedure. My hands go cold.

"Another time," Dr. Wendt says, disappearing into her lab.

I follow the technician out of the building and across to the birthing center. She leads me through the pink halls to a sterile suite where Dr. Malabar is waiting, a file in her hands. There's a rolling tray holding a length of thin, flexible tubing and a syringe. My gaze fixes on the liquid in the syringe which contains the blastocyst they're going to transfer to my uterus. I wiggle my big toe, comforted by the slight discomfort the pill beneath my nail causes.

"Your tests were fine," Dr. Malabar says, gesturing with the file, "so there's no reason we can't proceed."

In a moment of piercing revelation, I realize I don't have to break into the DNA database. Dr. Malabar is undoubtedly holding a copy of my DNA printout and everything related to it from the database. It's right there, in that file mere inches away. My parents' names. My genetic history. Who I am.

"No need to be nervous." Dr. Malabar misinterprets my suddenly shallow breathing. "The procedure is painless. We sedate you. It's not medically necessary, but we find most of the surrogates are more comfortable with intravenous sedation during the procedure. You won't be asleep, but you won't remember the details. Jariah here will help you undress and prep you for the procedure. I'll be back in a few minutes and then we'll have you on your way to the expectant mothers' quarters." She smiles, but it's an automatic reflex, part of her bedside manner.

I disrobe and get on the table. The technician covers me with a sheet and swabs the crook of my elbow with a germicide. It's cold. I resist the urge to yank my arm away when she tightens a band around my upper arm and painlessly eases a needle into my vein. Fluid begins to drip from a bag hung on a metal pole.

"Do you know the story of Moses?" Jariah asks in a low voice. "The Hebrew baby left in a basket in the reeds?"

Moses. The code word. My eyes widen. Jariah is Pharaoh's Daughter. I study her. She's maybe thirty and unremarkable as to hair, build, and coloring. Her hands are pretty, though, as they adjust a dial on the IV: slender, long-fingered, smoothly white.

"I'm not much of a Bible reader." I give the correct reply.

She nods. "Your friend is scheduled for an extraction tomorrow. She's been moved to the birthing suite. The timetable's been moved up. You break out tonight."

I've barely processed her words when Dr. Malabar strides through the door. She pumps a half-full syringe into the IV port and then picks up the prepared syringe on the tray. "Ready? Right then. Let's do it."

CHAPTER TWENTY FOUR

I awake in a bed. It takes me a moment to figure out it's not the bed I slept in last night. There's a window nearby and the sun slants in at a mid-day angle. None of my new roommates are present; they're probably lunching or in the lounge. Other than a little cramping, I don't feel any effects from the implantation procedure. In fact, I feel pretty good. Could pregnancy hormones be kicking in already, giving me this feeling of well-being? No way. A moment of clear-headedness tells me Dr. Malabar included some kind of hormone and/or chemical cocktail in my IV. I'm *supposed* to feel good, supposed to be happy I'm pregnant. I sit up and reach for my toe and the pill, but then hesitate. It's strange to think that right this minute there's new life growing inside of me.

The opportunity passes as Dr. Malabar comes in, my file in her hand. "The procedure went perfectly," she says, standing over me. "How do you feel?"

"Good. Great."

She checks my temperature and oxygen levels, makes notes in my file, and tells me they'll do more blood work in a week. Before she can leave, I ask, "Can I see the birthing area? I'd like to know what to expect." I have got to make contact with Halla.

A line appears between her brows. "There's plenty of time—"

"It's just that I'm so excited about it," I say before she can deny me. "I want to watch a birth and talk to surrogates who have given birth, so I'll do it right."

That makes her snort. "Almost all our births are assisted extractions, so there's no way *not* to do it right, but I don't see what it would hurt. I'm on my way there now; we have a surrogate about to give birth. You have a background in biology, I understand. You can come."

I hop out of bed and follow her from the room. Dr. Malabar detours into what looks like an office and slides my folder into a narrow slot above her desk. My teeth ache with my need to see its contents. She emerges and sets a brisk pace down the hall, lab coat flapping. I keep up and ask, "What's an assisted extraction?"

"Natural childbirth is too painful and we find it discourages surrogates from volunteering to carry subsequent fetuses," she says, not slowing. "In an assisted extraction, we use a laser scalpel to make an incision low on the abdomen and then through the uterus. We remove the baby manually and close the uterus and incision site with surgical sealant. It's much less traumatic for the mother and the baby." By now, we've exited the exam wing, traversed the nursery wing, and are on the hall with the birthing suites, with Dr. Malabar having used a card hanging by a lanyard to open each door. Iris scans take too much time, I guess, when you might be responding to a life-and-death emergency.

I almost bump into Dr. Malabar when she stops outside a sliding door.

"This is it."

Before we can enter, a voice crackles over an intercom system. "Dr. Malabar. You're needed in the nursery. Stat." The speaker's panic is evident even over the intercom.

"The preemie," she mutters and takes off at a half-trot.

She's forgotten me. This is my opportunity to find Halla. The first two rooms I look in—not bothering to knock—are empty. The third contains a woman I don't know. I find Halla behind the next door. My relief makes me careless. "Halla!" Only after greeting her do I remember Fiere's caution about always being under observation. I have to assume there's an imager in here.

She struggles to sit up, her face lighting. She looks healthier than she has in weeks and I can see that even a few days of good food and rest have helped her. The ripples across her belly indicate that Little Loudon is kicking mightily. Before she can say something that will totally give the game away, I rush in with, "I had my implantation this morning and Dr. Malabar said I could chat with some of the women about to give birth to find out about their experiences. You're Halla, right?"

Halla nods, obviously confused by my patter, but trying to play along. "I'm happy to tell you anything I can," she says, "but I haven't been here long. And this is my first birth, so I'm not exactly an expert."

I cut my eyes upward toward the lens in the corner they've made no attempt to hide.

Halla's eyes widen with comprehension.

"I'm Everly." I scan the room for something to write on and with. "You're having an assisted extraction tomorrow morning, right?"

Halla nods. "I'm afraid."

"I hear the procedure is very simple," I say, knowing she's really telling me she's afraid they'll take Little Loudon away. There's nothing to write on. Damn. I scramble to find a way to tell her about our escape. "I suppose they need to prep you for the procedure well in advance, though; they probably wake you about *four a.m.*"

Halla frowns, puzzled, but says, "I guess so."

"I heard they'll be here bright and early, at *four o'clock*, to get you ready to *go*."

Halla sucks in a breath and it turns into a hiccup. She nods vigorously. She gets it. We chat inanely for another couple of minutes and then I say, "I should talk to a couple more women. Thanks for chatting with me. I hope it goes well for you." I reach for her hand and she grips mine tightly. I think the contact makes both of us feel better.

"Nice meeting you, Emily," Halla says, eyes twinkling as she deliberately gets my name wrong.

I can't help but smile, so relieved that she's okay, that we're getting out of here tonight. "You, too."

I slip out of her room and decide I should really chat with another about-to-pop surrogate or two in case whoever's watching and listening is suspicious. I talk to one woman who's also having an extraction in the morning, and babble about how early they'll have to wake her for the procedure. "I am not a morning person," I say. I also talk to a woman who had an extraction earlier in the day. She says how much she's looking forward to serving at an outpost now that she's delivered the baby.

I leave her room, sobered, and find Dr. Malabar coming toward me. She frowns. "I forgot you were here. Surrogates aren't supposed to be in this wing unescorted." She has a technician escort me back to the dormitory, but I don't care. I accomplished my mission.

I eat dinner with my new dorm mates, shower, and climb into bed early. I have several opportunities to take my pill, but I don't. Every time I think about it, I hesitate. Maybe it's the hormone cocktail they pumped into me, but I can't yet bring myself to swallow the pill that will flush the baby—not even a baby, a collection of cells—from my body. The pill might have side effects, I reason, might make me too ill to escape tonight. I'll take it when I'm safely back at the bordello.

I've formulated a plan and once under the sheet I begin to put it into effect. Halla being in the birthing suite has complicated matters considerably. I can only think of one way to get into that building in the middle of the night. Consequently, I use the fork I smuggled out of the dining area to stab at my thighs and buttocks until I draw blood. I bite down on my pillow to keep from crying out and smear the blood on my sheet. I have to do some serious gouging. It takes far too long to get what I consider to be enough blood and I'm sore and frazzled by the time I'm done. Carefully folding Saben's drawing, I tuck it into my bra and wait for three-thirty. I occupy myself by obsessively running over my plan and the route we'll have to take from the birthing suite to the fence.

At three-thirty, I let out a loud moan. I sit up and double over. "Oh, God, it hurts."

A light comes on. The woman in the next bed looks at me with concern. "What's wrong?"

"Cramps," I bite out, hunching forward and wrapping my arms around my stomach.

Other women sit up and one comes to my bed. I strategically kick the sheet aside, supposedly in the throes of pain, and she spots the blood. "You're bleeding. Delania, fetch the technician on duty."

One of the women scuttles out. I'm desperately hoping that Jariah will show up, but it's a technician I don't know. She's fiftyish, several inches shorter than me, and at least twenty pounds heavier; her scrubs aren't going to fit very well. I let out something close to a scream when she comes through the door.

"Something's wrong," I sob.

"She's bleeding," my roommate observes helpfully.

The technician takes one look at the sheets, and helps me out of bed. "Let's get you over to an exam room and have a doctor look at you. You had an implantation today, didn't you?"

I nod and head for the door, clutching my stomach the whole way. The technician motions for the other women to go back to bed and follows me into the hall. It's quiet. No one else is stirring. I let her take me by the arm and lead me into the medical complex. Once she badges us inside, I make retching noises.

"It hurts so bad I'm going to throw up."

The technician hustles me to a hyfac. I rush to the stall and when she follows me, I reverse and slam the stall door into her. Dazed, she puts an arm out. I duck under it, get my arms around her, and bull her backward. She's soft and doughy in my embrace, and smells slightly sour. When I've got her up against the wall, I curl my fingers under like Fiere showed me and jab her in the solar plexus. She doubles over, and I crack my knee against her chin. Her head snaps back into the wall and she slumps down, unconscious. It's over in less than twenty seconds.

Only when she's out do I realize I've been saying, "Sorry, sorry, sorry," the whole time. The last "sorry" seems to echo against the tile. Conscious of time ticking away, I manhandle her out of her scrub pants and top, sweating and breathing hard with the effort. It takes too long. I pull the clothes on, free the badge lanyard from around her neck, and drag her into the stall. It's the best I can do. I don't suppose she'll be out for long; every second counts.

Trying to slow my breathing, I slip into the hall. No one's in sight. It's already four o'clock. Stripping the technician took much longer than planned—I need to go straight to Halla or we run the risk of not making it out before the Bulrush team has to pull back. I don't have time to hunt for my DNA data, for the folder that will tell me who my parents are. I chew my upper lip, torn by indecision. I can't stand the thought of being this close and coming away without the information I've yearned for all my life. I jiggle up and down, and then head to my left. The excess fabric of the jumpsuit bunches between my thighs, making my stride awkward.

At Dr. Malabar's office I knock, aware of the imagers. When there's no answer, I wave the badge over the reader's red eye. Nothing happens. It's not coded for access. *I shouldn't be here.* I should be getting Halla and leaving the building right now. But I can't go without my DNA report. It's right here. I can't pass up this chance. Angling my body so the imager can't see what I'm doing, hopefully, I wedge the slim badge between the door and the frame, wiggling it. Precious seconds tick away, but then the lock tongue slides back. I'm in."

I slip inside and turn on the light. I grab a handful of folders and flip through them until I reach one labeled "Jax, Everly." Letting the others drop, I scan the first document which seems to be details of the implantation, and thumb to the next. Immunological compatibility screening. Not what I want. *Get Halla, go get Halla,* my conscience shouts. My head feels pressurized. The third sheet is headed "DNA Structure and Genomic Analysis." I snatch it out, fold it, and tuck it into my waistband. Voices sound from the hall, and I jerk. Crossing the office on tiptoe, I ease the door open a half inch and put my eye to the crack. *Oh, no.*

Two women in yellow jumpsuits—a cleaning team it looks like. They've got a rolling cart full of supplies, and one of them holds a sanitizer wand, but they're not working. They're chatting, grousing about the effort it takes to sterilize an operating suite after an extraction. I can't leave the office while they're in the hall. It's ten nail biting, lip chewing minutes before their voices grow fainter. I peer through the crack to make sure they're gone, and see them headed toward the hyfac where I left the injured technician. I'm screwed. Even though they're still in sight, their backs are to me and I have to risk it. I ghost out of the room, leaving the door slightly ajar so the cleaners won't be alerted by the click. I can't make myself walk and only hope that any watchers will assume I'm headed to an emergency. I'm praying the badge will work as I approach the nursery wing. It does and I hear a baby's thin wail as I hurry along the hall, focused on the door that leads to the birthing suites and Halla.

I'm almost to it when a door opens behind me and a voice says, "Technician, I need some help here, please."

Without turning around, I make my voice gruff and say, "I've got a cold. I'm not supposed to handle the"—The what? Do they call them infants? Babies? Ex-fetuses? I'm sure there's a correct term, like making the surrogates say "fetus" instead of "baby," but I don't know it. I fake a sneeze, hold the badge to the reader, and am through the door as the now suspicious voice says, "Wait!"

She's going to call for help. If I'm lucky, she'll think about it for a couple of minutes, or have to do something with a baby first, but she's going to sound the alarm. I hear it in her voice. I pound down the hall to Halla's room and burst through the door expecting her to be alert and ready. Instead, she's curled up on her side under the blanket.

"Halla." Rushing to the bed, I shake her shoulder.

"Huh?" She blinks groggily.

"We've got to go *now*." I yank back the blanket. *Oh, my God*. My breath hisses out like I've been punched.

Halla's belly has deflated. She's not pregnant anymore.

CHAPTER TWENTY FIVE

They did the extraction early. That fact ricochets in my head. They could have done it while I was subduing the technician and searching Dr. Malabar's office. Hers was the extraction the cleaners were talking about. *If I'd come straight here* . . . I can't think about it now. Halla's still woozy from the surgery, in no condition to run. I spare only a brief sad thought for Little Loudon. He's locked in the nursery, imprinted with a tattoo that will lock the building down if I try to get him out. There is no way to get him now. None. My priority has to be getting Halla to the rendezvous spot. The bed's on wheels.

"Hold on."

Releasing the wheel lock, I grab the bedrail and back toward the door. Halla's sitting up, looking confused and nervous, as we trundle into the hall and I swing the bed so I can push it from behind. "Lie down," I suggest.

She reclines and I sprint down the hall. The bed is lighter than I expect and it almost pulls me off my feet once we build up some momentum. I can't stop it in time to keep it from bashing into the wall near the exit. Halla lets out an exclamation as I hurry to open the door. Wedging a corner of the bed through, I use its weight to hold the door open as I push the bed all the way outside. Fresh air!

A klaxon erupts behind me and I bite my tongue. As blood fills my mouth, I point the bed toward the rendezvous and shove. It takes more effort on the dirt path than in the polished corridor. *Whee-oo, whee-oo* pounds my ears, dizzying me.

"Everly. Four o'clock. Leave."

Halla sounds more alert and I'm grateful. "Are you okay?" The words come out in single syllable gasps. My thighs are burning as I use them to power forward. There's the lightning-split tree that signals the meeting spot, and the fence beyond it. "We need to climb a rope ladder to get out. Can you do it?"

"I think so. Where—" She makes an anguished sound. The moment I've been dreading has arrived. "Little Loudon," she keens. "My baby. We've got to go back for him."

"We can't."

Barked orders and running footsteps tell me the chase is on. I can only hope Alexander managed to blind the drones as he said he would. We must be getting close to the electrified border. I slow and Halla starts to slide off the bed.

"I'm not going without my baby."

"You're going to get us all killed." I push her back on the bed. She's weak and falls against the pillow.

Have they cut the power as promised? Grabbing the pillow, I fling it as far as I can. It's a white blur arcing toward the fence. Then, it lands and explodes in a poof of flame and charred fluff. The stench makes me gag. That would have been me and Halla if I'd gone another step.

A curse sounds from near the fence. "Got it," Saben's voice says. "Now."

A rock clatters to the ground, reassuring me that it's safe. I grab for the bed and realize Halla has wriggled off it.

"Over here!" It's a soldier's voice. It's close. Searchlights stab the darkness.

We're going to die. Halla's leaning against the bed, gathering the strength to run back to Loudon. *We're going to die.* I punch her in the temple. She falls back onto the bed, stunned, and I grab her legs and swing them up. Then, we're bumping over the no man's land to the fence. The bed crunches into the stone as a rope ladder slithers down beside us. *Clink.* Grappling hooks have snagged against the glass.

"Hurry," Saben calls.

A blast whistles past and a chunk jumps out of the wall, stinging my cheek. "Halla's unconscious," I shout. "I can't get her up."

Seconds later, booted feet appear on the ladder. Wyck jumps from half-way down and lands in a crouch. Then Idris appears. "Where?"

I indicate Halla. "She just had surgery," I caution them. A waste of breath. They need to get her over the fence any way they can; otherwise, she's dead. Another blast singes past.

They wheel the bed up against the fence. Wyck climbs onto it, and with Idris's help, gets Halla up and draped over his shoulder so her head hangs down his back. The pressure on her incision must be horrible. Alexander will know how to repair it.

"You first." Wyck's face is white with strain. "I can't get her over the top. We're going to need everyone possible on the other side to pull us over."

Idris nods and scrambles up the ladder, disappearing over the fence.

Wyck's got a beamer strapped to his back. I free it and motion for him to grab the ladder. He hesitates, then steps off the bed to put both feet on a rung half-way up, gripping a higher rung with one hand, while securing Halla with the other arm clamped across the back of her thighs. Halla dangles like a rag doll. "Pull," he yells.

The ladder starts to inch up. There's a blur of movement to my left. A soldier. Caught off-guard, I level the beamer and hesitate. The soldier falls and I look up at the wall, startled. Idris gives me a mock salute from where he's straddling the wall, beamer cradled in one arm. Wyck and Halla are almost to the top now. More yelling, sounding confused, drifts our way. One word stands out: "Fire."

I scan the compound, still dark, but with a lightening that says dawn is around the corner. An orangey glow flickers on the far side, past the lake. It's a fire. I'm as confused as the soldiers, but then I realize it's a distraction. Since it's inside the RESCO, I suspect Jariah is responsible. Booted feet pound toward the fire and someone issues orders for using lake water to douse it. Saben and a man I don't know have appeared at the top of the fence, smashing the glass insets with their weapons' stocks, then reaching over to grab Halla from Wyck. They balance her on her bottom atop the fence, facing into the compound. Then they maneuver her legs around until they're draping down the outside wall. Gripping her upper arms, they lower her, every tendon in their necks and jaws standing out. She scrapes along the wall and then she's out of sight.

The unknown man jumps down and then Saben helps an exhausted Wyck over with an approving thump on his back. He holds down a hand to me. "Everly. Hurry!" Slinging the beamer over my shoulder, I run for the ladder and grasp a rigid rung. The ladder sways as I step onto it.

A hand clamps around my ankle. I look down to see a helmeted IPF soldier. He's bleeding. He might be the one Idris shot. Balancing on one leg, I use the other to kick at his head. Saben, above me, has no clear shot. The risk of hitting me is too great. The man staggers, then renews his grip. My too-big pants start to slide down. I kick harder and the man's grip loosens. The scrub pants are at my knees. Something flutters. The DNA report! I grab for it. The soldier reaches up and snags my wrist.

Then, a hole opens on his right shoulder and blood appears. He falls backwards. There's a tearing sound and he's gone, half the report still locked in his grip. I look up and over my shoulder to where Saben shifted along the wall to get a shot at the soldier.

"*Everly.*"

I can't ignore the anguish and command in his voice. Made awkward by the sagging pants, I scramble the rest of the way up the ladder.

Saben claps me on the shoulder when I reach the top. "Let's get out of here."

"Ladies first," I say, flashing a grin. Despite the fact that we're still in horrible danger, everything feels like it will be okay now that I'm with Saben. Lowering myself to my stomach, I swing my legs over. The remnants of the glass cut through my top and grind against my abdomen. Someone on the other side braces my legs and helps me down. When I hit the ground, he takes off running, hops onto a scooter and zips north. There's no sign of Halla or the other rescuers who must have been here; they're all headed for safety, I hope. The headlights of IPF ACVs, at least three of them, streak toward us.

Saben grabs my hand. "Come *on.*"

We jump into a two-seater and Saben ignites it. I can tell immediately that it's been modified for turbo speed. That makes it faster, but also less stable. I grab the seat edge as we blast away. A round sizzles past us and smashes into a tree trunk. It topples as we slide beneath it.

"Too close," I breathe.

Saben doesn't reply, too intent on evading the IPF to talk. We're in a copse, weaving so quickly through the tree trunks that I hardly dare breathe for fear of unbalancing us. Skimming over a large rock, we roll, the instability almost capsizing us. Saben rights the ACV and, if possible, goes even faster. One of the ACVs on our tail fires again. The beam goes wide, but close enough to make us pitch. I bang my forehead on the dash. The beamer strapped to my back knocks my shoulders and I grab it, cursing for not having thought of it before.

A round explodes through the rear window, raining shards of polyglass on us. I swivel in the seat so I'm on my knees facing backwards. Two IPF ACVs are behind us, riding side by side as much as the forested terrain allows. I can see the helmeted heads behind the windshields.

"Hold this thing steady," I say, leveling the beamer. My index finger puts pressure on the touch pad to let off a blast. The pursuing ACV swerves and I miss by a mile. I wish I'd spent more time with Idris in the attic weapons range. The stock vibrates against my palms to let me know the weapon's charge has fallen to twenty-five percent. I only have a couple of shots left. I've got to make them count.

With the image of the falling tree that almost crushed us in mind, I aim for a magnolia's overhanging bough. Timing it carefully, I put two fast shots into the rotten wood seconds before the closest IPF skimmer surges beneath it. The heavy limb separates from the trunk with a loud *crr-rack* and smashes onto the ACV's roof. It spins out of control and we're pulling farther away as it skids toward its partner. The two vehicles collide and explode in a ball of flame and spinning metal parts. I turn my head away to protect my eyes from the glare.

"Nice shooting."

I nod, looking back to see if the third ACV is still pursing us. Not. He is slowing, intending to help his wounded comrades, I assume. I slide down into my seat, suddenly trembling.

"You okay?" Saben can't spare a look, not at the speed we're traveling.

"Uh-huh."

Saben takes a circuitous route back to Bulrush's headquarters, to guarantee we're not followed, and it's two hours before we dive into a tunnel entrance that's new to me and approach the brothel from the north.

"Thanks for getting us out of there," I say as we emerge from under a tile-coated trapdoor in a utility room. It smells like wet metal from the old furnace and air conditioning units rusting there. The idea that Alexander and Saben are trusting me with more of Bulrush's secrets pleases me, even though I'm almost too tired to experience any emotion. In the hall, Saben catches me by my upper arms. His grip is firm, his expression serious as he gazes into my eyes.

"If you'd been killed—"

Wyck charges around the corner, saying, "Halla's going to be—" He stops dead when he catches sight of me and Saben, his gaze going from one of us to the other.

Saben releases me. "You did great back there," he tells Wyck. "Halla wouldn't be here if it weren't for you."

A tic jumps below Wyck's left eye.

"Is she okay?" I ask, trying not to think about how badly I wanted Saben to kiss me. "Where is she?"

"Upstairs. Sedated. She was hysterical about the baby."

We hurry upstairs to the room where Alexander operated on Fiere. She's guarding the door and stops us before we can enter. Her dark hair is all which-way, as if she's been raking her fingers through it, but her face is composed.

"Alexander's still repairing the incision," she says, holding a hand to her own abdomen, as if in sympathy. "He says she'll be fine, though."

"I don't know what happened," I say. "The extraction wasn't scheduled until morning, but when I got to her room, they'd already delivered the baby."

"She probably went into labor," Fiere says. "They'd move up the extraction, if that happened."

"I couldn't get the baby. There was no way."

"I know," Fiere says, in a voice that says she really does. "You did great getting yourself and Halla out of there."

"These guys did the hard part," I say, motioning to Wyck and Saben. "Especially Wyck, carrying Halla up the ladder."

"I couldn't believe it when I saw you pushing a bed across the courtyard," Wyck says.

"A bed?" Fiere asks.

Taking turns and talking over each other, Saben, Wyck and I tell Fiere about the rescue. They talk about rounding up ten Bulrush agents for the mission and about contacting Pharaoh's Daughter to plan a diversion. I explain how I fooled the technician and stole her clothes and badge. I leave out my detour to Dr. Malabar's office, but become ultra-sensitive to the rasp of the paper against my stomach. Suddenly, all I want is some privacy so I can read the report . . . what's left of it. Fiere, though, insists on examining and disinfecting the gouges I made on my thighs to bloody my sheets. Shooing Wyck and Saben away, she takes me into a small bedroom and swabs the fork punctures and scrapes with alcohol.

"Nasty," she observes, "but clever." She lowers her voice. "You took the pill, right?" When I don't answer, she says, "They give you hormones, and something else, I think, some kind of mood elevator, during the implantation. You know that right?" Her tone is urgent. "What you're feeling, whatever urge you have to actually bear the fetus they implanted in you, it's chemically induced. You're a bio-chemist for heaven's sake—you understand that."

I do understand that, but I can't rationalize away what I feel. I know it doesn't make much sense, but part of me wants to have the baby. He or she is destined to be someone special, someone who can help Amerada, help all of us. Raising the baby scares me to death—no way could I take that on—but I can at least give it life and then leave it at a Kube. Like I was left. I wonder then if my own conception was unplanned, perhaps unwanted. Maybe. But even so, my mother didn't sweep me from her womb. She gave me life. Don't I owe this baby the same gift? I don't say any of this to Fiere. I pull up my baggy scrubs and say, "I need to find something to wear and then see Halla."

Fiere steps back, her eyes opaque.

I hide in the hyfac with the door locked and strip, peeling the albatross drawing and the DNA report carefully from where sweat has stuck them to my skin. I sit on the toilet. It's cold against my bare skin. Dragging in a deep breath, I clutch the document I took from Dr. Malabar's office. For a minute, I actually think about destroying the document, as penance for losing Halla her baby. No matter how badly I want to know who my parents are, this piece of paper wasn't worth sacrificing Halla's happiness. What's done is done, I tell myself, swallowing hard around the lump in my throat.

I unfold the page. It's headed with my name, age, and gender. Most of a DNA fingerprint appears below that information, colored bars graphing who I am at the molecular level. The paper shakes as my eyes travel down the page. Under the heading "Likely Parental Matches" there's a colon and then the words "No matches found." There's more, but my fingers go slack and the paper slips to the floor. All that risk, and still no answers. I let the tears fall. Soon I'm sobbing silently, hunched over, shoulders shaking. I'm thinking about Halla, about her anguish when she realized we were leaving without Little Loudon. But I'm also crying for me. I still don't know.

My crushing disappointment is tempered by disbelief. It's impossible. Everyone, *everyone*, is in the DNA database. Dr. Ronan's voice echoes in my head, urging me to be skeptical, telling me that of course not every bird has died off. "Every" is a big word in the scientific world. I try hard to get into scientist mode, to jettison emotion for logic. I scrub my face with my hands to wipe away tears and mucus. The evidence before me clearly indicates that *not* everyone's DNA has been entered in the national database. Everyone with a ration card has to supply a DNA sample before receiving one, so the data suggest my parents never received food or electricity from the state. Outlaws? I suppose it makes sense that children born to outlaws aren't registered. Even so, their parents should have been in the database. The DNA registry became mandatory shortly after compulsory insurance coverage. The system should have found my grandparents, at least. Something's not right.

I retrieve the page and smooth it on my knee. There's the first part of another genomic map; the rest is torn off. Below it, the type says, "Sibship Index, 16 Polymorphic Loci, 99.9998%, Confirmed. Sibling Match: One. Sibling Na" It breaks off there, the rest torn away. *I have a sister or a brother.* It's too much to take in. I re-read the five and a half words a dozen times. Older? Younger? Sister? Brother? Where is he or she? Who is he or she?

There's knock on the door. "You okay in there?" Fiere asks.

I quickly fold the page and tuck it away. "Almost done." My voice sounds congested.

I take the world's quickest shower, don a clean jumpsuit with the DNA report hidden in my bra, and turn the hyfac over to Fiere who gives me a strange look. I hurry back to the makeshift surgical suite. Entering, I can't help but compare it to the ultra-modern facilities at the RESCO.

The "operating table" has been scrubbed and smells of wet wood. A hint of rosemary perfumes the air and I imagine a former owner, Alexander's aunt, chopping and sorting herbs on that table. Those thoughts leave my mind when I see Halla lying on a cot, eyes closed. Her arms are outside the sheet that covers her, dark against the pale linen. I approach the cot on tiptoe.

"She'll recover." Alexander speaks from behind me; I hadn't noticed him sitting in a chair, keeping watch over Halla. He's slumped on his spine, legs extended, arms crossed over his chest. "The interior seals held up; I only needed to re-seal the exterior incision and repair minor tears. They do good work at the RESCO, I'll give them that. She lost a little blood, but she'll be up and about in a couple of days. Sore, but fine." He rises. "I need food. Don't stay long. You look like you could sleep for a week."

Giving him a grateful smile, I pull his vacated chair closer to the cot and take Halla's hand. It's limp and unresponsive in mine. I wish I could tell Halla about the DNA report, tell her about my sister or brother. But I never can because then she'd know how I betrayed her. It's physically painful to think that my actions, my selfishness, have put a barrier between us. A permanent one. We can never, ever be as close as we once were because Little Loudon's absence separates us. My gaze falls on a Bible half-hidden by the coverlet. I don't know if it's Alexander's or Halla's, but I reach for it.

Opening it at random, I read aloud softly, knowing how important the Bible is to Halla. "'My soul finds rest in

God alone; my salvation comes from him. He alone is my rock . . .'"

I don't know how long I read before her hand twitches in mine. I look up from the page to find her brown eyes fixed on me. There's an expression in them I've never seen before. I jerk away involuntarily and drop her hand.

"Halla—"

That's as far as I get in my explanation or apology or whatever I was going to say.

"Stop. Stop reading that. It's bullshit!" She swipes weakly at the Bible in my hand. "It's just . . . just *words*."

I set it carefully on the bedside table, hoping Halla will want it again soon, feeling almost sorry for the Bible that Halla has rejected it. Ridiculous. It's inanimate, unfeeling. I lean toward her, but she turns her face away.

"Get away from me," she says. "I hate you. You left Little Loudon. You let them keep my baby."

"There was no way to—I couldn't—"

"They didn't even let me see my baby. I never held my baby. Now I never will. It's your fault. Get out!" She shrieks the last word, rising up on her elbows.

"She saved your life."

It's Alexander's voice, quiet and compelling. He's standing in the doorway.

"Little Loudon *was* my life." Halla collapses back against the pillow, spent. Her eyes swivel to me, burning with fever and hate. "I will never forgive you, Everly Jax. Never." Her fingers brush the bruise on her temple. "You hit me. You kept me from going back. Little Loudon needed me and you—"

"They wouldn't have let you see him or keep him," I say, hoping my logic will get through to her. "They—"

She spits at me. The nasty glob splats on my cheek. I don't lift a hand to wipe it away. There's so much I want to say, but I know none of it will help. Not apologies or explanations or even the truth. Her pain is beyond all of it. The spittle slides wetly down my cheek.

Alexander helps me rise. My knees tremble. I try to speak, but he hushes me. "Not now. Give her time." He ushers me to the door and closes it. I linger, not knowing where else to go. A minute later he emerges, passing a hand over his sleek hair. "I gave her a sedative."

"She blames me." Rightly. It's my fault. By taking the time to search for my DNA report, I cost Halla her baby. I traded Halla's baby for a chance to learn who my parents are. I gambled her happiness and lost everything.

"She's hormonal and in pain. She'll see things differently when she's had some sleep and when the birth hormones recede. She'll understand that you had no choice but to leave the baby." He sees my doubt. "You had no choice."

"I did," I said. "I could have left her there, with Little Loudon."

"Don't be stupid," he snaps, sounding remarkably like Dr. Ronan for a moment. "If you'd done that, she still would never have laid eyes on that baby, and she'd have been forced into continued surrogacy, into a cycle of bearing babies she'd never get to hold. Leaving her was never a real choice. Don't confuse sentimental, false choices with reality. It's stupid and dangerous."

His brusqueness makes me feel a tiny bit better. "Thank you, I think."

His face relaxes into its usual gentle lines. "You did what you could, Everly. That's all any of us can do. You saved her life and she'll be grateful for that one day, even if she can't see past being separated from that baby for now." He grips my shoulder. "Stay away from her for a couple of days. She'll come around."

I thank him again. As a doctor, he knows more than most about DNA and the DNA registry, I suspect. Walking toward the main room beside him, I ask, "Hypothetically, can you think of any way that someone's parents' DNA would not be registered in the DNA database?"

He gives me a curious look. "Why?"

"Just asking." I shrug, knowing he's not fooled for a moment.

He gives it some thought. "Off the top of my head, I'd say it was probably more likely that someone removed the records than that they were never there."

That possibility hadn't occurred to me. "Is that possible?"

He shrugs. "Difficult, but for someone with the right access, not impossible. Do you want to tell me why you're asking?"

I shake my head, trying to process what he's told me. "Not yet. Maybe someday."

He lets it go and I feel a surge of affection for him. "Thanks," I say.

Dinner that night is subdued. Halla stays in her room with a tray. Fiere delivers it. When she returns, holding a peach-colored mug, she says, "You look like you could use some tea. I made a pot for Halla. Do you want some?"

"Thanks, Fiere." I accept the warm mug gratefully, and sip the precious brew slowly. It's got a wonderful golden-green color and gentle aroma. I know better than to ask how she got hold of rare tea leaves. We didn't even grow tea trees at the Kube dome because other crops were more necessary. She watches me until I finish the tea, and then takes the mug away.

"You're growing very domestic, Fiere," Idris says, observing us. She gives him the finger as she returns to the kitchen.

I wake with cramping that night, and when I get my period four days later, I know what Fiere did. I confront her in the ballroom when we're training. She's recovered remarkably quickly from her spleen removal. Alexander warned her not to resume hard training yet, but she replied that sparring with me wasn't any more debilitating than the daily walks he wanted her to take.

"The tea," I say, as we circle in a half-crouch, each of us looking for an advantage. She's got a single-stick and I've got a broom handle. I'm supposed to be learning to fight with whatever objects come to hand. "You put a pill in the tea, didn't you?"

One brow quirks up, like she's surprised I figured it out. "You're not meant to be a surrogate, Everly."

"That was my decision to make, not yours."

She strikes a sharp blow with the single-stick. Bracing the length of wood between my hands, I raise it to ward off the hit. "You're getting faster," she mutters.

"You slipped me that pill without my permission. You messed with my body. That's what the government does at the RESCOs—uses our bodies for their purposes, decides what's best for the country, and to hell with the individual's wants or needs. You set yourself up as wanting to help women, wanting to give them choices, but you're no better than the government. You took my choice away."

She goes white with fury and jabs and swings the single-stick in a series of quick moves. I meet each one with my broom handle and push her back on the last blow with a powerful upward shove of the broomstick.

"It was for your own well-being," she says, panting a bit. She hasn't regained her stamina since the surgery.

"You don't get to decide that." My own anger rises. "I am the only one who gets to decide what's best for me, what happens with my body. Not the government"—push with the broomstick—"not you"—swing at her head—"not anyone. Me." I lower the broomstick slightly, hoping she'll go for the opening. She takes the bait. I sidestep and drop low, ducking her thrust, and, holding one end of the broomstick with both hands, stab it between her legs, sweeping up. I catch her slightly off-balance, and her leg flies up. She lands on her back, hard. The single-stick skitters across the floor and thuds against the wall.

She doesn't try to get up or retaliate, just lies there, staring up at me, which I take for a Fiere-ish sort of apology. Throwing the broomstick down, I walk out.

CHAPTER TWENTY SIX

A week passes and Halla doesn't relent. When she's out of bed and feeling better, she avoids me, avoids all of us, really. The only one who can talk to her is Fiere, who is unexpectedly patient and gentle with her. I suspect she tolerates Fiere because Fiere has been there, sort of. She doesn't mention trying to see Loudon, although I know she hasn't forgotten him because she mutters his name in her sleep. Saben's away on a mission and I miss him, although it's easier to act normal with Wyck with Saben gone. I feel bad that my thoughts so often stray to Saben when I'm with Wyck and I try to be extra-affectionate with him to compensate. I continue my training, sometimes with Fiere (who never refers to our conversation and fight), sometimes with Saben, and occasionally with other Bulrush agents. Wyck trains with us most of the time now and he's far better than I am. It's ironic that he ran away from the Kube to avoid military service when it's becoming clearer and clearer that he has unusual aptitude for weapons and fighting. When I suggest it's time for us to pick an outpost and plan for our departure so we're ready when Halla's able to travel, he mutters that Cas is dealing with something and can't leave yet.

"We don't need Cas." I'm not even sure I want Cas along.

Wyck stiffens. "He's my friend, just like you and Halla are my friends. I'm not leaving without him."

We're slumped against the ballroom wall after a tough training session and I'm still, watching his profile. "You grew up with me and Halla—we've known each other for a decade. You've known Cas for less than a month." I try to keep my tone non-accusatory, but I'm hurt by his attitude.

"Friendship isn't about how long you've known someone," he says. "Sometimes it grows over time, and sometimes it's just there, like a gift. I'm certainly not friends with everyone at the Kube, just because I've known them for years. I don't care if I never see half of them again." He tacks a laugh onto the end of that statement, but I ignore it, zeroing in on an earlier phrase.

"You think of your friendship with Cas as a gift." He makes a show of stretching his muscles, leaning forward over his legs so I can't see his face, but I've known Wyck for a long time. "I see." I think I see. His affection for Cas explains his lack of passion for me. The kiss in the swamp was—what? The by-product of fear or relief, the uncertainty of surviving the day. It wasn't, as I thought at the time, a declaration of deeper feelings for each other. I suspect I know why he's ducked my kisses, why he hasn't pressed for greater intimacy. The memory of Saben's kisses makes me wonder if I'm not a bit relieved.

He turns his head, hands still gripping his ankles, and says sadly, "You see more than I do, Ev. Nothing is clear to me right now. I don't know—I'm confused. I care about you. I want to go to an outpost with you. I just want Cas to come, too. Halla can't leave yet, anyway. Why can't we wait a few more days before making plans?"

"Sure," I say. "Sure. We can wait."

Two women come through and I help ferry one of them, young and pregnant, to a station master with Fiere. The hand-off goes smoothly and the girl clings to me, thanking me over and over again, before continuing on her long journey to an outpost. I have to admit it's a rush, and, after seeing a RESCO up close and Halla's torment, I get satisfaction from helping this girl avoid that fate. I don't know how these girls and women find Bulrush, and no one's sharing that secret with me yet. I'm still very much on the periphery of the organization, I can tell, even though they seem to trust me more since the RESCO.

After the mission, near midnight, Alexander takes me to his office, the one with the computer. My eyes linger on it as he gestures me to a comfortable padded chair upholstered in worn green velvet, and seats himself in a rocking chair. He rocks gently as we talk, the chair emitting a sighing *squuh* with every backward rock. He's got a glass of the milky liquid and offers me a drink from one of the bottles arranged on an antique buffet behind him.

"Aunt Lorraine kept a well-stocked cellar," he says when I get up to examine the bottles.

"I'm surprised they weren't looted during the Between."

Alexander swirls the liquid in his glass so it coats the sides. "Since she ran an illegal business, Auntie had secret panels installed where her girls could hide if the place got raided. Closets behind closets, if you will. The same man who put in the panels walled off a section of the original basement for secret storage."

"I hope she didn't entomb him down there to keep the secret."

"Like the pharaohs with the pyramids, you mean?" He smiles.

I nod.

"No, I'm pretty sure she paid him a handsome fee and relied on his trustworthiness. Auntie was a good judge of character. So am I."

I pour a half-inch of amber liquid because I like the heavy glass bottle. Burying my nose in the glass, I inhale the aroma of caramelized peaches and alcohol, looking at Alexander over the rim.

"I want you to stay with Bulrush, Everly," he says as I take a small sip.

I cough, either from the searing jolt of the alcohol against my palate, or from his statement.

He suppresses a smile. "You're passionate, smart and resourceful. Your time at the RESCO has given you—I hope—some compassion for the women we try to serve. Saben and Fiere speak well of your fighting and your situational awareness on missions. They both said they'd trust you to watch their backs under fire." Correctly interpreting my look, he says, "Yes, Fiere, too.

"We don't recruit a lot of people. For obvious reasons, we keep our cadre as small as possible, but we've suffered losses recently. If you want to join us, you'd stay here for some months, learning the operation. Then, maybe we'd move you to a station, or keep you here, depending."

I wonder if the traitorous station master is the only loss, or if there are more I'm not aware of. Probably that. Did they lose anyone rescuing me and Halla? I'm ashamed that I haven't thought to ask that before. I ask now.

"No. One man nearly lost his leg when he crashed his scooter evading the IPF, but a comrade took him aboard and he's going to be okay. He may limp."

"What about Wyck and Halla?"

Alexander sets his glass down. "We still plan to help Halla move on. If her Loudon wants to go with her, we can help him, too. I don't think she's cut out for what we do, however, if that's what you're suggesting. As for Wyck—we're still evaluating him. He's certainly got useful skills, but . . ."

I don't try to make him finish the sentence. I don't want to hear anything negative about Wyck.

"This is a decision you need to make on your own, without regard to Halla and Wyck. I understand they're your friends and you are loyal to them. You fulfilled your promise to Halla by getting her to Atlanta, and you went above and beyond by getting her out of the RESCO, even if she doesn't yet see it that way. As for Wyck—" He repeats the phrase and hesitates, as if choosing his words carefully. "You're sixteen. You've known each other a long time and you've been through a lot together recently. There's room for a lot of growing yet."

I'm not sure what's he's trying to say, and I don't ask. All I know is I care about Wyck. He's important to me. The thought of remaining in Atlanta without him is painful.

I swallow the rest of my drink, enjoying the warm burn down my esophagus. "Can I ask how you got involved in Bulrush, how it got started?"

I can see him weighing his options. Finally, he says in a low voice, "The first thing you've got to understand is that the Between was a horrible time. Horror beyond anything you can possibly imagine. I was a brand-new MD when the new strain of flu appeared. My diploma wasn't even framed yet. I was doctoring in Minnesota, what's now part of the Ontario Canton. The cases started to pile up, the mortality rate was on a par with the most virulent strains of Ebola— in the high 70s. Unheard of. The CDC and the military got involved. There was talk that the strain had originated in North Korea, speculation that it was a bio-weapon. You'd think the country that came up with it must also have formulated a vaccine. If so, the flu had the last laugh on its creator, because there wasn't a single country on the planet unaffected. My patients fell dead around me. Mothers were so sure their babies would die that they didn't name them. I felt so utterly damn *useless*. I was of no more help to my patients than an accountant would have been, or a pastry chef. Useless."

He faces away, studying the wallpaper with its blowsy roses still surprisingly pink, twined around faded brown trellises. He regains control and turned back to me. His forefinger taps his glass relentlessly.

"I can remember, back when there were TV broadcasts and everyone got their news on the internet, seeing photos of the bodies piled up outside towns by the thousands, tens of thousands. Bulldozers and excavators working round the clock, digging mass graves and shoveling the bodies in. No ritual, no prayer, just—disposal." He gets up, pours himself a healthy dose from a squat bottle, and returns to his rocking chair. He takes a long swallow and then puts a fist to his chest. "By the time the second wave hit, the most devastating one, there was no one left alive to bury the dead. The bodies rotted where they lay. Then came the rats. Oh, my God, the rats. You can learn about it in a history class, but you can't understand it, can't feel it, unless you were there."

I keep silent, feeling small.

"Several states declared they were seceding, thinking that if they sealed their borders, they could stop the flu. They planted mines, destroyed bridges and highways. It didn't work, of course; it was too late. Even before the locusts and the famine, all kinds of crime and looting were rampant. There was no government, no law enforcement. It was every man for himself. Outlaw gangs formed; stores, homes and corpses were looted. Survivors protected themselves as best they could with guns and homemade weapons, by hiding. Factories and farms stopped producing because there weren't enough workers to man them. The country had no manufacturing, no central government, virtually no infrastructure. Then came the locusts. I had thought things were as bad as they could get, but by God I was wrong."

Alexander falls silent. I am hugging my knees to my chest with my feet on the chair, and I try to resume a more normal posture. He stares into his glass as if hoping to see the future in the amber liquid.

"Enough about that. Fast forward ten years. Huh, you don't even know what that means. There used to be movie viewing devices—never mind. Suffice it to say that when the Pragmatists began to consolidate power ten years later, raised a military capable of subduing the scavengers and looters and securing our borders, it was a huge relief to everyone. We brought order, developed the domes so people could eat, began to rebuild the infrastructure and regain some manufacturing capabilities."

"You were a Pragmatist?"

"Oh, yes. In on the ground floor. A founder of the movement. My wife and I, Oliver Fonner, Fabienne Dubonnet, twenty or so others. I was proud of the work we did in the early days."

I'm startled by his reference to Proctor Fonner and the Premier. "And then?"

"Then, once there was stability, we began to talk about ways of rebuilding the population. You've seen the result. Suffice it to say, I didn't agree with the establishment of the

RESCOs, with government licensing of reproduction. I argued against it. I lost. I left the movement, went into hiding a few steps ahead of assassination, I'm pretty sure."

My eyes round. "Really? They would have killed you?"

"Oh, yes." He says it without drama, accepting the obvious. "I fell into a bottle for a couple of years"—he hoists his glass with an ironic twist of his lips—"and took myself off the grid in the northern wilderness for another five. When I came back, Bulrush just happened. There was a pregnant girl . . . you don't need the details. Turns out I wasn't the only one against the reproduction laws and the RESCOs. There were others. Despite the government's best efforts to squash us, Bulrush is still here, still effective. And now there's you." He shoots me an enquiring look.

I feel clubbed by his story, dazed. "Can I think about it?"

"You must. There's no hurry, my dear. Take your time." He checks his watch and levers himself out of the chair. Steadying himself, he moves toward the computer. "You'll have to excuse me now." He powers up the device and I assume he's making pre-arranged contact with someone.

I'm dying to know what he uses the computer for, who he's in contact with, but I obediently leave, shutting the door quietly behind me. I've got a lot to think about, what with Alexander's story and his offer. What happened to his wife? Did she die? It all keeps me awake until the small hours, when the station master visits me in my dreams again, rasping accusations through the hole in his throat.

I don't tell anyone, not even Wyck, about the DNA report or Alexander's offer. I don't know what to make of the report, don't know what my next step should be. I'm at a dead end when it comes to finding my parents. As for my sibling . . . I don't know if I want to find him or her. Part of me is naturally curious, but part of me thinks it would be presumptuous of me to invade my sibling's life, especially when I find out I'm a wanted woman two days after Alexander's offer. Saben brings that news after a meeting with an IPF contact. Apparently, there's an arrest warrant out for me. I'm wanted for murdering an IPF officer during the RESCO escape and theft of a government zygote, a capital offense. I go cold when he tells me. We're in the tunnel with Wyck who is working on one of the ACVs that has a steering problem.

"Murder?"

"There's a reward for your capture."

The idea is so absurd that I almost giggle. I sober quickly when he adds, "Dead or alive."

Wyck sits up, tool in hand, and says, "You were right, Ev—we should leave now. For an outpost. We can get new identities, start new lives, like we planned."

I'm warmed by his willingness to go with me, after the way he was stalling the other day.

Saben's gold eyes cloud. He says, "That might be best. You'd be safe, Everly."

"Is there a reward out on you?"

He shakes his head. "I've been able to fly under the radar. We all have. Even Fiere. She wasn't pregnant when she got away from the RESCO, and it was a quiet extraction."

No blasts, bullets, or bloodshed, he meant. "So I'm endangering Bulrush by staying here," I say slowly. The idea crushes me. I'm taken aback by how sad it makes me. I'd been seriously considering Alexander's offer, I realize, even though I'm not one hundred percent behind what Bulrush does. I want to stay with these people. "I—"

A muffled *clink* sounds from around the corner.

"Did you hear that?" Saben is instantly alert.

Wyck scrambles up. I nod.

"I'm going to check it out," Saben whispers. He heads toward the bend in the tunnel and disappears from view. A moment later, he shouts, "IPF! Warn the—"

There's the sizzle of a beamer and his voice cuts out.

"Saben!" I start toward him, but Wyck grabs my arm and slings me around.

"You can't go up against an IPF squad. We have to warn the others, get them out of here. Go." He shoves me toward the ladder.

I shoot up it with Wyck behind me. I'm yelling as I come through the opening. "IPF! In the tunnel. Get out, get out."

Fiere emerges from the ballroom where she's obviously been training with Idris who peers from behind her. A single stick dangles from her hand. She takes charge. "Close the hatch," she barks at Wyck who hurries to comply, sliding the bolt into place.

Idris says, "I'll get Alexander," and takes off.

"Everly, warn Halla. She's in the kitchen. Everyone into a safe room or down in the tunnels at the back of the house. Where's Saben?"

I shake my head. She closes her eyes. After a moment, she opens them. Her jaw is tight and her lips barely move as she grits out, "Someone's sold us out. Right. Weapons."

A blast knocks the cover off the tunnel entrance. A helmeted head with a bio-chem mask making the face look like a giant insect, pokes through. Fiere lunges and swings the single stick with all her might. It thwacks into the head which lolls and then sinks below floor level. An arm emerges as Fiere tries to close the hatch again. It tosses a cluster of grape-sized metal spheres. They hover, dispensing a thin lavender mist that makes me cough uncontrollably and burns my eyes and the inside of my nose. I'm coughing and running toward the kitchen, determined to grab Halla and hide in the armory. My eyes stream. I don't see Wyck or Fiere. I hope they got out. Alexander and Idris, too. I bump into the door and then I'm in the kitchen.

Halla cowers on the floor, a blur to my stinging eyes. "Ev, what's hap—"

Two bangs sound in rapid succession, and the house shudders. "—fire the place and drive the rats out," a soldier says, voice distorted by the bio-chem gear. "Looks like . . . info was good."

Are they here for me? It's terrible to think I brought this down on Bulrush. I fumble toward Halla, get hold of her forearm and drag her toward where I think the pantry must be. Bulky shapes appear in the doorway, distorted by purple mist and tears. One raises its arm, flings something, and they back away. There's a flash that blinds me and a brutally loud metallic keening that disorients me. I think my eardrums are broken.

I hear Halla faintly, as if from underwater. "I didn't mean it, Ev. I don't hate—I didn't mean—!"

I'm on the floor, somehow, and rough hands are grabbing at me, dragging me up. I swing at the nearest helmet, and as my hand cracks into it, erupting in pain, another soldier grabs me from behind and flings me to the ground. My head clonks against the iron stove and I'm disoriented. My brain is scrambled. Wyck . . . Saben . . . Fiere . . . she said . . . what?

Suddenly, Fiere is there. A soldier half-turns, but too late. Her foot, driven with all her weight, slams into his chin and he goes down. She snatches up the beamer he drops and fires as another soldier lunges at her. He falls.

"We're getting out of here," she says, reaching down to me. "I'm not leaving without you." The sheer force of her will enables me to close my fingers around her hand. She pulls and I lever myself up. The grinding ache in my head makes it hard to think, my eyes won't focus, and I need to throw up. Concussion.

The kitchen door splinters. Sunlight and more soldiers pour through the hole. The light hurts my eyes. A beamer sizzles and Fiere is knocked back, her hand tearing away from mine, blood blossoming on her shoulder. She presses the heel of her hand to the wound. Her gaze locks on mine.

"If they take you, tell them whatever you need to, Everly. Just tell them. You don't know—"

Another blast silences her. The force propels her out of my line of sight. I scream her name; at least, I think I do. I start toward her, but soldiers rise up and block my way. They reach for me. I run. Slipping past the soldiers in the chaos of sound and swirling smoke, I make it through the kitchen door. A terracotta fountain, dry, and a wrought iron fence swing through my field of vision. *Courtyard. Gate.* I stagger toward the opening and see armored ACVs at either end of an alley. Soldiers boil out of them.

"—think . . . two are dead. Find the computer . . . more than one."

I refuse to think about who might be dead. Not Fiere. Not Wyck. No time. I run around the side of the house, and find myself in a narrow side yard bounded by a wrought iron fence and choked with four abandoned and rusted-out cars. I'm small enough to eel my way between them; the soldiers fall behind. I burst out into a front courtyard and pound toward the street, becoming aware of a powerful hum. Another weapon? I look up, scanning for threats, hearing the thud of booted feet behind me. A beamer blast zaps past me, missing, but raising the hairs on my arms.

I hit the street and turn right, stumbling over the chunks of asphalt and concrete. I'd give my right arm for an ACV scooter. My head hurts viciously.

A metallic clanking makes me start and I see a manhole cover rolling toward me. I hurdle it. An arm emerges from the hole, and then a blond head. Joy zings through me. Saben! I dart forward and grab him under the arms to help him out.

"Unh," he groans, flopping forward. He hauls himself to his feet but stumbles. "Hurt. You have to leave me." Blood oozes from his abdomen and he drops to his knees.

"Shut up." I crouch to work my arm around his back and wedge my shoulder into his armpit. I straighten, pulling him up, and move forward. It's getting darker and the hum louder. It almost drowns out the booted footsteps pounding closer. An approaching storm?

"Leave me," Saben says again, weakly.

"Not a chance," I grunt. His weight presses me down, but I make my burning thigh muscles propel us forward. His legs catch my rhythm after a moment and we're running together in an awkward lope, arms clamped around each other to keep him upright. I can feel the effort of will it takes him to keep going. I don't know how long he can last. We duck as another blast scorches overhead. I'm desperate for a hiding place. Then, I see it. Locusts. A huge swarm. Coming at us, obliterating the sky, blocking the light.

The soldiers behind us stutter to a halt, shouting confused orders. "Swarm. Inside!" "Get the girl—orders!" "Don't stop, you—" "Fire at will!"

The dark mass of locust bodies, all beating wings and hunger, is less than half a block away now. The air vibrates. Another blast singes past, scoring my side so I yelp and list to the right, jolting Saben. I glance over my shoulder at the soldiers. One is steadying his beamer, preparing to fire again. Another is running flat out toward us, gaining. Two more have dropped back.

"Everly."

I look up into Saben's face and he's actually smiling at me, although pain furrows his brow and makes him breathe shallowly. My chest tightens with emotion, with worry, with the strange exultation his smile elicits, and then with the blazing conviction that I am right where I'm supposed to be at this moment. With Saben. My smile answers his. We're insane.

Logic intrudes: *If we surrender, they'll treat Saben's wound*—. I cut the thought off because I know that's not what we're going to do. I feel Saben's muscles contract even before I take a step and then we're moving forward together. I tip my head back, eyeing the tidal wave of insects rising above us higher than I can see. Saben quirks a brow. "Ladies first?"

"The hell with that."

His arm squeezes my shoulders, and his laugh rumbles through me. Or maybe it's the locusts I feel, making my bones thrum. If only these millions of wings could lift us up and fly us far away. The best they can do is hide us, give us a chance, a small chance, to escape. Covering our mouths and noses as best we can, and shutting our eyes, Saben and I run as one to meet the swarm, letting it swallow us up.

END OF BOOK ONE

PREVIEW OF
INCINERATION
BOOK 2 OF THE INCUBATION TRILOGY

Prison is no place to spend your seventeenth birthday. I'm pretty sure today is my birthday, but it's hard to know since I've been here almost four months without access to a clock, calendar, window—forty-seven—or any other means of keeping time except by the regular delivery of meals. Swill. Vegeprote patties and the occasional fresh vegetable—I haven't seen so much as a radish in a week—pushed into my cell three times a day. Forty-eight. As much as I can when I am coherent and conscious, I keep track of the days by scratching faint marks on the floor beneath the bed. Forty-nine. There's a hundred and fifteen of them now, so happy birthday to me—fifty—happy birthday dear Everly . . .

"Jax!"

I pause mid-pushup and look to my left. The guard I call Bigfoot stands in the corridor beyond the electric field that keeps me contained. His face is as impassive as usual, but he's practically garrulous today. "Visitor."

I scramble to my feet, heart thumping hard and not from the exercise. I haven't had a visitor the whole time I've been here. Interrogators, yes, but they don't get announced by the guards. Rubbing the back of my hand where the IV went in last time, I regulate my breathing and concentrate on feeling calm. My heartbeat slows. I push the two inch scraggle of platinum hair off my face as Bigfoot deactivates the invisible barrier and motions for me to hold out my wrists. I do and he encircles them with maglock cuffs. Thus restrained, I follow him down the narrow hallway, the explosive bracelet on my left ankle making me feel lopsided. Sensors rigged on every window and door of this building will trigger the anklet and blow me to kingdom come. Needless to say, that has limited my escape fantasies since I haven't yet—despite hours of trying—found a way to detach the bracelet. If only Wyck were here—he'd have figured it out in ten minutes. We pass the hygiene cubicle where I get my thrice weekly shower, to a room I've never been in.

Bigfoot pushes the door open, his bulk hiding the room's interior. "Prisoner Jax," he announces, and steps aside so I can enter.

I hesitate, momentarily afraid this is a trap, a new twist on interrogation. Build up my expectations and then— wham! I realized weeks ago that the worst part of the torture is the mind games, the anticipation of pain or humiliation. What if—

Bigfoot thrusts me unceremoniously into the room, saying, "I'll be right outside, sir."

The room's sole occupant is plump and fiftyish, with mahogany hair slicked back from a widow's peak and tucked behind his ears, ruddy cheeks, and amazing violet eyes emphasized with black eyeliner. I've never seen eyeliner on a man. He's wearing a peacock blue coat with a stand-up collar, and heavy rings sparkle on every finger.

"No need, no need." He waves a dismissive hand at Bigfoot. "I'm sure young Everly and I will get along like a house afire." He glides to me, grabs my shoulders, and kisses me on each cheek with a loud smooching sound.

The door closes behind Bigfoot.

I blink. I've never seen this man before and he's treating me like I'm his favorite niece.

"Sit, sit," he says, motioning to the two loveseats set at right angles. "We need to discuss your defense."

I remain rooted to my spot. Defense? "Um, who are you?"

"My manners, oh, my manners," the man says, putting a hand with splayed fingers to his chest. "Loránd Vestor, esquire, at your service. Call me Vestor—we'll be old friends by the end of the trial." He beams, displaying the whitest teeth I've ever seen.

"Trial?"

"Of course your trial. You wouldn't need a defense attorney if you weren't standing trial, now would you?" He chuckles. "Oh, you're worried that I'm some court-appointed incompetent. No, indeed! I am the foremost criminal defense attorney in Amerada, and I'm offering my services—yes, completely without cost to you—because *I* believe in *you*, Everly!" More beaming, like he's bestowed an unimaginably wonderful gift on me. "Yes, truly I do, despite what they're saying. You're lucky to have me, you know. I have never—never!—lost a case or a client."

"Thank you?"

It seems to be the response he's expecting because he smiles again. I can't help noticing a dark mole on his cheek that gets compressed with wrinkles whenever he smiles. It's disconcerting because it seems to be winking at me. I tear my gaze away from the mole and finally let him persuade me to sit. I look around the room and notice a window. Sunshine pours through it and three potted geraniums in shades of pink and coral bloom on the windowsill. A lump rises in my throat. I haven't seen the sun in almost four months. The sunlight on the flowers' translucent petals is a gift.

Vestor's saying something, but I interrupt to ask, "Where are we?"

Delicate brows arch skyward. "Why, we're at the Central Detention Facility."

"No, I mean the city."

"Atlanta, of course. You don't think I would waste my talents in some outer canton, do you? No, it's the capital for me." He leans forward to peer at my eyes. "The interrogators haven't done anything with your memory, have they? That's strictly against the Laidlaw Conventions."

"I don't think so."

"Good." He pats my hand. "No more chit-chatting. We must get to work since the trial starts day after tomorrow. Lots to do, lots to do."

I hesitate, pretty sure I don't really want to know the answer, but then ask, "What am I on trial for?"

"Why, murder, my dear Everly. Murder of an Infrastructure Protection Force soldier and treason by way of theft of a zygote implanted at the Reproduction Support Community. Capital offenses. I only do capital cases in the capital city." He chortles again, clearly amused by his wordplay.

I'm not inclined to laugh. "Murder," I whisper. "Will they . . . execute me?"

He throws both hands up. "You have Loránd Vestor in your corner—of course not! *I* believe in *you*, Everly, and now *you* must believe in *me*. I will not allow you to be convicted and put to death. Why, think of the stain on my reputation." He sniffs.

"Wouldn't want a stain on your reputation," I agree sardonically. Despite myself, I feel a smile starting and become conscious of an unfamiliar feeling. Hope.

Vestor grins delightedly at my smile, tentative though it is. "Better, much better." He claps his hands. "Now, let's get to work."

He grills me about everything that happened from the time Halla and Wyck and I left InKubator 9 until I was captured and brought here. I am wary of telling him too much, and start with one word answers to his questions. I scan the room for recording devices and don't see any, but that doesn't mean there aren't any. Four months here have taught me to distrust everyone and everything.

Vestor starts me with a prompt. "So, you left Kube 9, you impetuous young girl, because Minister Alden suggested during an Assembly that she would like to have you work for her on locust eradication, right, and you were burning to get started, to put your science genius at the service of our great nation?" He cocks his head and raises his brows expectantly.

I really left the Kube to try and identify my biological parents and because my best friend Halla was pregnant and needed my help to reach her boyfriend in Atlanta, but I get the feeling Vestor wants me to agree with him. "Um, yes?"

He nods vigorously. "Yes! And you bravely helped your friend, Halla Westin, unfortunately deceased, escape from the outlaws who captured you and make her way to the RESCO where she was able to safely deliver her baby and give it over to the government for the good of Amerada."

"Yes," I whisper, squinching my eyes to keep back tears. They'd told me Halla was dead during my first interrogation session, but the mention of it still catches me like a beamer blast to the chest, leaving me hollowed out and empty. She died hating me and that's the most painful part. No, the worst part is that she's gone; I'd be glad of her hate if only that would bring her back.

It goes like that for hours, with Vestor supplying a favorable interpretation of everything that happened after I left the Kube, and me agreeing to it. He's obviously done his research and that makes me feel a little bit better about my chances. Bigfoot brings us food and drink midway through the session and it's the best I've had since being captured: fresh grapefruit and broccoli, rice and fish, even a fizzy beverage. I wolf it down while Vestor watches indulgently. He pats my cheek when he rises to go. "Don't forget: *I* believe in *you*," he says.

"Vestor," I say, before he can leave, "can you tell me where they are, what happened to them? Wyck and Saben, Fiere and Alexander?"

His brows twitch inward in the merest suggestion of a frown. With a warning in his violet eyes that I take as confirmation that our supposedly confidential session is being recorded, he says, "It is completely understandable that you should be worried that the outlaws might try to kidnap you again, or hurt you to keep you from testifying. You endured a horrifying experience, something that an adult would find hard to deal with, never mind a young girl like you. I can assure you, however, that your fears are groundless. I've been given to understand that you were the only survivor of the attack on the Peachtree Street house."

It takes me a moment to realize he means the former brothel that Bulrush used as its headquarters. I suck in an audible breath. "Dead? All dead?"

"Of course you're relieved to hear that. I'm grateful, too. Now, get a good night's sleep. We have lots of work to do tomorrow to make you presentable."

When he has gone and Bigfoot's replacement, a guard named Rute who occasionally offers a sentence or two of conversation, takes me back to my cell, I don't even try to sleep. I lie on the narrow cot and stare up at the ceiling. Heaven knows, there's not much else in my gray-painted cell to look at. There's a stainless steel toilet and sink in one corner and a single shelf where I have kept my *Little House on the Prairie* and my albatross feather and drawing since the interrogators finally became convinced the objects had no sinister purposes. I don't remember everything that happened in the interrogation sessions because of the drugs, but snippets of conversations, of questions about *Little House* being a code book for Bulrush, or even the Defiance, come back to me at odd times.

"It's just a book," I'd told them again and again. "A book my parents sent with me to the Kube." The feather I'd found on the beach, proof that birds were still alive somewhere. They returned it to me once they ascertained it couldn't be used as a weapon. The albatross drawing they sneered at and crumpled, but let me keep. Saben had given it to me, had drawn it because of the feather, and I treasured it.

I smooth it now, comforted by the familiar grain of the paper and the angle of the bird's wing in flight that sings with perfect freedom. It can't be true about Wyck and the others. They can't all be dead. Saben, gravely injured by a blast, had run into the swarm with me, but the force of the locusts had pulled us apart. I don't want to think about how weak he was. Surely at least one of the others made it to the tunnels, escaped. I'd seen Fiere get shot, so it was sadly possible that she had died, but the others . . . I refuse to believe it. They aren't dead. If they are, why did the interrogators spend so much time and effort badgering me to give up names?

Tears of shame trickle down my face as the memories come back, of the pain from the implanted electrodes, amplified by the drugs. The stench of bile and urine. I can still hear myself stuttering the names, and I am grateful that I didn't know many, and only first names at that. Alexander was right to keep details of Bulrush's operations away from me, because I vomited up everything I knew. It wasn't much, thank goodness. Fiere had shouted at me in those last minutes, told me to "tell them everything." I hadn't known what she'd meant until the second interrogation session when they'd switched on the electricity.

I shudder and turn on my side, burying my face in the thin pillow. The cameras are always on and I refuse to give whoever's watching the satisfaction of tears. I haven't cried since my first month here, since I decided I was going to survive and escape to find my friends. I started exercising that day, doing pushups, sit-ups, squats, and the other strengthening drills Fiere taught me, as many as I could, no matter how weak the torture left me. When I wasn't exercising, I sat on my bed, eyes closed, and went through every theorem and chemical equation I knew, reciting the Table of Elements in my head, envisioning each locust I'd dissected and working through different means of destroying them. That kept other thoughts at bay.

I must have slept at last because the next thing I know, Bigfoot is back with a tray and a command. "Wash."

He leads me to the hygiene cubicle after I eat and scratch another mark under my bed. He hands me a bar of soap and actual shampoo. "Hair, too."

I'm elated at the prospect of shampooing my stiff hair. They shaved it when I arrived and it's only two inches long now, but the harsh soap I've had to wash it with has left it dull and dry. I show no emotion, keeping my face as impassive as Bigfoot's when I enter the hygiene cubby. He removes my explosive bracelet and leaves, electrifying the doorway. I strip, feeling little embarrassment, even though I know guards are watching. I tell myself it's not too different than the decon drills we ran at the Kube. I was worried about being raped when I first got here, but it's clear the guards are chemically neutered. I suppose that's because even though I'm a prisoner, I'm still a breeder age female who could potentially bear a child for the state. There are too few wombs for the Prags to risk damaging mine.

Nonetheless, I turn my back to the doorway, and begin to wash in the spray that suddenly spurts from a dozen nozzles. It's cold. Goosebumps pimple my skin and I try to scrub them away. When I lather my hair, the lily-scented shampoo takes me back to the bordello and I feel like an avocado stone has caught in my throat. I let out a sound almost like a bark, and put a hand on the wall to steady myself. If there are tears, the streaming water hides them.

The water cuts off. Blowers switch on to dry me and then Bigfoot is back to re-attach my anklet. Dressed in my gray jumpsuit and with my hair damp, I am led to the room where I talked to Vestor. He's there, garbed in an emerald tunic, mole winking when he smiles. He swoops down on me and I get the double kiss treatment.

"Shoo, shoo, shoo." He gestures Bigfoot out of the room. When the guard has gone, he turns to me. "Sleep well? The under eye circles say not. Never mind. A bit of *tristesse* can be very affecting. We're playing to the jury and the cameras, you know." He hands me white garments that are draped over the loveseat. "Put this on." He turns his back.

After a moment's hesitation, I strip to bra and panties (and ankle bracelet, of course) and don the long white tunic and leggings. I clear my throat when I'm dressed. "Cameras?"

"Of course cameras. Yours is the biggest trial of the year. It'll be broadcast, suitably edited, of course, during a special Assembly. I'll be inconceivably more famous when I get you off." Vestor works his lips in and out as he studies me. "We're going for youthful innocence," he says, circling me. "No make-up. Pale. Sad but composed. Pretty, but not beautiful. Don't want to alienate any female jurors." He chuckles. "The long sleeves hide those unfortunate muscles. Your hair . . ." He runs a hand through it. "We'll even up the ends. That silvery blond is perfect—angelic. It's a shame they shaved it when you got here, but short like that it looks like a halo."

He summons Bigfoot and requests scissors, then snips at my hair to neaten it. "Al-most," Vestor says, studying me while tapping an index finger against his lip. "Your expression . . ."

"What about my expression?"

"It's too . . . confrontational, verging on combative, in fact. We're going for modestly downcast eyes, perhaps a whisper of puzzlement. You can't understand why you're on trial when you've done nothing wrong. Victim! Yes, we want victim. Can you give me victim?"

"No," I say uncompromisingly. I will not for one minute think of myself as a victim. That undermines my strength and I know I will need to be strong.

Vestor raises his expressive brows and I think I see a hint of amusement and even approval in his eyes. "Confused, then. Meek."

I look at my feet in my best approximation of "modestly downcast eyes."

"No, not sullen," Vestor says, sounding annoyed for the first time. "Hurt. Think of your friend Halla."

Pain lances through me and I look up involuntarily.

Vestor claps his hands. "Yes, exactly! Hold that thought."

I glare at him.

He bustles over and takes me by the shoulders, his face inches from mine. "This is not a game, Everly," he says in a low voice with none of his usual affectedness. "Well, it is a game—theater, if you will—but it is played for the highest of stakes: your life. You are on trial from the second you leave this prison. Your every move, word, and expression will be recorded, studied and evaluated—every eyebrow twitch, every upthrust chin."

He taps the offending chin and I lower it slightly.

"Your test scores tell me you are a very, very bright young woman. Well, you need to dedicate that brainpower to playing the role of injured vic—innocent, and you'd better put everything you've got into it because otherwise . . . Trust me when I say execution would look merciful compared to your likely fate if they convict." He steps back and pins a broad smile to his face. "Not to mention the crushing blow to my flawless record. Agreed?"

I nod slightly and work on looking timid and confused. With my brain worrying at what sentence could be worse than death, it's not too hard.

"Excellent!"

ABOUT THE AUTHOR

Laura DiSilverio is the national bestselling author of 15 mystery and suspense novels, and a retired Air Force intelligence officer. Her first standalone novel, *The Reckoning Stones*, was a *Library Journal* Pick of the Month. The third book in her best-selling Book Club Mystery series, *The Readaholics and the Gothic Gala*, comes out in Aug 2016. A Past President  of Sisters in Crime, she pens articles for *Writer's Digest*, and teaches writing in various fora. She plots murders and parents teens in Colorado, trying to keep the two tasks separate. *Incubation* is her first young adult novel.

Made in the USA
Charleston, SC
07 June 2016